# PRAISE FOR S...

*"Sean Grigsby has conce...
brilliant and harrowing series."*
John Hornor Jacobs, award-winning author of *Southern
Gods* and *The Incorruptibles*

*"Smoke Eaters is a thrilling, exciting, funny and
strangely heart-warming book, and Grigsby's experience
as a firefighter shines through on every page, lending
grit and realism to this rollicking ride of a tale in which
firefighters become dragon-slayers. It's exactly as bonkers
– and as brilliant – as you'd expect and I look forward
to more from this author."*
Anna Stephens, author of *Godblind*

*"This smoking debut is a shot of adrenaline to the
urban fantasy genre. Grigsby's knowledge of firefighting
combined with hot dragon action and blistering humor
create an irresistible romp of a read."*
Jaye Wells, USA Today Bestselling author of the 'Prospero's
War' series

*"Grigsby's world is vividly rendered and full of engaging
detail (dragons don't have wings as in the stories, their
victims linger on as ghostly spirits). As a romp, it delivers
by the gallon drum."*
Irish Times

*"This book is as fun as it sounds."*
B&N Sci-Fi & Fantasy Blog

SEAN GRIGSBY

# ASH KICKERS

ANGRY ROBOT
An imprint of Watkins Media Ltd

Unit 11, Shepperton House
89 Shepperton Road
London N1 3DF
UK

angryrobotbooks.com
twitter.com/angryrobotbooks
Burn Baby Burn

An Angry Robot paperback original, 2019

Cover by Lee Gibbons
Set in Meridien

This novel is entirely a work of fiction. Names, characters, places,
and incidents are the products of the author's imagination or are used
fictitiously. Any resemblance to actual events, locales, organizations or
persons, living or dead, is entirely coincidental.

ISBN 978 0 85766 797 7
Ebook ISBN 978 0 85766 798 4

Printed in the United States of America by Penguin Random House
9 8 7 6 5 4 3 2 1

*To Collin,*
*If life's struggles ever get you down,*
*may you rise again to meet them*
*and severely kick their ash.*

# CHAPTER 1

My give-a-damn was busted.

Now, if my mama had been standing beside me on the top of that Slayer truck, she would have said, "Tamerica Janeese Williams, why are you just staring at that dragon? Don't you have a job to do?"

I *was* staring at the dragon – this golden-brown bastard with a wingspan the length of two hover-buses – but I was also following it with the barrel of Slayer 10's non-lethal, Sandman laser cannon. Gliding twenty feet above the ground, the scaly circled us like a buzzard, and I spun the cannon on a swivel to keep it in my sights. I could have shot the dragon half a dozen times, blasted a laser into its neck and sent it tumbling into the ash-covered ground, unharmed and unconscious.

But that would have been too easy. Boring.

All I kept thinking about was how I hadn't had a good dragon fight in over a year. Smoke Eater Division's updated standard operating procedures, effective January 1st, 2123, didn't give a damn about my feelings, though. They specifically instructed me to take this scaly alive. Any dead dragon, unless it was beyond our control, would result in every responding

1

smoke eater crew to be fined. Headquarters couldn't afford to suspend us – they needed the manpower – but they could hurt our wallets. More captured dragons meant more dragon blood for the needy.

A quick injection could work miracles.

Even before I joined up, before found out I had the ability to breathe dragon smoke, I knew that "smoke eater" was just another word for "dragon slayer." I think what pissed me off more than anything was that Chief Brannigan had written the new SOPs, and he'd been the most dragon slaying mofo out of any of us.

It was sunset and one of those days where twilight shone blindingly blood red, so, other than the dragon, there wasn't much to look at that far out from Parthenon City, except ashes darkened by shadow and the distant, red-painted wall of smoke rising from where the dragon had burned a fledgling settlement. Most of the citizens had gotten away without any injuries and no one had died. That was good. There'd be no wraiths.

The small town had their own firefighters who could tackle the blaze while we handled the scaly.

"Williams!" my captain, Jack Kiesling, shouted from Slayer 10's front bumper. "Shoot the damn thing already!"

"I'm working on it," I hollered back.

The circling dragon craned its neck, locking its eyes on me as I kept the Sandman's sights trained on its middle. The gold of its eyes glowed like a laser sword. The scaly gave a quick roar that sounded like someone dumping a jug of gasoline on a campfire, then flapped its wings a couple times, cutting the air with a deep *whoosh* as it circled closer. Close enough to throw a rock at.

Captain Kiesling slapped both hands on top of his helmet. "Williams, Goddamn it!"

My captain was wearing a power suit and helmet, same as me and our driver, Zhao, but the captain's headgear always looked too big on him, like a little boy wearing his mother's fire helmet. My helmet fit great, thanks to my thick hair – my daddy always says our family originated from the Nubia region and that's where we get our good looks and even better hair. The smoke eater helmets were different from firefighters in that ours also had cheek guards, like Roman centurions wore way back when.

"What's taking so long up there?" Zhao asked through my helmet radio. He'd stayed in his seat at the wheel.

"Just trying to get a good shot." I swallowed at a dry mouth. The lie had already left my lips.

The propellerheads, the scientists working with us smoke eaters, had called this particular type of dragon a smaug. As we'd been driving out to the settlement it was attacking, the propellerheads radioed that it was a run-of-the-mill, four-legged, fantasy-type dragon. Nothing a single company couldn't handle.

Now, I'm not saying this dragon wasn't dangerous. Fire breath, slashing claws, and jaws that could snap a redwood in half is nothing to thumb your nose at. But I'd dealt with scalies in the past that shot gooey wads that would pin you to the ground before they ate your face off, and aqueous types that boiled the water within ten feet around it.

All I'm saying is that this dragon was within my comfort zone to battle, and I wanted some action. Wanted? Hell, I *craved* it. The smaug must have had the same idea, because its circular pattern was getting smaller and smaller, and it never stopped glaring at me. It even flexed its brow, bunching the muscles underneath its horns in a "Let's do this, motherfucker!" sort of way. All I had to do was wait for it to land and charge me. Then I'd tear it up with the laser cannon fixed to my power suit's right arm.

"Come on, bitch," I whispered to the dragon.

"What did you call me?" Zhao asked.

"End cast," I said, cutting our radio connection. This was none of his business. This was between me and the smaug.

"Williams." Captain Kiesling stomped around Slayer 10, trying to get my attention. "If you don't shoot that dragon right now, I'm going to write you up."

Shiver me timbers. What a threat.

As Kiesling finished his grand ultimatum, the smaug suddenly raised one wing, turned away from us, and soared off into the sunset, its pronged tail flicking at the wind.

Kiesling crunched across the ashes toward the fleeing dragon, as if he'd take flight himself and chase after it. He stopped and yelled toward the dying red sun. "Just great. Now we have to start over." He turned and pointed up to me. "Get down from there, Williams. What the hell is going on with you today?"

Truth be told, I'd been feeling this way for over a month. I thought I could get used to being, basically, a scaly dog catcher, but I missed the feeling that flooded my body after a successful dragon fight – like orgasmic, hot ice. It didn't matter how exhausted I was after the effort. Actually, that just made it even better. It put me in a trance-like state, where I could relive the fight without leaving the couch.

I'd forgotten what it meant to truly be a smoke eater. We were born with the ability to breathe dragon smoke and resist heat. Now we drove around sniping scalies without any of the fun, without any dragonfire warming my face. Things had changed and not for the better.

I began to make my way off the top of the Slayer, but Kiesling wasn't done grilling me.

"When we get back, we're going straight to Chief Brannigan's office."

I hadn't decided if I was going to apologize and play the supplication card or if I was going to smart off. I didn't get the chance to do either.

First came the blazing roar of the smaug. Then there was the distinct whiz of air, the sound of something flying very fast and speeding toward us. I only had time to say, "Oh, shit!" and hit my power suit's jump button before leaping off Slayer 10 as the smaug plowed into it headfirst. My suit's thrusters lowered me to the ground and I turned to see what had happened.

Slayer 10, black-painted with purple emergency lights, rolled several times across the ground. Its windows shattered and tossed pieces of glass everywhere.

Zhao's voice screamed into my helmet. "Mayday! Mayday! Mayday!"

He was trapped inside.

Captain Kiesling was flat on his stomach, having hit the ground as the smaug sailed over him. The dragon shook its head like a dog drying itself off and leapt back into the air. It flapped its wings to hover just above Slayer 10, which had stopped rolling and now lay overturned on its side. When the smaug inhaled deeply and stretched its jaws open, I knew what was coming.

"No, no, no!" I ran toward the Slayer; I had to get Zhao out of there. I would have power-jumped, but I'd just used it and would have to wait until my thrusters were charged again.

The smaug loosed its breath, engulfing most of the Slayer truck in a cone of flames. Even from where I was running, I could feel the heat. The average dragon can breathe fire continuously for up to twenty seconds at a time, and that was twenty seconds Zhao didn't have.

"It's burning me! It's burning me!" Zhao screamed, over and over again.

I pumped my legs as fast as they'd go. When my thrusters *dinged* to signal the power was back, I leapt into the air – just as the dragon finished its fiery assault. Slamming against the side of the smaug's head, I grabbed hold of its horns. My body covered its eye on that side, and the dragon thrashed its head to and fro, trying to figure out what kind of big fucking bug had flown in to pester it.

The smaug raised one of its claws, moving in to swipe at me. I climbed onto its snout as the claw scraped past where I'd just been. Both of the dragon's eyes looked forward and crossed a little as it spotted me on top of its nose.

Now, the maneuver I performed was extremely dangerous. I wouldn't ever recommend it to anybody if they were in the same situation. For the average Jane, getting hit with a claw is much better than getting a mouth full of teeth. But what I did was a move smoke eaters do all the time – or did, before going soft. We called it the widowmaker evolution.

As I expected, the smaug opened its mouth, at first trying to snag me in its teeth. I held tight to the top of its snout and dodged the bites. When the scaly figured it couldn't get me off the old-fashioned way, it opened its jaws wider and inhaled hard, like someone who'd been underwater too long. Being this close, I could hear the high-pitch squeal at the back of the dragon's throat, the ignis gland revving up to shoot flames.

What the dragon didn't know was that I wanted it to breathe fire, or at least try to. When it opened its mouth, I dropped onto its bottom lip and shot a sticky white stream of foam down its throat with the gun on my power suit's left arm.

"Spit or swallow?" I said, and jumped onto the side of the overturned Slayer truck.

The smaug hacked and scratched at its throat, stomping away backwards. It wouldn't be breathing fire any more. Not for a few minutes any way.

With the smaug distracted, I bent over Slayer 10's driver's-side window and looked down. Zhao was out of his seat and lying on his back across the broken window resting on the ground. His skin was a little red, but he looked okay as far as I could tell.

"Can you move?" I asked.

"It hurts," he croaked. "Got as far away from it as I could."

I nodded. "I know it hurts, Zhao. But you're a smoke eater, you'll be fine. We have to get you out of here quick."

Zhao winced when he tried to raise his arm and then dropped it back across his chest.

"Come on, man. You better get moving or I'll shoot you with a laser long before the dragon gets you." I shook my gun arm.

That got his ass climbing.

After crawling over the truck's doghouse, Zhao stretched his arm up to me. I had to lean through the window to grab his hand. I pulled and he screamed – louder than the hacking dragon a few feet behind me. I had to use two hands to do it, but I managed to pull him out.

Zhao rolled onto the top of the Slayer truck, groaning and breathing heavy.

I stood and nudged him in his side with a boot. "Hey, we ain't done yet. Power jump down and get somewhere safe if you can't fight."

His red cheeks jiggled as he nodded. Several grunts later he got to his feet, power jumped to the ground, and ran for cover.

When I turned around, Captain Kiesling stood in front of the dragon with his laser sword extended. The dragon was still dry heaving from the foam in its throat, but it was no longer in a tizzy. Now it had its sights on Captain Kiesling.

I'd never seen Kiesling in a fight. He'd just been

promoted and I'd been forcibly transferred to his crew so Captain Jendal could train a new rookie. The way Kiesling was trembling in front of that dragon told me all I needed to know.

"Williams get over here," he called through my radio.

"I'm coming, Cap," I said. "Don't attack it straight on. You saw what its head did to our Slayer. It's got a thicker skull or something."

Not to mention the teeth and claws were still in use.

Kiesling ran to the left, his laser sword thrumming through the air. The smaug got down on all fours and pounced in the same direction. Was it toying with him? Skidding to a stop, Kiesling turned and ran the other way. The dragon followed again.

"Quit trying to fake it out," I said, huffing as I ran toward them. "You're just getting it excited."

Kiesling stopped, but turned his head to the overturned Slayer truck and smiled. "I see the Sandman," he said. "I'm going for it."

"No!" I shouted.

But he'd already started running. The dragon roared and bent its chin down. With another quick pounce, it flung its head forward, ramming Kiesling with its skull and sending my captain twirling through the air.

The captain landed in a heap. His groans echoed inside my helmet as the smaug used its wings to sail over to where he lay.

"Hold on, Cap!"

Snatching one of Kiesling's legs in its teeth, the dragon rose to sit on its ass, lifting the man – upside down and completely limp – ten feet off the ground. I had about two seconds before the smaug tossed Kiesling into the air and swallowed him on the return trip. Dragons like to do that playing-with-their-food shit.

But the smaug didn't do that. Instead, it spread its wings and raised them as if it was about to take flight. I'd never heard of a dragon taking its meal on the road before, but I'd also learned in my two years as a smoke eater that scalies can do all kinds of unexpected things.

Captain Kiesling woke from his stupor and screamed, squirming in the dragon's teeth.

I shot my laser at full blast, focusing the shots on the dragon's closest wing. The shots flew wild as I ran, streaking through the air in a barrage of *pew, pew, pew*. That sound always got my blood pumping and, I'm only a little ashamed to say, it felt goddamned amazing to fire my gun at a live scaly again.

A few of the lasers hit the ash at the dragon's feet, but it got the smaug to flinch and turn toward me, providing a better target. The other lasers bit into the waxy flesh of the dragon's wing, ripping big, unsymmetrical holes through it, reminding me of bleeding Swiss cheese. While it still tried to fly, the scaly quickly found it was going nowhere.

"You need both wings to fly," I shouted.

I like to talk the dragons while I fight them. Just 'cause.

The smaug dropped Kiesling. He landed with an "Oof!" and power jumped to the other side of the Slayer. He was limping before he leapt, but our thrusters don't necessarily need our legs at full function to work.

Now it was just the smaug and me. I planted my feet and readied my laser for a killing shot. The dragon whimpered – or as close a sound as I can describe it – as it looked over its damaged wing. I almost felt bad for the damned thing. It was just an animal after all. It wasn't sentient. Nor evil. It was just following its nature. Then again, before cancer was wiped out fifty years ago, it had been following a natural design, too.

My compassion sizzled away when the dragon snarled, its nostrils trembling and puffing out smoke. It gave me goose bumps. The good kind.

"Come on, baby," I said. "You know you want it."

The smaug inhaled and puffed out its chest. When it tried to breathe fire it hacked against the foam still stuck in its throat. I laughed and put my hands on my hips, where I remembered my new toy was holstered in a container on my power suit. The device, what the propellerheads had dubbed a "haymo" after some famous dragon slayer, was round and the size of a tomato. I pulled it out as the dragon growled and kicked ash away with its hind claws. I pressed the button on the top of the haymo and charged toward the dragon, hollering as hard as my lungs would let me.

This excited the dragon. It sprayed spit with another of its roars and galloped for me at full speed. Claws kicked up ash. Golden eyes flickered with hunger. Teeth, dripping with drool, spread wide before surrounding me on both sides.

I chunked the haymo into the smaug's mouth and power jumped away before the jaws clamped down.

But I hadn't properly directed the jump and was soon pointing headfirst toward the ground. My helmet took most of the impact, but that didn't mean much to my aching body, especially my neck and back. It felt like a herd of scalies had done the cha-cha right on top of me.

And then the smaug *was* right on top of me. The haymo hadn't worked. All I could do, as the scaly reared back to chomp, was lay on my back and say, "Fucking propellerhea–"

Fierce blue rays of light shot from the smaug's neck. The dragon froze mid-bite and remained motionless as the blue rays began to spin… just like a propeller.

*Nice touch,* I thought, rolling out of the way.

With a heavy and wet flop, the smaug's head fell to the ash beside me. Its golden eyes were no longer glowing, replaced by the stare of a dead fish. The scaly's body stayed upright for a second longer before tipping over and landing harder than a drunk white girl at a club.

"That's how we do it," I said, but it came out sounding too tired to be cool. Besides, there was no one there to high five.

As I got to my feet, the haymo plopped out of the dragon's severed neck, rolling across the ground and collecting ashes in the sticky blood. It stopped at my power suit's right boot. I picked up the device and turned to my approaching captain and driver. Kiesling, guarding an arm across his chest, limped and frowned. Wincing from his burns, Zhao was wide-eyed and looked at the scene as if he was on another planet.

I held the haymo above my head. "I love this thing!"

Flames erupted behind me.

I spun around, grunting against the pain in my neck, ready to shoot more lasers. How the hell could a decapitated dragon could breathe fire?

The smaug was still dead. Flames sprang from its body and severed head. I had to back away from the blaze as it grew and hungrily ate away at the dragon. I'd never seen such a thing. Night was pretty much upon us and the bright flames seemed to be the only thing that existed. After a few seconds, the smaug had been reduced to a pile of glowing yellow embers.

Then Kiesling spoke.

"You're in so much damn trouble, Williams." He tried to point at me with the arm he'd been coddling, then cried out in pain. "I think I broke my arm."

I bent over to look. "I can make you a sling for the ride back. I've seen Yolanda fix worse in a day or two."

"Ride back?" Zhao said. "The Slayer is trashed."

I turned and looked at our apparatus. It looked like a crushed and burned can of soda. "I guess we're going to have to radio for someone to come get us."

Kiesling's voice trembled with a serious heaping of anger. "If you think you can do whatever you want, that you can't get fired because we need smoke eaters, you're dead wrong. We can *make* smoke eaters now. You almost got us killed today, and I'm going to have your badge for it."

"Fuck all that," I said, turning to Kiesling and hiking a thumb over my shoulder. "Did you not just see that dragon burst into flames?"

# CHAPTER 2

I don't know what it is about deep voices on the other side of closed doors, but it drives me crazy. Sunk into a blue cloth chair – it felt like wool – outside Chief Brannigan's office, I wasn't able to understand anything Captain Kiesling and the chief were saying. I mean, I knew they were talking about me, but that sure as hell didn't put me at ease.

Was Brannigan defending me? Was Captain Kiesling being diplomatic and not burying me in too much shit? Maybe he'd dumped all his anger on the ride back?

After the smaug had self-destructed out in the wastes, Kiesling radioed Smoke Eater headquarters and asked them to send somebody to pick us up because a member of his crew had gotten Slayer 10 demolished. The propellerheads, as calculating and even-tempered as ever, didn't ask him to go into any more detail.

That wouldn't stop rumors spreading like a plague. About me, about what had happened. Smoke Eater Division is an offshoot of the fire department, and from everything Chief Brannigan told me about his days with the FD, the traditions are the same. Gossip just happens to be one of those traditions.

Want everyone on the planet to know something? Tell a smoke eater. It had probably reached every ear before the smaug's head hit the ground. It would get blown out of proportion, too, more than likely. By the time it got back to me, they'd be saying I rammed the dragon with the Slayer truck, lit Zhao on fire, and shot Kiesling in the arm.

I'd hoped like hell headquarters wouldn't send Captain Jendal and Renfro, and whatever rookie had taken my spot on their crew, to pick us up. It was slowly creeping in that I might have screwed the pooch, and I didn't want to face my old crew until my guilt had faded to a manageable level.

Kiesling didn't wait around for the en route apparatus to arrive. Without a word to either me or Zhao, he limped off toward the road. Of course, Zhao and I followed. Kiesling said nothing the two miles or so we walked until Cannon Truck 8 – a smoke eater crew I knew but never worked with – showed up and gave us a ride back. That's when Kiesling released all the words he'd been holding in.

His verbal assault went on and on, which made me feel worse. The other crew listened with wide-eyes as he ranted and raved about how I'd taken my sweet-ass time shooting the dragon and that I was a loose cannon, yadda, yadda, yadda. The usual shit.

I chose to keep quiet, which wasn't my regular way of doing things. Usually, if someone comes at me or is throwing shade where I can hear, I go on the offensive. That wouldn't have improved things at all in the back of Cannon Truck 8. Neither would blubbering out excuses and apologies.

I'd been fully-prepared for the cannon truck crew to crack jokes about me, if only to lighten the mood, but they never asked for my take on what had happened, didn't even respond to Kiesling after he'd finished bitching. Kiesling seemed to be cool with that, because after he was done he stared out the window until we pulled up to the front of headquarters. The cannon truck folks told us to have a better day before they drove off.

Outside Brannigan's office, I'd been yanking on a loose thread in the blue chair. I was getting bored and needed a distraction from the muffled voices, so I pulled out my holoreader to see what was new on the Feed. There was a chance I made the news, slaying the smaug. If it made me look good, I'd show Brannigan. If not… well, I hadn't seen any news drones flying around. Then again, I'd been busy doing my job, and plenty of Ohio smoke eaters had been captured on film without them ever knowing.

I clicked on the news thread. An anchor lady hovered above my holoreader's screen. "It was only completed a few months ago, but the Theresa Renee Parker Memorial Wraith Enclosures have brought about a huge spike in immigration to Parthenon City."

What a mouthful.

Theresa had been a firefighter under Brannigan, before he became a smoke eater. She'd been eaten by dragon at a house fire they'd been fighting. Later, she was also the first wraith Brannigan trapped in this weird, Canadian ghost remote we now use. Brannigan had plans to pass out wraith catchers to the general public and have us smoke eaters teach them how to use it in the unlikely event they ran into one of those ugly fuckers.

Wraiths are the ghosts of people killed by dragons. My mama and daddy never understood it and would always ask me to explain wraiths to them, since I had to learn about them in smoke eater academy. After a lot of trial and error, I came up with a simple explanation that seemed to satisfy my parents.

Everybody thought dragons were make-believe until they emerged from below ten years ago. I figure it's the same with ghosts. They go together like a crocodile and the plover bird that cleans its teeth. Dragons need wraiths to protect their ash nests while they go back underground, or fly, or crawl off to burn down some more shit.

I hadn't given the smaug a chance to use it, but all dragons can shoot electromagnetic pulses. It kills our equipment, forcing us to use ancient backup like lances and shields. And if you consider human souls to be made of energy, it's easy to see that a dragon could manipulate it to basically create an electric ghost guardian that would claw your throat open if you got too close.

That's not what I finally told Mama and Daddy, though. To them I said that dragons were created by the devil and if they kill someone, they enslave their souls.

They accepted my explanation, but that's because they're all about the churchy shit, and don't really watch the news. But it created a new problem: Daddy didn't want me to be a smoke eater anymore.

"It'd be terrible enough to lose you," he'd said. "How do you think I'd feel if some ugly-ass dragon turned your everlasting soul into one of those things? Our people were slaves long enough."

He had a point. It hurt to hear my daddy beg me to quit being a smokie, mostly because I'd been thinking about it myself and it just made it that much harder not to turn in my resignation.

The newslady on my holoreader said, "We met up with Ted Sevier, who led construction of the enclosures, along with input from Chief Cole Brannigan of the smoke eaters, and newly-elected Mayor Tilda Ghafoor."

A wraith wall appeared on my holoreader. It was like a long aquarium tank where the ghosts floated around inside, baring their electric teeth and clawing at the glass. Where legs should have been, the wraiths only had tattered flesh that trailed under them like a beat-up flag.

"This is it," said a skinny white guy with thick blond hair that touched his shoulders.

The words that floated under his image told me it was Ted Sevier, but I knew him well enough. We'd seen him every so often when we'd dropped off sleeping dragons.

He spread his hands as he stood in front of the glass-encased wraiths, smiling like he was showing off a brand-new hover-car. "It's one of four enclosures, but we see all of them acting as a single unit. North, south, east, and west."

The Feed cut to a news drone's view of the enclosure from above. Shaped like a hexagon, the top of the enclosure was covered by –

"Reinforced steel and a laser-field cover the top so no dragons can fly out," Sevier kept yapping as the image moved to show each enclosure at different points surrounding Parthenon City. "The ground is obviously open so the dragons can emerge when they're attracted to each enclosure's wraith energy – we have plenty of that – and the dragons can return below if they want. But we've found something very interesting as we've studied them inside the enclosures. Most of the dragons stay. They mate, fight, live their scaly lives. I think they feel safe with all of the wraiths in the walls. They don't have to kill people, we've provided the wraiths for them. They sometimes cannibalize each other for food, of course, but we let nature take its course. When we need to, we tranquilize the dragons and go in to draw blood for the hospitals."

I shook my head. These people were trippin'. Sure, dragon blood saves lives. I'm not against that. But this was going to go to shit someday and the scalies were going to make up for lost time and kill way more people than their blood had saved. I just hoped I'd be long gone when it happened.

The Feed cut back to Sevier, who was still grinning smugly. "Now, a question we get a lot is how we refill the wraith walls when they disappear, especially when dragon fatalities are at an all-time low. The answer is that we don't. We've instituted a constant electrical current within the walls to keep these same wraiths floating around for good."

Wraiths out in the wild tended to disappear within a couple months of being created, kind of like a battery running out of juice. By then, the scalies' eggs are hatched and there's no more use for the wraith to prowl the ash heaps.

"We're the first city in the country to implement these enclosures," Sevier said. "Many other cities, even internationally, have been in contact with us so they can have their own wraith enclosures. I do have to give credit to Canada for providing us with the means to do this, although we're unable to contact them to give our thanks."

Brannigan was the reason for that when he attempted to stop one of Toronto's dragon sacrifices. Canada had given us the means to take down dragons without killing them, but they shut their doors to us for good after that. A little bit later, they decided to do the same to everybody else. Chief B must have really given them a bad impression about how the rest of the world acted. Then again, the rest of the world didn't hold a lottery to see who would be dragon victuals.

The news lady reappeared in the air above my holoreader. "And since Parthenon City is the sole source of both dragon blood and the means to keep dragon attacks to the lowest anywhere in the world, many from all over the country are flooding in to receive the benefits."

A man wearing a Robot Football League polo replaced the news lady. He held a little, frizzy-haired girl in his arms who couldn't stop staring at the camera.

"I came here for my family," the man said. "There are too few cities spread out nowadays. Everything else is just ash. I came from Little Rock. They did their best, but they couldn't stop these monsters. And my Sadie here," he nodded to the little girl, "she was born with a heart defect. She's needs the medicine they make with the dragon blood. Nothing else can help."

Back to the news lady, "That's just one family, but there are hundreds more that have recently arrived. More are expected. Mayor Ghafoor, in a statement this morning, had this to say."

The mayor, a small woman in a pink hijab, floated in front of my face, standing behind a podium. "Parthenon City welcomes our new citizens. We hope you find happiness, and I look forward to all of us working together."

I liked our new mayor, especially compared to the asshole in office before her, who'd nearly gotten me killed. Ghafoor had taken a page from her predecessor's book in implementing fire droids, much to Brannigan's disappointment. But the robots were being used as supplemental manpower instead of replacing firefighters and leaving them jobless. It was a compromise even Brannigan agreed to, despite his hatred for metal men.

What I liked about Ghafoor was that she actually seemed to give a damn, even if I didn't agree with how she went about things sometimes. I guess that's the thing about politicians: you never get the perfect person to represent you. But Ghafoor listened to us and other emergency services, to the civilians. That went a long way with me.

"However," the news lady reappeared, "not everyone is optimistic about the influx of new Parthenians. Former Droid Factory executive, Duncan Sharp, has formed a group he calls PC First."

A man in a black turtle neck stood in front of a line of men who looked exactly like him: hair longer in the front than the back and slicked to the side, cheeks red with fury, and neon holotorches in each of their fists.

"Not that asshole again."

I paused the Feed and looked up to see Patrice Johnson, a smoke eater on Slayer 4, poking her bald head through the doorway.

"Hey, girl!" Smiling, I jumped up and pulled her into a hug.

She danced me around in a circle. "You all right? I heard you knocked your captain the fuck out and then drove your Slayer into a dragon hole."

"You know damn well that's not what happened." I plopped back into the blue chair.

Patrice sat in the one across from me, laughing. "Ah, I'm just fucking with you."

She was shorter than me, but stout. She could easily throw me over her shoulder and run a mile before her legs gave out. Everyone called her Dynamite.

One day, when Patrice walked in on her crew talking about shaving their heads as a sign of brotherhood, she'd been excited to join in. But the dudes on her crew told her she was excused from participating. Only the men had to do it. Next shift, the crazy bitch walks in with a head as smooth and bald as a fire droid's. And what's better, the men had been too chicken shit to do it themselves. Patrice kept the bald look ever since. It worked for her, honestly.

I nodded toward the man's image floating above my holoreader. "So, you know this guy?"

"Know *of* him. We had a false alarm at the Conlin building the other day. Him and his people were across the street running their mouths. Talking about putting Parthenon City first. Hating on the folks moving in from other cities. You know the type."

"Yeah," I said. "I do."

"Fool starts calling these new people rats. Rats, T. Saying they're this generation's greatest plague, eating up all the food, taking all the medicine. Talking 'bout how the mayor is too soft and won't protect the true citizens from dirty out-of-towners."

I shook my head.

"I couldn't believe my ears," Patrice said.

"What was his name again?"

She rubbed her bald head, remembering. "Shoop? No, Sharp. Duncan Sharp."

I'd read somewhere that all villains think they're the hero of their own story. Bullshit. They just don't care one way or the other. Everybody has to stop and do some self-reflection to make sure they don't trip up along the way and become an asshole. That's the difference between villains and heroes. Heroes have the ability to stop and examine if what they're doing is the right thing, even if it'll make it harder to get what they want in the end.

I'm not claiming to be hero, and I sure as shit ain't a villain, but I'd been doing some serious self discovery these last couple of months.

Patrice's snorted a laugh. "We got his ass, though."

"What did y'all do?"

"When we were leaving the scene, we passed by all of them out there in their dumbass turtlenecks. Right when that Sharp dude was really getting worked up on the microphone, my driver laid on the air horn." Patrice clapped her hands, threw her head back, and laughed so loud I was sure Brannigan could hear it in the next room.

I couldn't help it; I burst out laughing with her, tears coming to my eyes.

"And they start scattering everywhere," she said, "covering their ears and searching for cover. My driver ain't letting up, and all of us are cracking up in the Slayer. The only one of 'em left out there is Sharp, and he's just glaring at us with hands up like this."

Patrice turned her elbows toward the ceiling. Hands at each side of her head, she scrunched up her face, as if she was trying to be menacing, but was too uncomfortable to get the job done.

"Patrice." Her captain appeared at the door. "We have to go."

"Alright, Cappy." Patrice stood and patted my knee before bouncing out into the hallway.

Her captain followed behind her, but slowed long enough to point to me and say, "Nice going today, Williams."

I sighed and grabbed my holoreader. Duncan Sharp hovered there, frozen in a snarl, fist raised in the air. How people could take him and his ideas seriously was ludicrous. But it was happening. The Feed, instead of ignoring this xenophobic circle jerk, was giving it a larger platform.

I slapped away the hologram. "*You're* the rat, motherfucker."

When I looked up, the chief's office door was open with an arm-in-a-cast Kiesling and Brannigan standing there, eyes on me.

With a cocky grin, Brannigan said, "That mouth is going to get you in trouble, Williams. You weren't talking about me, were you?"

# CHAPTER 3

"Can I get you some coffee, water, or anything?" Brannigan asked, closing the door behind me.

I stood there with hands in my pockets. "I'm good."

My uniform was coated in sweat and smelled like a fireplace someone had used for a urinal. I needed a shower.

The Feed projected from the chief's wall, but was muted. An advertisement for popup, dragon-proof tiny houses was on. I'd seen it more times than I cared to count. The guy in the ad danced some strange pachanga as he opened a large crate. All four sides fell down and revealed a thick, gray square. With a ridiculous smile, the man hit a button on a small remote. The square unfolded and built itself, finishing into a small home. After the man shook his booty into the front door, a phone number appeared on screen, claiming discounts for newly-arrived citizens of Parthenon City. Businesses were seeing opportunity with the influx of people moving in. For them, it was time to exploit and make bank.

Brannigan walked around to his chair behind the desk. He was wearing the orange shirt of a chief.

Golden, crossed lances were pinned to his collars.
His shield, secured above his left breast pocket,
reflected the ceiling lights. It was still weird to see
him dressed like this. It didn't fit, like a businessman
wearing b-boy clothes. I wondered if Brannigan was
bored with his position, slaying paperwork instead of
dragons. Maybe that's why he was making all of us do
unsatisfying work, too. Misery forces company.

He sat down and extended a hand to the chair in
front of him. "Relax. I just want to know what's up."

I breathed deep through my nose and took the seat
he offered. "Chief, I just want to say–"

"Get the hell out of here with that chief stuff,"
Brannigan said with a laugh. "It's Cole or Brannigan,
or old ass – and you used to call me that a lot. I
might be running shit, but that doesn't mean I'm
above you. Hell, I probably wouldn't have made it
through rookie school without you."

We both knew that wasn't true. Brannigan was
a steamroller. When he set his mind on something,
especially if you told him he couldn't, he'd bust ass to
accomplish anything.

I couldn't tell if he was trying to put me at ease
or was being genuine, but Brannigan was the kind
of guy where what you saw was what you got. He
had no filter and didn't give a damn what anybody
thought of him. I always wanted to be like him in
that way, but sometimes I worried I was only *trying*
not to care what anybody thought and that secretly,
unknown even to myself, I was insecure as fuck.

"Cool, Brannigan."

He eyed me for a second, like a concerned father,

even bunching up his gray eyebrows as he did it. "So Afu tells me you think you might have lost your passion for the job."

Goddamn it.

I huffed and rolled my eyes.

"Is it true?"

"I told him that in confidence."

Brannigan nodded. "I guess he's just worried about you."

"No, he just wanted to get back at me for breaking up with his goofy ass. Probably thought it would make him look good."

"You and Afu broke up?"

"Didn't tell you *that* did he?" I leaned forward in my seat. "Anyway, I don't feel like talking about this, Chief. I mean, Brannigan. Aren't we here to debrief what went down with the smaug?"

Brannigan stuck his tongue behind his upper lip. I'd noticed him do this a few times since becoming chief. It was a tick that helped him retain some tact before he spoke. Otherwise, he would have just let loose with whatever he was thinking. He had to keep his cool. Act like somebody he wasn't. That had to be frustrating.

"Yeah." He leaned forward, too, resting his forearms on the desk. "We're here to talk about what happened out there today, but I think this shit about you losing your passion is related. True or false?"

He had me there. But I shrugged a non-answer.

"What is it?" Brannigan asked. "Is it because I became chief? Are you wanting to focus on your DJing? Are you mad because I haven't been able to come out to any of your gigs? I can't take Bethany to

27

a club. She's seven. Although she'd probably be able to kick all of the bouncers' asses."

I'd intentionally not invited Brannigan to my DJ gigs, if only for the fact that I played music at the clubs while wearing my power suit. It was my gimmick, and I was both glad and surprised that it hadn't gotten back to the department. There was no official rule against it, but I was sure it would be frowned upon.

"It has nothing to do with any of that." My voice came out louder, angrier than I'd intended. But oh well. "I voted for you to be chief, DJing ain't paying the bills just yet, and I understand you're busy with your family and work. So, don't make this about you. You really want to know what I think?"

He nodded and waved his fingers like a fighter saying, 'Bring it on.'

Alright, I brought it. "I think this bullshit with keeping scalies alive is a mistake. Soon there's going to be too many of them to fight and no amount of wraith walls or Sandman lasers is going to be enough. I didn't get into this job to be high-end animal control."

"Why did you get into this job?" Brannigan asked.

"I wanted to help people." Such a cliché answer. It's what everybody says. Didn't make it any less true. But besides this catchall statement, every smoke eater has an additional reason, the *real* reason, and not because they were born to breathe dragon smoke.

Brannigan, as usual, caught my bullshit. "Give me a break, Williams. It's me, for fuck's sake. If you were only about helping people, you'd be fine with how things have changed. The dragon blood, ieiunium curate. *That* helps people. The enclosures help people.

28

Be honest."

"I want action." I slapped Brannigan's desk as I said it. The release of built-up tension felt good. I had to sit there and appreciate it.

A knowing smile spread across Brannigan's face as he leaned back into his chair. "You sure got some action today, didn't you?"

Well, my good feeling didn't last long did it? Figures.

"I feel like shit that the Slayer got wrecked," I said. "And that my crew got hurt."

"Give me your version of what happened today."

I did, although it was strictly the facts. I might have skipped the part where I taunted the dragon instead of shooting it. Brannigan listened. He never made a face, or gave any impression that he was pissed off. I wondered what he thought of the smaug bursting into flames.

"It just caught fire?" Brannigan asked.

"Yeah, for no reason. Never seen anything like it."

"Maybe the ignis gland erupted when you cut its head off."

"I thought about that, but if that's what happened, I would have seen the fire start in the throat, and everything from the neck up was separated from the rest by a good three feet or so. The whole dragon ignited at once." I snapped my fingers. "Hot as shit, too. I'd say even hotter than the usual dragon fire. I know that sounds crazy."

"No," Brannigan said. "Nobody believed me when I thought Mayor Rogola had something to do with the wraith fires. We need to get the propellerheads on this so it doesn't bite us in the ass. After we're done here, I'd like you to go out there with them."

"The location is in the report. They don't really need me, do they? What's left of the smaug is near the overturned Slayer truck." I dropped my head, shaking it in defeat. I'd gotten so caught up in talking about the combusting dragon I'd almost forgotten why I was sitting in front of Brannigan. "And if I'm suspended for what happened today, what's the point?"

He cleared his throat. "When I was an engineer with the fire department, this was, like, almost twenty years ago. I was speeding in the engine, on the way to a fire, way over what our SOPs allowed. It had just rained and I should have disengaged our pump's exhaust brake. I didn't. Coming around a curve, we hydroplaned. I did my best to correct, but it was out of my hands at that point. We spun around twice, jumped the curb, and hit three parked cars. Five-inch hose spilled everywhere. Every vehicle involved was totaled, including the fire engine. The only reason we didn't roll over was because we'd hit a fire hydrant too. It got stuck under the pump and helped prop us up."

"Damn," I said.

"It could have been worse. Those cars could have been occupied. Our engine could have rolled, and injured or killed everybody on board. Accidents happen, but I can look back and see what I did wrong that day."

I sighed – more of a groan. "So what's my punishment? One shift without pay? Three?"

Brannigan laughed. "Did my bad habits rub off on you or were you always so to-the-point? I can't remember."

I laughed, too – a small one. More like a sputter of the lips. I still felt like the world was crashing down on me. "I just hate the waiting. If something bad is going to happen, I'd rather just get it over with. What's it going to be? If not a suspension then, what, a fine? Termination?"

"You really think I'd fire you?"

I shrugged. "Captain Kiesling said—"

"Kiesling is a 'Yes' man. And sometimes I think if I ever stopped walking abruptly, he'd fly right up my ass."

I smiled.

"But I also have to look at what you failed to do on that dragon call. You *wanted* a dragon fight, and you made up your mind that you were going to get one no matter what the rules say or what your superior officer thought. Hearing both you and Kiesling's accounts tells me there were plenty of times you could have hit that scaly with the Sandman and called it a day. I know you miss the adrenaline rush, Williams. Hell, you think I don't?"

He didn't give me time to respond.

"There's no way I'd rather stay cooped up in an office all the time when I could be plunging my laser sword into one of those ugly bastard's heads," he said. "But I was given a shit ton of responsibility after Chief Donahue died. I didn't even want it, but you and everybody else chose me.

"You know what separates firefighters and smoke eaters from regular people?"

"Imaginative use of four-letter words and a higher mortality rate?"

The side of Brannigan's lips curled up. Real

31

recognizes real, and smartass recognizes smartass.

"Ain't that the truth," Brannigan said. "But we can also adapt to sudden change much better. We have to. I want to treat what happened today as a learning experience. I want you to see that, even though we don't get to do all the cool shit we used to, in the end it's better for everybody. I don't want anyone dying on my watch.

"You know, when we went to Canada, I thought all of those Canucks were crazy. Keeping dragons alive? Containing them? I thought it was a wasted effort with no benefit."

"What changed?" I asked.

"The Canadians were doing it for their reasons. We're doing it for ours. I fully give you permission to shoot me dead if I ever try to start up a dragon sacrifice program, but, Tamerica, we've discovered a miracle in scaly blood. I know you hate the new protocol, but wouldn't you feel worse if some kid died when they could have been saved with a simple shot of the blue shit. It's more important than getting our jollies slicing and dicing."

"Becoming a dad has changed you." I didn't mean for it to come out so harshly.

"It's given me better perspective." He pulled out his holoreader and poked through pages floating in the air. "Kiesling has asked me to remove you from his crew."

I didn't like working with Kiesling, but it was a hit to my ego that he'd made it mutual.

"So what now?" I asked. "Am I going to trade spots with another smoke eater?"

Brannigan looked up from his holoreader. "No. We're giving Kiesling one of the new rookies."

Huffing, I said, "So I'm going to be stuck doing office work?"

The only thing worse than playing Sleepy Time Scaly was being cooped up in headquarters, typing my life away.

"Just give me a damn minute," Brannigan said. "I have to make it official on our roster."

"Make what official?"

Brannigan gestured for me to zip my mouth. I waited until he was done using a single finger to type. The old bastard was going to take forever while my career hung in the balance. I'd probably be cleaning toilets for the next six months. I was mentally kicking myself. Had knocking off that smaug really been worth it?

Yes. Yes it was. Worth every damn minute.

"Okay," said Brannigan. "It took a little maneuvering, but everyone should get a Feed message and it'll go into effect tomorrow at shift change."

"What'll go into effect?" This old white man had lost his mind.

Brannigan stood and held out his hand for a shake, grinning like the pachanga-dancing tiny house guy. "Congratulations…"

Standing, I shook his hand, not knowing why.

"…Captain Tamerica Williams."

"What the fuck?"

"Look over the Feed message I sent," Brannigan said. "It lists your crew and your apparatus assignment. You've been moved to tomorrow's shift. I'd hate to make you work forty-eight hours in a row, and your old Slayer truck is out of service anyway, so take the rest of the shift off. Might as well sleep here tonight, yeah?"

My head nodded in agreement.

"I really hope this will reignite your passion," Brannigan said, "but I understand if you come back in here some day to say goodbye. After you clean up, get with the propellerheads about what you saw happen to the smaug. Then, tomorrow at 0700, you'll be calling the shots on your own rig."

I stared at Brannigan, my mouth hung open. This was worse than getting fired or pushing holographic paperwork. He was punishing me under the guise of a promotion. Wasn't this some sneaky ass shit?

"Brannigan, I don't–"

Before I could go into my tirade about how Brannigan was torturing me with this new position, the Feed hovering off the wall caught my attention. It showed a smoldering house. Fire droids and firefighters were extinguishing the remaining embers. The words across the bottom read, 'Recent Fires, Suspected Suicide Arson.'

Brannigan turned on the volume before I had to ask.

"First assumed to be unrelated," the news lady's voice said, "fire marshals are now suspecting that no fewer than three recent fatal house fires were caused by suicide arsonists."

Photos of three different families appeared on screen. An elderly couple, two women holding a toddler and an infant, the last was a Latino family of five. My stomach sank before the news lady confirmed what I already knew.

"Each of these families died in their homes, unable to escape the blaze. Fire crews responded efficiently to each incident, but were unfortunately too late."

Three more pictures appeared: one of a middle-aged white man with a goatee, a young Asian woman with long hair, and a black man who looked like a bald-version of my Uncle Teddy.

"Now, investigators are revealing that, in each case, an individual seemingly unknown to the family was found inside. Strangers with no connections to the victims. Most startling of all, evidence indicates that these strangers were the cause of the fires."

"Fuck…"

"…me." I finished.

The fire chief appeared on screen. An unseen reporter asked, "Why have you waited until now to reveal your findings?"

"We wanted to make sure this was, in fact, what we suspected. It appears that these three individuals entered the victims' homes, two of them in the middle of the night, and, using an accelerant of some kind, lit themselves on fire.

"We're working with police, but at this time we have no motive. There doesn't seem to be any connection between the victims or the perpetrators themselves. We don't want to scare anyone, but right now, we're encouraging every citizen to be vigilant. Lock your doors. If you see something suspicious, or anyone who shouldn't be in your neighborhood, don't hesitate to report it."

The reporter asked, "You said some kind of accelerant was used. Do you know what specifically?"

Rubbing the back of his neck, the fire chief said, "Honestly, an accelerant is the best thing we can guess at. We didn't find any trace of gasoline or anything else, but there's no other explanation as to how these fires grew so fast. Maybe an incendiary device, much like a bomb. I'm… I'm at a loss. I…."

The last image of the fire chief was of him shaking his head, bunching his lips, and clearly holding back tears. He rushed away, waving off the reporters.

Appearing again, the news lady said, "We've learned that one of the arsonists, Gerald From," - a picture of a white guy came up "had recently moved to Parthenon City from Denver, just before it was destroyed in last month's drake swarm. And it seems tension surrounding the arrival of immigrants is growing worse."

# CHAPTER 4

"Sometimes I think the Feed tries to rile people up on purpose." A driver named Holland's voice echoed off the tile walls.

Tucked fifty feet away in the shower at the very back of the locker room with my back under the high-pressure stream of water and I could still hear his loud ass. He was talking to another smoke eater named Feingold, and I guess they didn't realize how much acoustics the locker room had.

"Yeah, man," Feingold said. "But one of those arsonists was a refugee."

"They're not refugees."

"Sure they are. They left their cities to come here because we have things they want. I bet you anything the other two aren't originally from here either."

"Feingold, you're from fucking Kansas."

"Well," a long moment passed, "that was years ago. This is a new problem."

"If it doesn't involve a dragon," Holland said, "it isn't my problem."

"That's not very compassionate."

Exiting the shower, I used my favorite big, fluffy towel to dry off. When I first came to Smoke Eater headquarters, I was worried about the coed locker room. Some female smokies even roomed with men during rookie training. Brannigan had shared a room with Captain Jendal. When I told Jendal – Naveena, I call her – that I didn't feel comfortable about it, she said she understood my feelings, but that it was a way to make things fair for everybody and to instill that we were a unified force. We were to behave professionally. If two dudes could room together without fucking, so could members of opposite sexes. Several smoke eaters are transgender, too, so it just made it easier to say, 'This is where we shit, shower, and shave. Period.'

Although we can be crude, smoke eaters are held to an extremely high standard. Harassment of any kind would be handled with extreme prejudice. What that meant exactly, I didn't know. It never came up. But heaven help you if you ever failed to put the toilet paper on the dispenser roll.

I was about to get dressed when Holland's voice carried through the locker room. "Holy shit, have you read your Feed messages?"

"I don't ever look at that stuff," said Feingold. "Why? What's going on?"

"Look."

I didn't even have to guess. They were looking at Brannigan's message about me getting promoted. I hadn't even looked at it yet. I keep my holoreader in my locker when I'm on duty. Too many smokies have gotten their devices burnt or smashed carrying them around in their pockets on dragon calls. Being a captain would change that. I'd have to keep it on me all the time.

"You've got to be kidding me," Feingold said.

I wrapped the towel around my torso and crossed my arms. A hot ache formed in my chest. Feingold and Holland didn't even know I was back here. I didn't like being talked about, but if people were going to talk shit, I'd rather it hear out of their own mouths and have them look me in the eye while they did it. So, slowly, I walked toward where my fellow smoke eaters were having their little bitch session.

"I know," said Holland. "It's such bullshit. You hear what she did today?"

"Everybody's talking about it. I'm sure the smokies in Memphis have heard about it. If I'd known wrecking a Slayer and nearly getting your crew eaten was how you got promoted, I would have done it already."

"I'm surprised that fat ass of hers can fit into a power suit."

They laughed, and I picked up my pace. All I had on was a towel, but I didn't give a damn. I'd kick their asses anyway.

"And they promoted the bald chick, too!"

"Let me ask you something," said Holland. "Do you think these women smokies can do the job just as good as us?"

I rounded the corner and leaned against a locker. "I've breathed more smoke, slain more scalies, and trapped more wraiths in a week than either of you two punk bitches have done in your entire career."

Holland was dressed and straddling a bench, while Feingold was naked and held a towel in front of his junk. Both of them snapped their heads toward me, eyes wide. Feingold's towel slipped. He cupped his privates with both hands.

"And that's not even counting the robots I chopped up when Rogola attacked headquarters and tried to kill us all," I said. "Remember that? Oh, wait. You wouldn't. Because you weren't there."

Holland swallowed. Feingold remained frozen with a handful of nothing.

"And like you saw in Brannigan's message, I'm now a captain. That's right, me. A black woman whose stellar booty fits perfectly in her power suit thank-you-very-much, who has no tolerance for bullshit and who now outranks you. So I'm going to give you three options." For emphasis, I raised a finger for each. "I can either write up your asses, kick your asses, or both of your asses can go wash every single apparatus in the bay right now. What's it going to be?"

Feingold gathered up his towel and fought Holland to be the first out the door. Both of them shouted, "Sorry, Captain!" as they left.

I sat on the bench and sighed.

A while back, Brannigan had sent me a holobook about women in the fire service. Holland and Feingold's gum-flapping was nothing compared to what the first female firefighters had to go through. For them, every single day was hell, just to do the job they loved.

In the old days, when a woman firefighter would walk into a firehouse kitchen, all of the men would walk out. The women were ostracized, hazed, had their reputation shit on. Everyone said they were too weak to do the job, even civilian women.

Thinking about it now made me feel guilty for wanting to leave smoke eating. Those women firefighters didn't quit and they had to fight against more than just dissatisfaction.

"The Captain is in the house!" the deep voice boomed through the locker room.

I looked up and there he was, Afu Kekoa, my ex-boyfriend. His green duty shirt stretched across his chest as his dark tattoos peeked out from the collar and short sleeves. He'd tied his long black hair into a bun. That always used to turn me on.

*Used* to. Right.

I rolled my eyes at him and trudged back to my locker to get dressed. The propellerheads were waiting and I really didn't want to get caught up in an ex-lover's spat.

Afu followed on my heels. "Hold up, teine."

Teine. It was one of the only Samoan words I remembered.

"I'm not your girl," I said, slipping on panties under my towel. Afu had seen me naked a hundred times, but I'd revoked that privilege.

"What's with the attitude?" he said. "You broke up with me, remember? I'm not the one acting like we can't still be friends."

I turned my back to him as I pulled a duty shirt over my head. "Friends don't go tell the chief that I lost my passion for the job."

"Ah, shit."

The locker room was silent as I finished dressing, tying off the last boot. Afu could have walked out, as far as I knew, even though his heavy steps were hard to miss. The man was built like a hover-train. But when I turned around, he was still standing there, hands on his hips and a slight, guilty smile on his face. At six foot three, he stood a good eight inches taller than me, and had shown, more than once, how easily he could lift me with one arm.

"I'm just looking out for you," said Afu. "I don't want you burning out. You're one of the best smokies on the job. I don't know what I was thinking. I guess I thought Brannigan wouldn't think less of you. That he'd be able to help. He's probably seen this kind of thing before."

"What kind of thing?" I thinned my eyes. Maybe if I tensed hard enough, lasers would shoot out and set that long hair on fire.

Afu shrugged. "I don't know. Depression?"

"I'm not fucking depressed. I'm bored and unsatisfied. There's a big difference."

"Yeah, well, I was right, though. Brannigan didn't think less of you at all. He promoted you!" Those big teeth appeared with Afu's fifty-mile-smile, white as wraith fire. "Captain Williams. Wow. This is crazy. Just don't go bossing me around too much, yeah?"

"You don't have to worry about that," I said, looking for a gap on either side of him to slip through. The big bastard took up the whole space between the lockers. "We won't have to deal with each other outside of… these kinds of run-ins."

Afu's two bushy eyebrows bunched together. "T, didn't you read the Feed message?"

Oh, hell no.

I threw open my locker and grabbed the holoreader lying under a bra. With a finger press against the notification in the top right corner, Brannigan's message floated up from the screen. My eyes darted over the message, too frantic to read the whole thing through. Congratulations to Captain Tamerica Williams, blah, blah, blah. Following transfers will take effect tomorrow…

Shit. It floated there in holographic green. Official. Practically irreversible.

The new crew of Cannon Truck 15: Captain Yours Truly, Dynamite Patrice Johnson as driver, and – I had to read it five times before I finally accepted it – Afu Kekoa as smoke eater.

"And how about that?" Afu said. "They promoted your girl, Johnson. We're going to be a hell of a crew. And we can all hang out off shift, like we used to."

I turned off the holoreader and shoved it into my pocket. "This isn't right. This has to go against some kind of conflict of interest rule."

"We aren't dating anymore," Afu said. "And the way you're acting, it's like you don't want to be friends either."

He looked sad. Puppy dog eyes came easy to Afu. What sucked is that it was always sincere when he did it. I don't think he had a manipulative bone in his body.

I relaxed my face, dropping the ache of irritation I'd built up in my cheeks and around my eyes. Could I work with Afu on a crew? Supervise him? Was I seriously thinking about this?

"Tammy," my mama would say, "looks like you don't have much of a choice."

I tried, but failed, to conjure a smile. "This'll be… fun."

Afu must have thought I was throwing an olive branch at his face, because he was grinning. Then again, Afu had the emotional memory of a goldfish.

He never stayed sad or upset for long. Eventually, no matter what was happening, he'd revert back to his usual jolly-ass self. I hated that about him.

"You still DJing at Infinity Saturday night?" he asked. I nodded.

"Cool. I'll come out. Buy my new captain a drink. Might have a bag of sparks with me, too."

Sparks. Little pills of bottled static.

I didn't do that shit any more. It was a safe drug, but after a while, I got weirded out about putting hologram tech into my body. What if someone could figure out a way to hack into it and make you do things? Afu had said I was paranoid, but he'd quit sparking while we were dating out of respect. I guess he'd returned to the habit. Well, I might not have been his girlfriend anymore, but as his captain I could put a stop to it quick, fast, and in a hurry.

Afu turned and left me to the deafening quiet of the locker room, where I stood for a few more minutes before heading over to meet with the propellerheads.

This may sound crazy coming from someone who traps dragons and ghosts for a living, but thinking about all the responsibility Brannigan had dumped on my shoulders, the void of the unknown lying in front of me like an endless pit, the people on my crew I had to look out for and make sure didn't die, I was scared. I'd never been so goddamned scared in all my life.

# CHAPTER 5

"You say it was right here?" Yolanda, one of the
lead propellerheads, pointed a long metal pole at
the ground. She wore enough gear for a two-week
excursion and was monitoring at least three different
devices. The sphere at the end of her pole chirped as
Yolanda hovered it over glowing embers that clung to
the ash like wet paint. We were back at the scene of
my crime, where the smaug had burned away. It was
too dark to see and too early to care.

The embers on the ground looked like a neon stain in
the outline of the smaug, like how cops used to draw a
white line around dead bodies. The embers were yellow,
glowing more eerily than natural. This wasn't the usual
type of fire – the embers would have faded already – and
that included anything burned by dragon fire.

"Yeah, the smaug was right here," I said. "Can't
you see the radioactive dragon outline?"

A flashlight drone flew down to hover behind
us, whirling blades keeping it in the air. Yolanda
had sent it fifty feet above to get an aerial view of
the scene. It shined its light wherever Yolanda's gaze
went, wirelessly connected to her goggles, and now it
blinded me as the propellerhead tilted her head in my

direction. I held up a hand to block the light.

"Come on, now," Yolanda said. "I'm a scientist. I don't assume anything, even when it seems obvious."

I'd gone straight to Yolanda after I'd left the locker room. Not only was she one of the few other black women at headquarters but she was also, in my opinion, the smartest of the propellerheads. She'd basically invented ieiunium curate from dragon blood, and reverse-engineered the nonlethal laser cannon we'd gotten from Canada to create more for every apparatus in our fleet. But I didn't hold that against her. A lot of people would say she single-handedly brought on the current period of peace.

When I'd gone to talk to her about the smaug, Yolanda was busy in the watch room, helping other propellerheads monitor seismic activity deep below Ohio. Some goober had named it OSAS, for Ohio Seismic Alert System. It was how we were able to detect possible dragon emergences. Yolanda had expanded the technology by shooting monitor needles deep into the ground at different points all over the state. It had cut smokie response time in half.

She'd listened to what I had to say about the smaug, but said she would have to get back to me about it later. So I went to check in on my former engineer Zhao. He lay in a lab room in nothing but his boxers. Blue, sticky ieiunium curate had been slabbed all over his reddened body.

I apologized my ass off, but he only laughed and said, "That was the most action I've gotten since rookie school. Plus, this blue stuff will have me back to normal tomorrow. No hard feelings. Pinkie swear."

His words had taken the edge off my guilt, but I still felt like shit. I'd gotten him burned and tossed around inside a ton of metal. He might have already let it go, but I wasn't going to.

I've always been hard on myself.

Exhausted, I'd gone to my room and fallen asleep without bothering to take my uniform off. I was going to be wearing it in a few hours anyway as a captain. At five o'clock in the morning a loud rapping hit my door. My shift roommate, Jessica, only grumbled in her sleep as I got up to see who the hell was inviting a punch in the face.

Yolanda stood there in full yellow-coated propellerhead attire, a pair of goggles strapped around her forehead. "You ready to show me where this dragon burned up?"

I'd seriously considered slamming the door in her face and grabbing another hour and a half of sleep. But I was feeling penitent about what I'd done to Zhao, and the smaug had been turning to ash in my dreams all night anyway.

A few minutes later, I'd stepped into my armored power suit, had it seal itself around my body with a *click*, and was looking over what remained of the smaug.

"You know you didn't have to bring your power suit," Yolanda said. "We're just gathering data."

Said the woman wearing enough gear to send someone to Mars.

"I don't feel right out here in the ashes without it. Plus," I tapped the side of my helmet, "I like to stay in radio contact if any good dragon calls come in."

Yolanda nodded and the hovering drone bobbed its

light in sync, wobbling in the air. "I guess that kind of dedication is what will make you a good captain. Congratulations, by the way," she said, as if I'd just told her I'd had a great cup of coffee that morning.

That's how most propellerheads were; not really aloof, just "meh" about anything non-sciencey, especially the red tape of smoke eater administration.

"Thanks, Yo-yo," I said. "So what are you thinking happened to the smaug?"

"I'm picking up a butt load of voltage in these embers," she said, studying her holoreader. "First hypothesis that springs to mind is that the dragon's EMP reacted with the haymo grenade you threw. Maybe the ignis gland, as well?"

"You don't sound convinced by that."

The sky began to lighten in the east. I'd have to be getting back to headquarters soon for my first day as a captain.

"Well, it just doesn't make any sense," said Yolanda. "And we don't have a dead smaug to study. We just have these never-ending embers." She dug into the pack hanging from her shoulder and tossed me a jar. "Mind scooping some of that up for me?"

Our power suits had been built to withstand all kinds of hell, but opening that jar with my metal-covered digits was damn near impossible. Without a word, I handed the jar back to Yolanda. She twisted off the top and handed it back, trying hard, but failing, not to laugh. As I bent over to gather the coals into the jar, the heat pelted my face as if it were a full-on inferno. That was something new. Being a smoke eater, I could resist heat a lot more than the average person.

"The heat coming off of these embers is ridiculous," I said.

"Really?" Yolanda said. "That *is* interesting. I'll have to study the embers when we get back to headquarters. Then I can find out why. You haven't been feeling weaker lately have you? Has any smoke felt hard to breathe?"

She reached out to check my forehead. I slapped her hand away.

"I'm not losing my abilities. The fire that burned up the smaug was more intense than the flames coming out of its mouth."

"Maybe certain dragons, like the smaug, have an anatomical booby trap if killed…"

"Yolanda, I have to get back to headquarters."

"… like a surge of all their internal power bursting out at once. Maybe this has something to do with… but, no."

"What?"

She tongued the back of her teeth. "OSAS has been picking up some strange activity recently. Seismic of course, but also a strong frequency coming from underground. We sent smoke eaters to each point of activity to check it out but, by the time they arrived, the occurrence had gone and also no dragon. Lot of residual heat, though. At first I just put it off as an anomaly in the monitoring system…."

She was back in her own world, head twirling above the clouds. I was about to yell her name when my holoreader rang. It was Brannigan.

"You ready for today, Captain Williams?" Chief's holographic head materialized above my holoreader.

"Yeah," I said. "I'm just out here with Yolanda getting extra crispy dragon samples."

I pointed Brannigan's head toward Yolanda. She waved, grinning so wide it made her cheeks puff out.

"Hey, my favorite lady in yellow," Brannigan said. "Williams, I appreciate you looking into this, but we need you back at headquarters. Slayer 7 was scheduled to give a presentation to some Cub Scouts, but they just caught a run for a slimy Shenron making its way from Louisville."

"So you're sending me to tackle some kids."

"If it makes you feel better, you guys got the tougher job out of the two. You think dragons are mean? I sent the location to your holoreader. Basic stuff: what to do if you find a dragon egg, stop, drop and roll. You'll do fine."

"I'll be making Afu do all the talking."

"Perks of being a captain." Brannigan smiled.

"So why are you calling me and not dispatch?"

"Well—"

"I don't need a babysitter, Brannigan."

"I know we say 'sink or swim' but it's your first day as an officer – and you're going to do great – I just want to be here for you, since I'm the one who put you in this situation. Sometimes you need a lifeguard."

Maybe I should have been glad I wasn't being thrown to the wolves. Any captain would have told you they'd have loved having the chief act as a crutch for their first time being in charge. But I could walk just fine on my own, and I didn't need a daddy looking over my shoulder. I already had one who stuck his nose into my business every chance he could. And a mama who did that, too.

"Just do me a favor," I said.

"What's that?"

"Don't make this a regular thing."

Brannigan's digital head tilted to the side. "Watching over you or sending you to kids programs?"

"Both," I said.

# CHAPTER 6

"Oh, yeah, baby!" Patrice 'Dynamite' Johnson, my new driver, clapped and laughed. The sharp sound of her connecting hands bounced off the walls of the apparatus bay. "This is the dream team right here."

Her green uniform looked fresh off the loom. As I jogged closer, I saw that the smoke eater emblem on her shirt – two crossed lances behind a dragon skull – had the glossy look of fresh embroidery. Where it had said *Smoke Eater* above her right breast the day before, it now said *Driver*. She stood next to Afu, who'd already stepped into his power suit.

Behind them waited Cannon Truck 15. Its black storage bins were outfitted like every other smokie apparatus, but with the added artillery of a big-ass cannon on top, kind of like a fire department aerial ladder if the ladder could shoot dragons out of the sky. The cannons used to be awesome and lethal, able to level twelve story buildings. Now they were Sandman lasers like all the rest. The truck also had a smaller barrel, on the underside of the big one, which shot a metal chain net. It was manually cranked, which would be handy if it got hit with an EMP and lost power.

I blew Patrice a kiss she snatched out of the air and

tucked into a pocket that wasn't there. "You got you a new uniform, Patrice?"

"New clothes for a new promotion." She turned around and wiggled her ass.

"Enough of that shit," I said. "We've gotta go."

"Alright, T." Patrice smiled and hopped into the driver's seat. "I mean, Captain Williams."

The truck's engine snarled as Afu gave a thumbs up. "This is going to be fun."

I couldn't think of anything to say that would sound more like a captain than an ex-girlfriend, so I tucked in my lips and gave him a single nod. As usual, Afu didn't catch anything amiss and climbed into the back seat with a shit-eating grin.

I did a quick walk around of the truck, opening bins and looking over our equipment. The previous driver had done a great job keeping it clean and maintained. The purple and green lights, the black paint of the truck body, the conical length of the cannon, it all glistened. When I got to the front, I noticed a glossy black square in the center of the grill. I had never seen it on any of the rest of our fleet, and I knew Slayers and cannons inside and out.

When I leaned in for a closer look, the truck's sirens whooped. I must have jumped ten feet in the air.

"Motherfucker!" I covered my ears and glared at Patrice through the windshield.

"Sorry, Captain." She wasn't a damn bit sorry. She bounced in her seat, cackling. "I was just checking the audible warning signals."

"You ever do that again," I said, "and the next audible warning signal is going to be the swift sound of my foot up your ass. Let's go."

Patrice continued laughing.

Opening my door to the awaiting captain's seat, I hesitated. This was it. Placing my ass in that seat was officially taking the responsibility thrown at me. Thankfully, my body climbed into the rig before I could talk myself out of it.

My door shut with an explicit click and Patrice zoomed us out of the bay and into the open air, where the sky was filling with fat clouds that looked like moldy cauliflower. I tried not to take them as a bad omen.

"Maybe it'll storm and we won't have to do this stupid presentation," I said.

"Cappy?" Patrice asked. I was nowhere close to being comfortable with someone addressing me as Captain, or any of the cute shortenings of the title. "Can you tell me how to get there?"

"Oh, yeah," I said. "I guess that would help."

All smoke eater apparatus are equipped with a holoreader that receives alarms. It shows us where to go and sometimes they even send a short profile on the suspected type of dragon. Firefighters back in the old days had to memorize their districts.

I poked at the device's floating keys to get the Cub Scouts' address.

"What are your expectations of us, Captain Williams?" Afu asked from the back seat.

"Don't fuck up," I said.

After Patrice leaned over the steering wheel and laughed loud enough to break the windshield, I amended my answer.

"Look, this is all new to me," I said. "I would have been happy staying a smoke eater the rest of my life. Money is good enough in any position and I didn't want any of the headaches of supervising other people."

Patrice raised an eyebrow and took a few glances my way.

"Yeah, even cool people like you. So, we'll take every call individually and do what we do. You see something I need to know about, say something. We're a team. I don't want puppets waiting for me to pull on their strings. I know y'all and what you can do. We'll be alright."

"Damn," Patrice said. "She's even sounding like a captain now, Afu baby."

"Well, hell yeah," said Afu. "She sounded like a captain the whole time we were dating."

*Don't respond to that*, I told myself. Instead, I told Patrice the directions to the Cub Scouts.

If Patrice heard me, she didn't acknowledge it. "Afu, you need a strong queen telling you what to do, anyway. I'm surprised your big ass can put your power suit on the right way."

"Hey, I've been doing this longer than you," said Afu.

"Just not as good, bro. That's why I'm in the driver's seat and you're back there getting ready to be assaulted by a bunch of five-year-olds."

Afu laughed. "I'm never getting promoted. I don't want to sit on my ass behind a wheel. I want to be in the action. You got me fucked up if you think I want anything less."

"Hey, I'm just trying to set myself up for retirement. I'm going to find me a good man, have lots of babies. Maybe get a house out near one of those new settlements outside the city. Hell, I'll even raise sheep."

"Why not chickens?" Afu asked. "Who the hell wants sheep? There are all kinds of stories about dragons eating people's sheep."

Patrice shook her head hard and fast. "No way in hell. I hate birds. *Especially* chickens. And maybe the department will let me keep my power suit, so dragons won't fuck with my farm."

This banter went on for the next thirty minutes, while I sat there trying not to listen to any of it.

It was a Saturday, and the Cub Scouts met at a small metal building in the northern part of Parthenon City. When we pulled up, a large group of kids and a lone adult stood outside. The Cub Scout leader was a tired-looking woman in a gray sun dress and flip flops.

Patrice turned on our emergency lights and hit the air horn a couple times. The kids went wild, breaking away from the adult and waving their tiny arms like limp noodles in the air.

Patrice slammed on the brakes to avoid hitting the oncoming horde. "Are these little bastards trying to get run over?"

"Just park here," I said.

We hopped out and the kids immediately started talking all at once.

"My daddy is a garbage man."

"Do you keep a pet dragon at your house?"

"I want to drive the truck!"

A taller kid, older than the others, way too old to

be a Cub Scout, strolled up to the back of the group. "Are you guys in league with the po-po?"

He wore a green t-shirt showing off the rapper, Daddy Doody. If nothing else told me this kid was a little shit, his taste in music sure did. He smirked, as if what he'd said was hilarious, but I didn't understand what the hell he was getting at. I decided to ignore him.

"Afu," I said. "This is your show."

My smoke eater smiled proudly. Afu loved kids. I was sure he wanted at least four of his own. Our relationship had ended before we'd crossed that wobbly bridge, but it would have been one of many other nails in our coffin. I didn't want kids. Never have. I would have gone and gotten my uterus scooped out if it didn't cost so much. Plus, the procedure would have taken me out of dragon slaying for at least a month.

"All right, everybody," Afu said, raising his arms to get them all calmed down. "How are you doing?"

All the kids shouted, "Good!"

The older jerk in the back said, "Bored."

The Cub Scout leader took our arrival as an opportunity to lean against the chain link fence and puff on her bubble vape. She was going to be no help.

"We're the Ohio smoke eaters," Afu said, "and we're here today to talk to you about some important things you need to know."

"You guys came to my school," one of the kids said. "You told us all about it."

In a mishmash of cute voices, the others shouted, "Me, too!"

"Then this should be easy," said Afu. "Now, first I want to talk about what you do if you're in your house and you feel the ground shake."

"Get out of the house," one of them responded.

"That's right. You want to get out of your house as quickly as possible. Dragons like to emerge inside homes. So if you're outside you're safer. You also want to talk to your parents about having a meeting place, where everyone knows to go. Where's somewhere your family can meet up?"

"The mailbox!"

"Very good," Afu said. "The mailbox is a great place to meet and make sure everyone is out of the house."

"Unless the dragon eats your parents." The older kid snickered.

The Cub Scout leader shook her head as she exhaled a blue bubble.

The smaller kids whined, clearly upset at the thought of Mommy and Daddy dying upon the teeth of scalies.

"Well, it's our job to make sure that doesn't happen," Afu said, trying to console the younger scouts. "And if the house is smoky before you can get out, you want to do what?"

"Get low to the ground!"

"Yep," Afu said. "Heat and smoke rise, so you want to get as low as you can while you're making your way out of the house."

Oh, fuck. The older kid raised his hand.

"You have a question?" Afu pointed to him.

"Yeah, what happens if one of these refugee arsonists breaks into your house and locks you

58

inside?"

Afu looked like he'd been kicked in the nuts. "That's not–"

"And they burn you up. And all your toys." The older kid was addressing the little ones, trying to scare them.

It was taking all I had not to jump in and put the little bastard in his place.

"That's just scary stuff on the news," Patrice said. "And we handle dragons."

The older kid pointed to my driver. "Why is she bald? Did a dragon burn her hair off?"

I waved at the Cub Scout leader, trying to get her attention. She moved lazy eyes toward me.

"You mind if I take this older one around the truck."

The woman flapped her hand. "He's all yours."

"Come with me," I told the Daddy Doody fan.

Smiling like he'd earned a prize, the kid ran a greasy hand along the side of our truck. I led him to the other side while Afu started in on what to do if you see a wraith.

"I've seen all this stuff before," the kid said. "You guys come to my school every year."

"What's your name?"

"Toby."

"Well, Toby, have you ever seen this?" I raised the door to the bin housing my power suit.

"Duh. The dumb guy talking to the little kids is wearing one. It's not that special." He looked me up and down. "How do you get your big butt inside one?"

I grinned, swallowing the scream that wanted to break out. Popping open a pocket on my power suit, I ejected a wraith remote and handed it to him. "Know what that is?"

"No."

I grabbed his thumb and pressed it into the red button at the base. "Don't let go of that. It'd be very bad for you."

"Why?" His question dripped with attitude, but he kept his thumb pressed to the button.

"See, what you're holding is a wraith trapping remote. The black button traps the ghost. Can you guess what the red button you're pressing does?"

His eyes widened.

I nodded. "If you let go of that button, it's going to release the wraith I caught earlier today. If that happens, I'll jump over this truck to get the other kids to safety. The other two smoke eaters will help me. I don't think your Cub Scout leader will want to stick around. That'll just leave you and this nasty dead thing out here to get to know each other better. Can you feel it buzzing under your thumb, just waiting to get out, biting and slashing anyone who's around?"

Toby swallowed and stared at the remote.

"I don't like you scaring the other kids," I said. "I don't know why you have such an attitude problem, and I frankly don't care. Now, if you want me to take that remote from you and prevent an unnecessary bloody mess out here in the parking lot, you're going to do what I tell you. For the rest of the presentation, I want you to be on your best, and I mean *best*, behavior, alright?"

Toby said nothing. I smiled. "Now say, 'Yes, ma'am'" Toby trembled. "Yes, ma'am."

"Careful now." I pressed my thumb to the button and pulled the remote away.

His breath shook as if I'd just defused a bomb in front of him.

"Now get back to the other scouts and remember what I said."

When he disappeared to the other side of the truck, I let go of the button. The remote's display showed it empty of any wraiths.

Fucking kids.

I returned to where Afu was talking about never touching or playing with a dragon egg, to go straight to an adult and tell them about it. I doubted these kids would ever have to heed that warning. The enclosures had made it unlikely, and before that, wraiths guarding dragon ash heaps had dissuaded anyone from going on an egg hunt.

Patrice leaned over and whispered in my ear. "Whatever you did to that kid, it worked. He's shook."

I smiled and looked at Toby. He stood straight, listening attentively to everything Afu said.

My holoreader rang and I climbed back into the captain's seat of the truck to answer it. Again, Brannigan's head appeared.

"Ready for me to make your day?"

"We're back to killing scalies and no more of this Sandman bullshit?"

"Nice try. Wrap up your thing with the Cub Scouts. OSAS is picking up seismic activity in Sandusky – God, I hate that name."

"OSAS or Sandusky?" I asked.

Brannigan puckered his lips, thinking about

it. "Both, I guess. They're telling me the dragon emergence is going to happen within an hour. If it hasn't already. No one in Sandusky has called anything in because it's pretty much a ghost town, but we've put out an evacuation notice to be on the safe side."

"So if anybody is there, it'll be a few nosy rednecks who listen to our radio traffic," I said.

"Hey, like I always told you: empires fall and seasons change…"

"…but dumbasses are eternal," I finished.

"Also, the police and fire chiefs have asked all smoke eaters to be wary of any strange people around. They're grasping at straws on this arsonist thing."

"Because arsonists can also cause earthquakes." I rolled my eyes.

"It doesn't make sense to me either, but, if it puts their minds at ease, I'm telling you like I promised them I would. There might come a day when we need their help on something. Just focus on the dragon."

Something inside me could always tell when a dragon call was going to be good. Whatever was going down in Sandusky, it conjured goosebumps all over my body, and a pressurized heat filled my head, as if all my focus was coming to a single point right between my eyebrows.

But damn. This time I was in charge. This time I had to follow protocol and put any dragons we might find to sleep, then cart their asses to a wraith enclosure. I had two people under my command. The added weight of responsibility doused the initial adrenaline surge.

Abusing my position, doing my own thing and getting into another dragon fight would be an absolute no-can-do. Brannigan knew that. That's why he promoted me. This was some elaborate, fucked-up lesson he was trying to teach.

Well, the joke was on him and everybody else who might have been talking about me behind my back. I'd take my heftier pay check and follow every smoke eater procedure to the letter. Tamerica Williams was going to be the best captain in smoke eater history, even better than Naveena Jendal. Not just in Ohio, but every state in this burned down US of A.

"Oh, and Williams?" Brannigan said. "Remember that water training we did in rookie school?"

"Yeah."

"You're probably going to need it."

# CHAPTER 7

"Seriously, Afu," said Patrice. "I think you should have been a daycare worker."

"Don't be mad that I have more of a motherly instinct than your triflin' ass."

"Can we focus here?" I said.

"Oh damn." Patrice pointed ahead.

Chubby whacks struck the windshield. It had started raining.

We pulled into Sandusky an hour after leaving the Cub Scouts. Through sheets of water dumping from the sky I saw smoke drifting up over rooftops, but I couldn't see the point of origin. The smoke was light and coming from somewhere close to the Lake Erie shoreline. If there was a dragon – and my gut said there was – it had fucked up by picking an uninhabited town to invade. I just hoped Brannigan was wrong and I wouldn't have to go swimming, even though I was going to get wet either way.

On the ride over, I'd done well to remain stone-faced and only spoke in order to give directions while Patrice and Afu continued to joke and talk about shit they were planning to do that weekend – first among them was coming out to see me DJ at Club Infinity.

I wished I could relax, be the kind of captain I'd want to work for. But it was so damn overwhelming, and having Afu in the seat behind me didn't help at all. I felt like I had to paint on an extra coat of professionalism.

Brannigan had called Sandusky a ghost town and, while I knew what he meant, I was keeping a special eye out for any floating, electric spirits. The enclosures surrounding Parthenon City had pretty much put a stop to wraith sightings out in the wastes, but you could never be too careful.

Most of the buildings in Sandusky had been turned to ash, but we were coming up on a cathedral that had stubbornly resisted the demons that had torched everything else. A sign said it was Saint Peter and Paul Catholic Church. Movement up high drew my attention in time to see a huge stone fall from one of the four pointy tops. The stone crashed against the street just outside my door, splattering grit-filled water against my window.

"Damn!" Patrice shouted. "Was anything up there, Captain?"

"No," I said. "Just gravity, but be careful driving through here."

I instructed Patrice to drive us toward the flashing circle on the holoreader. When the truck stopped, we were sitting outside one of those stilt houses that hovered above the lake. Except the back half of this one was in the water and the house rested on the remaining front poles at a sharp angle. Smoke churned out of the broken windows and the doorless entrance while the rain flowed in.

"Just great," I said.

It was much safer for a dragon to come to you. Any time you enter a structure where the dragons are waiting, you're entering their domain. You're at their mercy.

With a touch to the button on the side of my helmet, my therma-goggles extended and rested over my eyes. The scene turned gray, except for a blue blob deep inside the house. The color of the blob told me what it was before I even saw the human shape.

"What the hell?" I said. "There's a person inside that house, but I don't see any dragons."

"I thought this was supposed to be a ghost town," said Patrice.

With a stretch, I popped my neck. "Lots of shit is 'supposed to be.'"

"What's the plan?" Afu asked.

I retracted my goggles and stared at the broken stilt house. "Afu, you're with me. First thing we have to do is get that idiot out of the house. Maybe they can tell us something. Patrice, you set up the cannon. When the civilian exits, put him in the back of the truck. If there's a scaly in there, we'll try to draw it out so you can get a clear shot."

"And what if you can't draw it out?" Patrice asked.

"Sink or swim." It might have been tempting fate to say our unofficial smoke eater slogan near a large body of water. But since it was already said, I hopped out and told Afu to grab two extend-struts.

While he grabbed the devices, I brought out my goggles and scanned the house and water again for dragons. Still nothing. Maybe my gut had been wrong. Maybe this had been an earthquake – there were still plenty of them – and some squatter had gotten themselves trapped inside the stilt house. Trying to stay warm, he'd lit a bonfire inside like a dumbass. No dragon here. Lucky for the squatter, I guess.

"Where you want these struts?" Afu carried one on each shoulder. To the uninitiated, the struts would look like big rectangles of red metal with claws at each end.

I grabbed one from him, a shit ton heavier than he made it seem. "Let's prop these on the underside of the house."

We set the struts on the ground. The press of a button shot a claw deep into the dirt to keep the strut in place. The next button I pressed extended the other end of the strut into the house's underside. Staying somewhat in sync, Afu extended his strut. Now we could enter the house without worrying about it crashing to the ground or sinking into the lake with us still inside.

I power-jumped through the doorway. After another quick scan through the smoke, I stepped aside and waved at Afu to follow.

When his boots hit the floor, the house shifted and whined like a dying whale. I gripped both sides of the corner I'd backed into, glaring at Afu. He had his therma-goggles extended and looked around at the dark, oblivious to the fact that the house had almost collapsed.

It wasn't Afu's fault, of course. I had no suggestion for how a six-foot-plus Samoan could gently jump into a weakened, half-drowned house. And his abundance of muscle had gotten me out of a lot of scrapes… and under a lot more sheets than I could count.

But fuck me, he was playing seesaw with an entire building.

"Watch your step there, Tinkerbell," I said.

Retracting his goggles, Afu put two fingers to the brim of his helmet and said, "Just be careful not to get any of my fairy dust on you."

"That better not be an innuendo."

"Hey, wouldn't it be a lot easier if we made all these dragons swallow clocks so we could hear them coming?"

I rolled my eyes. The smoke had begun to dissipate as I called out to whoever was in the house. "Smoke eaters. Is there anyone in here?"

The only response I heard came from the rain outside and unseen lake water bumping against the living room walls.

"Great." I turned to Afu. "Now we have to go find this fool."

As I reached up to turn on my helmet's flashlight, I took a step forward and…

…It was one step too many. My foot slipped against the steep angle and sent me to the floor. I slid fast toward the darkness. Afu flung one of his armored hands toward me, but I wasn't quick enough to grab it.

Distance is indiscernible in the dark. It felt like I slid for miles. My hand, still extended from trying to grab hold of Afu, caught against the edge of a doorway – at least, that's what I was hoping it was, and not the tooth of a sea serpent.

I remained still for a second, trying to gather myself and inspect my surroundings. When I moved my boots, they trailed water. So, I was nearly in the lake. Other than that, I couldn't see shit. I nearly slipped when I extended my goggles, but they showed nothing waiting in the water to gobble me up. I was ready to try to climb back toward Afu when a muffled voice, as cold and wet as the lake below me, spoke.

"It's very patient."

"Tamerica!" Afu's voice echoed from high above.

A blue blob crept toward me. I was hanging on the outer door frame of the kitchen, and had to bump my helmet into my shoulder to retract the goggles. In the middle of the kitchen, a wrinkled hand held a glass stick filled with glowing, pink liquid. His other hand held tight to a hammer he'd plunged into the wall. The man shook the glow stick and raised it to illuminate a masked face. The man wore an ancient firefighter air-mask, the kind with a breathing tube that looked like an elephant's trunk. White tufts of beard poked out from the mask's underside.

"Sir," I said, "are you alright?"

"One of them came for me as soon as I got here. I always knew it would be this way. But it's patient. It wants me to come willingly." This dude looked and spoke like a wannabe wizard. He was wearing one of those novelty t-shirts that made it look like he was wearing a cartoon bikini with women's breasts. Holes were scattered throughout the fabric.

"Are you saying a dragon attacked your house?" I turned to face him better, making sure I didn't lose my grip and sink into the water.

He shook his head. "Not my house. I'm a volunteer. This today is going to make me just like you, though."

I hated dealing with crazies.

"But this is my town," he said. "Mine. I've claimed

the whole thing, and I welcome the beast from the lake. I don't want to fight it anymore."

"Sure," I said. "Whatever you say. What's your name?"

"James Wilkins, the Third."

"Okay, Mr Wilkins. Let's get you out of here."

"I can't."

I huffed through my nose. "I know it's a tough climb. But I have a power suit. I can jump us out of here."

"No, no, no!" His voice was angry now, and he was shaking his fist holding the glow stick as if he was stabbing somebody with it. "You just want all the glory for yourself. I have a right to face the dragon same as you!"

"Just relax."

I'd been fortunate in my career to have only had to rescue a few of these damaged individuals. Alcoholics or pill heads, usually. They were always uncooperative and dragged a quick operation into an all-night headache.

"It's here!" The man pointed toward the water, where my boots were submerged.

I shifted my weight in order to turn on my helmet's flashlight. The light beam struck the water below me, where smoke bubbled into the house from below the surface. I'd never seen shit like that before. It was a definite phenomenon, but I was more concerned with what was pushing the smoke out of the water. I scraped my boots against the slick floor to keep them out of the lake.

Extending my left hand to the old man, I said, "Sir, you better come with me right now or you're going to die."

In the glow stick's pink light, he removed his mask and smiled, showing teeth the color of dirty paintbrush water. He hacked against the haze of smoke as he said, "Looks like... you're the one... out there hanging like... a worm on a hook."

Oh hell no. I was ready to leave this son of a bitch and jump back out to where it was safe in the rain.

But that wasn't the smoke eater way. And I would have hated to mark a civilian death on my first day as a captain, especially when I could prevent it, even if this idiot thought he could survive without an air mask. I'd just have to knock him out and drag him from the house against his will. I power-jumped to sail into the kitchen, but something very big burst from the water below me and threw me off course.

The kitchen's door frame had barely enough room for my boots to stay atop, but that's where I landed. Bare wall was the only thing my hands could claw at; if I didn't want to fall into the lake, I had to keep flat and lean all my weight against it.

Slowly, I turned my head toward the water.

A huge head, like a seahorse, rose from the water. Against my helmet's light, its scaly skin shimmered where it didn't resemble dead, human flesh. But this was no water-logged cadaver, and it sure as shit wasn't a seahorse. It had a long, thin snout with rows of needle-like teeth visible from the sides of its closed mouth – like one of those angler fish or a gharial crocodile I'd seen at the zoo as a kid. Its eyes were pure white, like it was blind and the body was long and curved like a snake, no arms or legs.

My brain, even in a paralyzed quicksand of fear,

raced through the information I'd learned in class with Sergeant Puck so many years ago. The dragon was a Scuttlepreen... no, something with an 'L.' Lewdalien? Leviathan! That's what this type of dragon was called. It wasn't as big as they could get, but it probably hadn't eaten in a long time either.

Fucking Brannigan, jinxing me with a water scaly.

The leviathan locked its eyes on me. It opened its mouth and puffed out a blast of steam, instantly turning the house into a sauna. Slithering its middle forward and rearing back its head, the scaly was about to either snatch me in its jaws or boil me. I raised my laser arm and took aim.

Before the dragon or I could attack, old-man-Wilkins, hiding in the kitchen, shouted a greeting: "Welcome! Welcome!"

The leviathan rasped and flicked its slimy neck toward the inside of the kitchen.

"Hey!" I yelled. "Over here. You want me, not him."

I shot my lasers, but the scaly had already thrust its head into the doorway. My shots flew over the dragon, blasting holes into the roof. Gray daylight poured in, providing a touch more visibility. The leviathan snaked out of the kitchen with the old man clamped between its jaws. Wilkins, the dumb bastard, was still holding on to his glow stick.

"I'm going to be a wraith," he screamed. "I'm going to live forever!"

Rumbles of gas sounded from inside the scaly's belly, expanding the skin, stretching the scales to where they would rip, before the pressure escaped the leviathan's mouth, steam hissing like a cappuccino machine. Billows of boiling vapor bombarded the crazy old man as he coughed up blood. His scream matched pitch with the high-pressure heat.

I'd been wrong about how the leviathan liked to attack. Turned out it snatched and steamed at the same time. The steam removed any sight I'd gained from the holes in the roof. I looked back toward the front door. Afu wasn't there.

"Cast!" I shouted into my helmet's radio. "Afu, where the fuck did you go?"

"Hold on," he said. "I'm coming back."

Hoping to get lucky, I blasted a few laser rounds, but they only illuminated the steam in brilliant blue before disappearing. None of the shots would have been fatal, but maybe they'd make the dragon second-guess attacking me.

A different kind of light responded to my lasers. White and flashing like electric flames, casting the leviathan's shadow from behind the steam. A blood-curdling shriek came next as the light formed into a single, floating body.

"Oh, fuck," I said.

The old man's wraith flew from the steam, clawing and screeching toward me, fast as a bullet. I power jumped out of its way, but had nothing to grab hold of. I flew upward, but when the arc reached its peak, I hit the slanted floor and slid back toward the leviathan and the oncoming wraith.

Punching open the metal pocket in my leg, I ejected a wraith remote and aimed as I slid down the middle of the house. The wraith rushed to meet me. It was like a horrible game of chicken. The ghost roared and spread its arms. I roared back. All it took was a press of the remote's trapping button and a coil of light sucked the wraith up easy peasy. Wilkins' dragon-formed spirit was gone in a blink.

But it wasn't over. When the ghost vanished, I saw what was waiting for me at the end of my slide. The leviathan rested its chin against the floor, mouth wide open, ready to receive me. I spread my legs and planted a foot on the dragon's top and bottom jaws. My first instinct was to shoot foam in to the scaly's throat, but that would only result in scalding wads of bubbles being shot back at my face. Lasers or a haymo would be great if I was trying to kill it – and oh, did I want to – but I had to prove to Brannigan that I could do the job. The new way.

Power jumping was the only option I had left, but the thrusters were still charging. The leviathan didn't need to recharge its steam and my mind was scrambling for a way out.

A joyful war cry came from above me.

Afu sailed over my head and landed atop the dragon's head. His power suit clinked as he pounded his armored fist into the dragon's eye, holding on to one of its rounded horns with the other hand.

"Go," Afu said in a wobbly voice as the dragon tried to shake him off. "Patrice… has the cannon ready. I'll be… right behind you."

Afu had tied a rope outside and laid it where I could grab hold. I engaged my thrusters, and snatched the rope. Hanging there, I watched my ex-boyfriend play rodeo on the leviathan's head.

"Quit playing with it," I said. "Let's draw it outside."

Then, as quickly as it appeared, the leviathan hissed and dropped below the water... with Afu still hanging on.

# CHAPTER 8

"Y'all alright in there?" Patrice asked through my helmet.

"The fucking dragon just dragged Afu underwater."

She said something else but I didn't hear it. I was too busy grabbing my aqua respirator from another pocket. Brannigan had suggested that I might have to do some water aerobics shit like this. Well, here it was. I should have told Afu to be ready to swim. He was horrible at holding his breath at the best of times.

*Please be okay*, I thought.

I strapped the respirator around my nose and mouth, and then extended my therma-goggles to create a seal around my face. Smoke eaters can breathe smoke, sure. But water is a little more of a bastard.

I let go of the rope and shot feet first into the lake.

The water was as warm as a Jacuzzi, so I had a hard time detecting any blobs of heat signatures, but I could see a bit better than inside the house. I swam through chunks of wood and other debris. The back part of the structure had been completely ripped off. I passed over a cluster of glowing translucent sacks that were huddled together. Eggs. I didn't have time to destroy them, and given leviathan biology, there was no way to know if they'd even been fertilized yet. The dragon had made only one wraith so far… that I knew about. Along the way, deeper into the lake, I bumped into the gnashed and boiled carcass of old-man Wilkins. His glow stick was still shining from his ragged hand.

The only reason my power suit wasn't dragging me to the bottom was because the thrusters sensed we'd gone into aqueous operations and puttered out a very low level of power to propel me through the water. I could have swum faster in my own skin, but at least I wasn't sinking. Afu and the leviathan were nowhere to be seen.

Swimming in an expanding circle, I tried to figure out how I would save Afu or get revenge on the leviathan if I couldn't. Afu was too heavy to drag, and lasers were shit in water. I needed to get Patrice to come look with me. It would take too long – more time than Afu or I could afford – to search by myself. My respirator prevented me from radioing a call to him.

What a shit captain I was turning out to be.

Shifting toward the shore, I puttered along slowly until I got to where I could crawl out onto the beach beside the wrecked stilt house.

"Patrice!" I called as soon as the goggles and respirator were off my face. "We need to look for Afu. He's in the lake."

"Uh oh. Uh oh," Patrice repeated in heavy breaths.

Big splashes came from behind and I flipped around with my laser ready to sear off chunks of scaly flesh.

Afu was on hands and knees, removing his own aqua respirator. I ran and grabbed him in a bear hug.

He was almost as tall as me on his knees.

I laughed, nearly crying. "Fuck, I thought it got you."

Then, realizing what it looked like I was doing, I dropped my smile, wiped my eyes, and backed away. "You didn't kill it did you?"

Afu quickly got to his feet and began chugging for the cannon truck. "No, it's still out there. Probably coming–"

The full force of the leviathan came roaring out of Lake Erie – an enormous gray snake of a dragon. It slithered onto shore, dripping its slimy spit onto our helmets. Instead of wings, it had blue-green fins on each of its sides.

"Patrice," I said low into my helmet mic.

No answer.

"We're going to have to slay this thing," Afu said. "It's not like there's a pool at the wraith enclosures to dump it in."

The leviathan snapped its teeth twice and raised its head to the rain, chugging out a bubbling call from its throat.

"We can't kill it," I said.

"What?"

"It's not even attacking us," I said.

The leviathan remained raised on its eel-like middle, singing its siren song like a drunken accountant on karaoke night.

"Patrice, shoot this thing already. What's the hold up?"

"I was getting suited up to look for Afu," she said. "Stand by."

Afu put a hand to my armor and pulled me

backwards with him, away from the crooning serpent. "This ain't good," he said. "Something isn't right."

"I got this," I said. "Just–"

The lake surface exploded again.

Slithering out of the water to snap and snarl beside the one leviathan came a second.

"Hurry, Patrice," I said. "There are two of them!"

"I'm moving as fast as I can," she said.

The leviathans circled us, swollen bodies blocking either of us from escaping. Afu extended his laser sword, and I didn't stop him. The dragon in front of me attacked, snapping for me with a hungry mouth. I power jumped out of the way and landed outside the scaly blockade.

But now Afu was sandwiched between the twin leviathans and both of my weapons were useless unless I wanted to clip the dragons' fins or coat them in foam – both of those weren't going to do shit.

"I have to kill them, T," Afu said.

There have only been a few moments in my career as a smoke eater where I didn't know what choice to make. Oh, I've cautiously paused to evaluate a situation, hesitated even, but there on the Sandusky shore, watching two sea monsters surrounding my ex-boyfriend, I was at a loss.

I hated being a captain already.

"Cap?"

"Fine," I said. "We don't have another choice."

Afu laughed and power jumped to get eye-level with one of the dragons. He wrapped himself around its neck and began plugging its flesh with his laser sword while I fired shots at the other scaly's back.

A few chunks of flesh dropped to the ground like charred fish, but it wasn't doing enough damage to be fatal. Afu's dragon fell to the ground. The other big eel-like monster hissed and flopped around to face me.

A huge green laser flew over my head and pelted the remaining leviathan in the face. It swayed to and fro for a second before falling toward me. Afu dove out of the way in time, but I'd been too slow, only able to turn and land on my face. The dragon's weight crashed onto me, beating me into the sand. Afu ran over and began digging granules away from my face.

"Are you okay?" he asked.

I grumbled, but gave him a thumb up. Not only had Patrice robbed me of a justified dragon slaying, but Afu had gotten one without me.

Patrice sauntered over like the hero of the incident, singing a song that went, 'You ain't never seen a badder bitch than me.'

"What's next, Captain?" Afu asked.

I turned my head toward him – or as much as I could with a fish-gut-stinking, unconscious dragon on top of me.

"Get this fucking thing off me."

# CHAPTER 9

All smoke eater apparatus had been recently fitted
with extendable hover-trailers that were stored
underneath the chassis. They operated the same way
the business end of a tow truck would. Patrice backed
the cannon truck up to the sleeping leviathan and
we slid the trailer under it. After the living, sleeping
dragon was secured to the trailer with magnetic ties,
the dead one burst into flames.

Patrice flinched so bad, she fell on her ass. "What
the hell just happened?"

"Goddamn it," I said. "Not this again."

"You seen something like this before, Cap?" asked
Afu.

I stared at the yellow flames and the disintegrating
dragon. "Yeah. Same thing happened to the dragon I
fought yesterday. I killed it and then *poof*. All burned
up into ashes."

Afu raised a bushy eyebrow as he looked at the
leviathan strapped to our truck's trailer. "This one
isn't going to do that is it?"

"I sure as hell hope not," I said. "Only seems to
happen to the ones we kill."

I was about to tell my crew to hop into the truck

so we could get the hell out of Sandusky, but an engine growl in the distance interrupted me.

Patrice got to her feet and tried unsuccessfully to brush off the wet ashes that had caked onto the seat of her armor. "Now what?"

A pickup truck rounded the corner and headed straight for us. Two men stood in the truck bed, carrying rusty poles with sharpened ends. The pickup truck parked just in front of us and the two men in the cab got out.

"How do you do?" said the one who'd been driving.

"Just fine," I said. "But you guys need to clear out. This is a dragon scene and we're closing it off for further investigation."

They all looked like miners that had just crawled out of a hole, wearing hard hats with lights strapped to the base. They were dressed in flannel shirts and dirty jeans, dressed too similarly to be a coincidence. These were uniforms in some weird way.

The two in the bed hopped to the ground and jogged over to form a line with the others.

Removing his helmet and holding it under his arm, the guy who'd been driving scanned a finger over me and my crew. "You guys smoke eaters?"

I looked to the leviathan on the hover trailer, our black and purple cannon truck, and a shrugging Afu and Patrice in their power suits. "Yeah. We are. But like I was saying—"

"I'm Harold Pinch," he said. "These are my men. We're volunteers."

*Ah*, I thought. *Jolly volley firefighters. Makes sense.*

"One of our guys," Harold said, "Wilkins is his

name, came out on his own when we first felt the quake. He's not all there in the head, but he's passionate about the job. Wondering if you might've seen him."

Shit.

I stepped closer to Harold and kept my voice down. "He was wearing a cartoon bikini shirt."

"Yeah," Harold said in a gruff smoker's voice, not trying to be as discreet as I was, "he never took that stupid thing off."

Sometimes you just can't take a deep enough breath before giving bad news. "I hate to tell you this, and I tried like hell to save him, but… Wilkins passed."

Harold dropped his head. The other guys in his mining unit – or whatever the hell they were – caught the gist and either kicked the ground, covered their mouth with a grimy hand, or loosed a whispered swear word.

"How'd it happen?" Harold asked, nearly crying.

"I…" Did he really want to know? "Well, he was in the house over there for some reason and a dragon got him. This one right here, in fact."

Harold cleared his throat and straightened his stance. "Has his wraith shown up yet?"

Now that was a weird question. "Um… yeah, but we took care of it."

"We'd like to have it, please," Harold said, as serious as could be.

"Captain, we should get back, yeah?" Patrice said, trying to help get me out of the heartbreaking bear trap I'd stepped into.

Afu added, "Yeah, we need to hurry before the Sandman wears off."

"Look," I told Harold, "we really have to load up. I'm afraid I can't release his wraith to you. It's for public health."

"That's his soul!" Harold shouted. "You don't have the right to it. If any part of him is staying in this life, it should be helping his brothers in the cause he cared so much about."

The others nodded and shouted their agreement. Oh boy.

"Harold," I said, "I get it. Volunteer firefighters like you have the same camaraderie as smoke eaters, but—"

"We're not firemen," Harold said.

"Oh." I blinked, confused. "Sorry, I thought you said you were volunteers."

"Yeah," he said. "We're volunteer smoke eaters."

Patrice's laugh cracked over the Sandusky ash like a bolt of lightning. Afu was doing only a little better with an armored hand over his upturned lips.

"What's so funny?" Harold was now pissed.

"Don't mind them," I said. "It's just… we've never heard of volunteer smokies."

He raised his chin. "We're the first."

"Okay," I said, throwing in the towel. "That's not my jurisdiction to decide, but we're going to get out of here."

"Hold up," he shouted to my turned back as I made my way to the cannon truck. "Give us Wilkins' wraith! And what's with these embers burning? You just going to leave 'em like that? They could start a fire."

"Don't touch those," I yelled back.

"We out?" Patrice asked, following beside me.

"Hell yes," I said. "I'm done with these wastelander wannabes."

When I got into my seat, Harold was yelling for the others to jump into their truck. Patrice floored it and had Cannon 15 zipping down the road out of Sandusky, but a minute later Harold and his goons were racing along my side of the truck.

"Give us Wilkins!" Harold shouted through his window.

The guys in the bed of the truck pumped their weapons in the air while Harold and the man next to him continued to shout angrily.

Now, I don't know if it's because my daddy had told me stories about what used to happen in this country to people of my particular pigmentation at the hands of people who looked and acted just like Harold and the other rednecks, and it definitely didn't help that I'd just fought two dragons and didn't get the release of permanently ending either of them myself, but whatever the case, I wasn't about to take any kind of bullshit from these motherfuckers.

"Stop the truck," I told Patrice.

She did. And when Harold's truck stopped beside us, I let him have it.

"Now look here," I said. "I'm starting to feel threatened. So, if you sonsabitches don't leave us alone, my crew and I will use everything at our disposal to fuck you up. Do I make myself clear? You're obstructing our duty."

Harold frowned, thought about it for a second. A rusty pole versus a laser sword should have been a no-brainer. "We're going to talk to your chief about this," he said.

"Feel free to do so," I said, resting my arm more

comfortably on the window frame. "But you better heed the words painted on the back of our truck and keep back at least three hundred feet."

After securing my wraith remote inside our truck's lockbox, I flicked two fingers toward the road ahead. Patrice nodded at the signal and we were back on our way with a leviathan in tow.

Unfortunately, Harold and the wannabe smoke eaters followed just behind.

# CHAPTER 10

"These white boys aren't backing off," Patrice said, taking glances at the side view mirror.

Groaning, I looked into the reflection on my side. Sure enough, Harold and the boys were keeping their distance, but steadily following, all of them glowering like kids in the back seat who'd been told to shut up while grown folks were talking.

Brains in mirror may be smaller than they appear.

"There isn't much we can do," I said. "They can talk to Chief when we get to headquarters. If I know Brannigan, he'll give them a swift kick in the ass."

"And that's if he's in a decent mood," Afu said.

Patrice shook her head. "Still makes me nervous having a tail like this."

"I'll call Brannigan," I said.

Cannon 15's holoreader beat me to the punch, chirping with an incoming call. With pitch-black hair hanging to her shoulders, Captain Naveena Jendal appeared. Yolanda paced behind her. Something in me wanted to hang up on my old captain, claim it was a mistake if I ever saw her in person again. I knew I'd have to face Naveena at some point, and hear again how I'd screwed up on that smaug call.

But instead of ending the call, I said, "Um, hi."

"Are you guys all right?"

A big bump vibrated from behind the cannon truck. I was about to cuss out some rednecks for ramming my apparatus, but looking in the mirror, Harold's truck hadn't changed position.

So what the hell was it?

"Cap," Afu said. "I think the leviathan just moved."

My throat tightened. "Hold on, Naveena," I said, leaning out of the window for a look at our quarry. The leviathan lay as unconscious as ever. Maybe we'd just run over a big rock in the road. I told Afu as much.

"Sorry," I said, turning back to Naveena's hologram. "Now what were you saying?"

"I'm checking to see if you guys are okay."

I tried to answer politely. Naveena and I had been on tons of calls together and spent a bunch of time hanging out off shift, too. But it felt like she was sticking her nose into my business, seeing if the new captain wasn't already fucking up.

"We're good," I said. "We've got some obnoxious hicks claiming to be volunteer smokies following us, but they're no biggie. Snagged a leviathan, though. Bringing it back now."

Yolanda turned and ran over, nearly shoving Naveena out of the holofield. "You caught a leviathan?"

"Would've been two," I said. "But Afu had to kill the other one and it burst into flames like the smaug."

Yolanda scrunched up her entire face. "Well, that makes no sense."

"It happened once. Why not a second time?

88

Maybe this is a new scaly trend taking off."

"Yeah," said Yolanda, "but leviathans don't have any EMP ability and their ignis gland is packed inside a bladder full of water. This throws out my hypothesis."

"We're getting off track," said Naveena. "The reason we called to check on you—"

"Goddamn it!" I yelled. Another bump from behind. I again leaned out of the window, and this time the leviathan was definitely moving, writhing against its restraints. "Shit. I'll have to call you back, Naveena."

"There's something following you underground," Yolanda shouted.

"Huh?" I said, snapping my head back to the holoreader.

"Something is coming in hot, heading straight for you," Naveena said. "The propellerheads have been monitoring it since you left Sandusky."

"Why the fuck was that not the first thing you mentioned!?" I appreciated the propellerheads more than anybody, but sometimes they forget that we're the ones out here risking our asses for everybody else. Naveena should have known better, too.

"We weren't sure what it was," Yolanda said. "And it's not creating new burrows, it's using old ones, so no quakes. It's not moving like a dragon at all."

"Then what is it?" I asked.

The leviathan thrashed even harder. Any more jerking around and it could overturn the hover trailer. Then we'd be back to square one fighting the stupid dragon, on top of having to fight off the wannabe smoke eaters so they didn't end up like their wraith pal, whilst dealing with a subterranean mystery guest.

"Um, Captain?" Patrice tapped my thigh. "These volunteer fools are trying to pull some shit."

Outside Patrice's window, Harold's red truck zoomed past with the guys in the open bed hugging their metal poles like teddy bears. With a quick jerk, the truck swerved into our path, forcing Patrice to slam the brakes. We hit a dead stop as Harold's brake lights blared red, but the truck never came to a complete stop, not until the earth blew open and yellow fire exploded from the ground beneath them.

Our cab filled with a mixture of swear words and screams.

The heat was so intense it shattered our windshield and warped the mirrors, and even the dash. In hindsight, the burst of flames and dirt was perfectly circular, like a cookie cutter made from a flamethrower. The blast was probably twenty feet in circumference, but at the time it seemed like the whole world was ablaze. It was the first time I'd ever felt pain from heat. Though, compared to the tiny cuts the pieces of windshield made across my face, the heat was nothing.

Harold's truck had disappeared in the fire, but when the flames died down, a charred hunk of metal – completely unrecognizable as a pickup – dropped from the sky in a smoldering heap. One of the guys who'd been sitting in the back of the pickup lay a few feet away from the crater left by the explosion. His whole body was covered in a thick, dark layer of char, steadily smoking into the wind. He tried to army crawl, but soon gave up, rolled to his back, and lifted a smoking arm to the sky, pointing – maybe blaming

God for his current predicament. I was amazed he was still alive.

"Williams?" Naveena's hologram said. "Williams, what happened?"

Gagging against the taste of sulfur on my tongue, I wiped tears from eyes. "Send… backup. Now."

"We're on our way." Naveena and Yolanda disappeared.

"You two," I brushed glass from my shoulders and looked at Patrice and Afu, "knock the leviathan out again. I'm going to go check on that man out there. Get ready to fight another dragon. Whatever it is, I don't think it's emerged yet."

"You see that fire?" Afu said. "I say we run and wait for backup."

"That's not an option," I said.

Patrice patted palms against her bald head, as if she was checking for burns. After a big breath, she said, "I'm ready, girl."

All three of our doors popped open, just as three straps behind us snapped in sequence. The metal of our truck's roof bent in and wobbled from something heavy slithering on top. The little of the windshield that remained fell in jagged pieces.

The leviathan slid off the front of Cannon 15, shifting its head left, then right, hissing like an angry snake on crack. Its entire body quivered and writhed as if it was in pain or listening to a really bad heavy metal song. Then it spotted the surviving volunteer.

"Fuck," I said.

Securing my helmet, I hopped out and ran, but the leviathan was already speeding across the ash, as fast on land as it was in water. Power jumping put me a couple feet away from its tail, but I was still too late.

The leviathan scooped the dying man into its jaws. The poor guy in the dragon's mouth was too hurt and exhausted to even scream. The scaly hissed and convulsed seizure-like; it must have had a bad reaction to the Sandman laser. No dragon had ever woken up from the tranq gun before.

I grabbed the scaly's tail and yanked, but all it only made the bastard turn and glare at me; the burned man's legs still sticking out of its mouth. With a flick of its tail, the leviathan tossed me toward the deep pit that had opened underneath the pickup truck.

I dug both boots and all ten of my armored fingers into the dirt to stop myself at the edge of the crater. And thank Christ, because I'd never peered down such a deep hole. There was no end that I could see, and patches of flames burned in random places all the way down, so it wasn't for lack of light. And that was another thing.

What made the hole? When a scaly emerges, it's there in all its ugly, horned monstrousness. It doesn't make a hole, turn around, and decide to come back later. But I couldn't worry about that. I had to deal with the spazzing dragon right in front of me.

I heard the snap of bones and a puff of boiling hot steam before I ever got to my feet and turned to face the leviathan. When I did, electricity sparked from the beast's jaws and a newborn wraith used its gnarly hands to claw out of the leviathan's white-flaming mouth. The air filled with hisses and shrieks.

Goddamn it. Not again.

I opened the container in my power suit and

reached for my wraith remote… which wasn't there.

Double goddamn it.

It was in Cannon 15's lockbox. Patrice and Afu ran toward the leviathan, laser swords extended and *phumm-ing* with each swing of their arms.

I fumbled toward them on aching legs. "Toss me a wraith remo—"

Something swift slammed into my back, sending me into the dirt. By the time I flipped over, the wraith filled my nose with the smell of burned flesh, shrieking with its electric teeth in my face, and its white speckled claws swiping down, about to puncture my skull and finish me off.

The wraith's dagger-like fingers had to have been less than an inch from my eyeball when the ghost burst into flames.

But they weren't the white flames the wraith was born from. They weren't even the canary, neon yellow that had exploded under Harold and company. These flames were black, the same black that shot from a wraith remote when trapping them.

I'd heard of wraiths disappearing out in the wild, but I'd never seen it myself, and it was usually a few weeks until they vanished from their given territory, not forty-five seconds.

With the wraith gone, though, and my eyes toward the sky, I finally saw what the last of Harold's men had been pointing at before becoming a leviathan snack.

A giant, flaming bird was in the air, and barreling straight down for us.

I rolled onto my feet in a dead run toward the

cannon truck. Patrice and Afu were doing a waltz with the leviathan, trying to dodge its attacks and find an opening to power jump in for some slicing and dicing. But the dragon was behaving erratically, like nothing we'd seen before.

Casting to their radios, I yelled, "Get out of there! Head for the truck."

"What?" Afu said. "We've almost got this thing, Cap. Give us a chance."

"This bitch is bugging like crazy," said Patrice.

"Big fucking fire bird coming down on us. Jump out of there right now, damn it!"

They looked to each other and instantly retreat-jumped toward Cannon 15.

It was a good thing, too, because half a second later, the bird impacted into the earth clutching the leviathan in its talons and emitted a wave of flames in a giant ring that crested just over the top of Cannon 15.

More damaged apparatus on my record.

With an ear-stabbing shriek that would make a wraith wince, the bird raised its beak to the clouds and squawked out a victory as the leviathan writhed helplessly under its weight.

"What the hell kind of dragon is that?" Afu asked.

"That's no dragon," I said. "It's a...."

# CHAPTER 11

"Phoenix!" Patrice finished for me.

That didn't make any sense. But dragons did? Ghosts did? The realm of possibilities had already been blown wide open a decade ago. We just had to adapt to them and keep the human race going one day at a time. Sense didn't have anything to do with it, not when it was burning right in front of me and my crew, piercing its beak into the leviathan's belly.

A phoenix. Shit, I guess it was. The bird was covered entirely in yellow flames. Even its predatory eyes were like bonfires curling toward the sky. Where a cluster of feathers would have been blowing in the wind, instead it was flickering flame. When the bird spread its enormous wings, they became sheets of flight-giving combustion.

The leviathan tried to fight back, snarling and snapping at its attacker. But the phoenix shoved one of its talons in the scaly's face, holding it down as it ate the dragon alive. Poor sea serpent didn't ever have a chance, not against something three times bigger and constructed almost completely of fire. Then, as casually as if it had been a twig, the phoenix snapped the leviathan's neck.

Instantly, the dragon caught fire and turned to ash. Just like the other leviathan. Just like the smaug.

Afu swallowed, his shaking, armored hand jangling against the side of Cannon 15. "Do... do we kill it."

"Get your hand off the truck," I whispered to Afu through gritted teeth. "It's making too much noise."

He did as he was told. "And if we do, won't it just resurrect? That's what they do, right?"

I tried to slow my breathing down. I was shaking, too. "We won't kill it if we can get it back to the propellerheads alive. They can study it so we won't get caught with our pants down if there are others. Patrice?"

No answer.

I turned toward my driver. Her mouth hung open, eyes glued to the phoenix.

"*Patrice!*"

She flinched and whispered, "Sorry, Cap."

"Get the Sandman trained on the bird," I said. "Go as slow and quietly as you can." I knocked knuckles against the dragon skull emblem on her power suit. "Sink or swim."

"Sink or swim, baby," she said, but it lacked her usual enthusiasm.

I radioed the propellerheads and requested Jet 1 for an immediate airborne attack – extra foam if they could swing it. They gave me a thirty-minute ETA.

All that was left of the leviathan was a pile of yellow, glowing embers which the phoenix began scooping into its beak. With each swallow the bird grew in size. The flames of its wings crackled as they burned bigger and brighter. Hotter. By the time it had finished eating, it would be double its original height and width. And it was already two stories tall.

It wasn't that farfetched. The behemoth we'd fought not long ago was an apex predator dragon, feeding off its own kind. But this was different. The phoenix turned scalies into coal for its anatomical furnace.

"What do you want me to do?" Afu asked beside me. "I don't know what to do!"

I looked into his big brown eyes, and for some goddamned reason I was so happy to be here with him. There was nowhere else I'd rather be. Then, I could have slapped myself. Afu and I were over and there was an inferno bird just a few feet away.

"We need to focus," I said, too sternly, more to myself than him. That was always my flaw; I projected my own shit onto other people, people I loved.

*Used* to love!

There was a slight pout to Afu's lips, even though he was trying hard to keep his head in the game. "I'm doing my best, Captain."

Pointing to the phoenix, I said, "We'll surround it, hold it off until Patrice can put it to sleep. Something starts going south, I'll focus on its flames with my foam. Grab a shield from the truck, and use your laser sword as a last resort. And I mean that, Afu. Don't kill it unless you absolutely have to."

"Okay, okay," he said, raising a defensive hand. "No more monster killing."

Patrice spoke through my helmet radio. "Cannon is in position, T."

As Afu and I stepped lightly to either side of the phoenix, the air smelled cleaner than I could ever remember, absent of the funk that dragons and wraiths brought with them. I guess that's what happens when everything is incinerated. Fuck, I could imagine what this bird could do to a city. *My* city. We couldn't let this flying cataclysm escape. Not on my watch. Too many people had died already; stupid people who'd done it to themselves, but still.

Finishing its meal of dragon coal, the phoenix chirped like a satisfied sparrow, which was weird for something the size of a jumbo jet to do. It turned its head to Afu and then me, unconcerned. Flapping its fire wings, the phoenix lifted into the air.

"Patrice, now!" I shouted.

Cannon 15's Sandman sang as it fired the tranq laser across the horizon. It hit the phoenix under its right wing. And then, in the most fabulous way…

…Not a fucking thing happened.

"It didn't work!" Afu said.

*Thanks, Smokie Obvious.*

It wasn't true that *nothing* happened. The phoenix got pretty pissed, shrieking and flapping faster to hover just above us. If it had seen our presence before as random spectators, we'd just upgraded ourselves to prime enemies.

"We can't kill it," I yelled to remind Afu.

Instinctually, I power jumped and blasted the phoenix's nearest wing with a foam stream. The flames sizzled and died down when the foam made contact, causing the phoenix to zero in on me. But a few seconds later the wing was back to its full blaze.

"Oh shit," I said. "Patrice, we need the chain net."

"Hold it off for a second," she said. "I need time to crank the gun."

We didn't have a second.

The phoenix aimed for me, cutting through the air like a hot knife. I dove out of the way, but at the last second, the bird flicked its wing and batted me in the side. I stumbled, but landed on my feet just fine. My power suit, however, was on fire.

"Oh, goddamn it!" I slapped at the flames rising from my suit's armpit, but it was doing as much as a one-legged droid in a foot race.

I blasted the fire with my foam, but the white suds only sizzled away no matter how much I dumped onto it. The fire wasn't going away.

"Afu, help!"

I was freaking out. Normally, I would have kept my cool and figured something out, but this was beyond my capacity to understand, to get a handle on. And I was so damned exhausted already.

Afu power-jumped over to me as the phoenix, half a mile away, swooped around to come back for a rematch. "Get out of the suit," he said.

Out of the suit? That was suicide.

The phoenix's oncoming shriek quickly changed my mind. I hit the latch in the front of my suit and fell to the ground. Afu heaved me onto my feet and we ran for the truck.

I felt the heat at my back and knew the phoenix was right on top of us. The bird's shriek came next, stabbing my ears so badly I had to cover them with my hands and lose speed – not that my running was doing shit to save me. Then I made the mistake of looking over my shoulder.

The phoenix's talons were spread open, ready to snag

me and Afu. It wouldn't even have to bite us to finish the job; the flames would do us in way before that.

A loud *phloom* shot through the air as Patrice fired the chain net out of the cannon. It struck the phoenix, enveloping the bird and cinching around it with quick, magnetic ease. It spiraled through the air away from me and Afu, then thudded through the dusty ashes on the ground, continually squawking.

When the netted phoenix came to a rest, I marched toward my power suit that was still burning and cracked it open like a discarded oyster.

"We should stay back, T," Afu said. "Yeah? Wait till backup arrives?"

"You're probably right, Afu, but I've got to do this."

I kept walking. This bird had officially pissed me off. I wasn't going to kill it, but I was going to make it very uncomfortable. The flames on my power suit had died down, but I had to kick ashes onto the foam arm so I could grab it and drag the suit toward the phoenix. I didn't need to get that close, not for what I had in mind. Maybe just ten or fifteen feet away.

"What are you doing?" asked Afu.

Huffing from the strain, I kneeled and aimed my power suit's foam arm toward the phoenix. It stared at me with those flaming eyes. For a second I hesitated, because the bird wasn't looking at me like it wanted to eat me or burn me to smithereens, it looked worried. Scared.

I wondered how scared Harold and his guys felt when they were blasted fifty feet into the air.

I jabbed the foam button on my suit and soaked the phoenix with the white goop. It always worked like a charm with dragon breath. The phoenix fire, though, was too damn hot and unkillable. The foam was useless, but dousing the bastard was making me feel better, so there was that.

The phoenix gargled all high-pitched against the foam, and I was careful not to accidentally drown the thing. It sounded like a cappuccino machine frothing up steamed milk.

Then it switched to the sound of a tea kettle about to blow.

"I don't like this, Tamerica." Afu only said my full first name when he got serious, and that was close to never.

I dropped my power suit's arm and looked back at him. He was in a full run, headed my way, as if he was going to tackle me. Behind me, the phoenix trembled faster and faster, fire flashing like a strobe light.

Then Afu did tackle me.

It was just in time. He'd seen something I couldn't – not while I was neck deep in my rage-fueled birdie bathing. The phoenix exploded, firing molten pieces of chain net like bullets. They scattered everywhere, pinging against Afu's power armor as he covered me, some dinged off my helmet that I'd thankfully left on. But one of the pieces of shrapnel caught me in the arm.

I screamed into Afu's ear, and it was a credit to his composure he didn't roll off me and leave me to the mercy of the flying hot metal.

When the last of the explosion had subsided, Afu sat up and hissed at the sight of my arm.

"What?" I said, voice hoarse. "It's not that big of a deal. Just a scratch."

But I hadn't seen it yet. It hurt like a motherfucker,

but so did a paper cut. Dropping my head to the injury… well, there it was. My arm was pouring blood. If there was a metal piece in the gaping gash of my flesh, I didn't see it. My head got dizzy and the surroundings seemed farther away, both in sight and sound. I felt hungry and in desperate need of a nap.

"Stay with me, T." Afu took out a rapid tourniquet and slipped it above the gash that was steadily spewing blood. He hit a button and the strap cinched tight.

I screamed. But I wasn't bleeding to death anymore.

"Patrice," Afu called through his helmet. "Get the medical bag."

"You know," I said, sitting up in the ashes. "You always had the prettiest eyes."

What the fuck was I saying!?

"Then focus on my eyes," said Afu. And he focused his on mine.

"Wait," I said, snapping out of my delirium. "That fucking bird."

I jumped to my feet, wobbling like a drunk. Afu tried to sit me back down, but I shoved him away. The net that Patrice had snagged the phoenix with was gone, completely melted and shattered into bits. The phoenix had cremated itself. All that was left of the bird was a pile of glowing, neon-yellow ashes.

My anger returned. This fucking thing couldn't even stay alive while we were trying to keep it that way. I swung a foot into the ashes, scattering the glowing mess across the ground. I was stomping on them, kicking them. I fell back, too weak to stand.

Afu caught me in his arms, always there for me, even when I'd been such a shit to him. "What the hell are you doing?" He was angrier than I'd ever seen him. "The thing is dead. Gone. There's no point kicking its ash."

"Hey," Patrice said, walking over hefting our truck's medical bag. "But that's just what we are, boo. We're ash kickers."

Jet 1's engines filled the air as it crested the horizon. Afu took the lead and told them we'd taken care of things, but needed immediate evacuation for me. He must have gotten the message in too late, though, because when Jet 1 was directly overhead, they dumped a fuck ton of foam on top of us.

All of us looked like we'd been shit on by a very big bird. I looked at Afu and spat out a wad of foam before saying, "I don't know who's flying that plane, but theirs is the only ash I want to kick right now."

# CHAPTER 12

It was Renfro.

"You get transferred to another crew and the world goes to shit." Renfro walked down the lowered hatch of Jet 1, spreading his arms, like he'd won the day all by himself. His smile made his ruby red eyes sparkle even in the cloud-blocked sunlight. "What's up with that?"

Ever since E-Day, when the dragons first emerged, certain people had developed a rare ability to see in the dark, which changed their eye color to blood red. Doctors called it *dracones tapetum*, but everybody referred to the condition as dragon eye, and it was even rarer than being born a smoke eater. Renfro was the only person I knew with both qualities. There were plenty of times he'd spotted an emergency means of egress inside a house or a deep hole in the floor that our therma-goggles didn't catch.

Renfro had also taught me most of what I knew about shooting foam and lasers – banking them off walls in tight spots and such. I wouldn't say this to Afu or Brannigan, but any dumbass can swing a laser sword around. Us foam-and-laser shooting smokies had to be more accurate with our weapons.

Afu and Patrice helped me toward the jet as

propellerheads poured out with equipment and flying video drones that buzzed around them like over-sized flies.

I scooped a big handful of foam off my chest and flung it into Renfro's face. "We had it handled and pretty well cleaned up before you dropped this shit on us."

Renfro laughed, wiping the foam out of his eyes. "I'm just messing with you, T. I'm glad you're okay. And I'd already dropped the foam when Afu radioed me. Sorry."

I flipped him the bird. And maybe it was because of blood loss and exhaustion, but I wondered if you lit a raised middle finger on fire, you could call it "giving someone the phoenix."

"She needs to rest," said Afu.

"I'm good," I said. "This is nothing."

Patrice gave a scolding hum. "Girl, you need to sit your ass down and take it easy for a while. Hell, I do too. I'll slab you with some of this curate, but then I'm done for the day." She patted the med bag on her shoulder, which was still covered in foam. "So quit trying to be Captain Tough Bitch."

Renfro raised his eyebrows and stared at Patrice with those eyes that were probably a lot scarier for someone not used to seeing them.

"Um," Patrice said, "I mean, Captain Williams."

"Right," said Renfro. "Get her inside and treat her wound. You both need rehab yourselves it looks like. This must have been some dragon."

He jogged off to catch up with the propellerheads before any of us could correct him on that last part.

Oh, well. It was going to come up soon enough.

My crew sat me down on a seat at the side of the jet and began working on cleaning and treating my arm.

I watched them for a minute before saying, "I love y'all."

"She must have lost a lot more blood than I thought," said Afu.

"No." I shook my head, but the motion was way slower than I had meant it to be, like life was a gelatin mold and I was barely moving through it. "You both did great work today. I don't think I've ever had to face such an avalanche of shit in my entire career. I'm glad that I had both of you beside me. Sink or swim."

They both nodded. I think Afu might have even teared up a little, the big pussy.

"I'm still so confused," Afu said.

"What's new?" I laughed, trying to brighten the mood.

"Seriously," said Afu. "What the hell is going to claw its way out of the ground next? That phoenix wasn't like any dragon, even though I kept telling myself to fight it like one. And did you see how that leviathan was acting?"

"And I don't think that was the Sandman wearing off." Patrice coughed and sighed, her eyes getting heavy. "That big ass bird… was messing with its head somehow. Scaly… was trippin'."

"The phoenix ate the dragon, though," I said. "Barely even had to move. Wasn't even a fight, it was a goddamn execution."

Afu held out a contemplative palm, as if the answer he was looking for would flop out of the sky and into his hand. "And another thing, birds don't come from underground!

"Bats live in caves," I said.

He dropped his chin at this and puckered his lips deep in thought.

"Burrowing owls," Patrice said. "They love underground."

Afu and I both turned to her, impressed and confused.

Patrice shrugged. "I watch old animal shows on the Feed sometimes... when I can't sleep."

She moaned and touched her head.

"Are you okay?" I asked.

"I don't know," she said. "I think some of those ashes got in my mouth when you were kicking them around."

Fuck me. I'd been too angry to notice what my dumb actions would do to my crew. There was no telling what kind of toxins were in those ashes.

Sirens filled the air outside and the green and purple strobes of Slayer 5 followed shortly after that. Naveena jumped out of the captain's seat, fully suited up and rushing around the dragon scene looking for something to do.

The rookie that had taken my spot on Naveena's crew got out of the driver's seat and followed behind his captain. His name was Harpo – no, Harribow, or something like that. He never said much and constantly looked around at the world like it was going to bite him.

Maybe he had the right idea.

He wasn't a born smoke eater like most of us. Like Patrice, he had joined up after a dragonblood infusion gave him smoke eater abilities. We didn't treat created smokies like him any differently. We needed the manpower, and the scaly juice allowed them to do everything we could. So what did it matter?

Giving up on talking to the propellerheads, Naveena ran over to Renfro, who pointed her toward me in the back of Jet 1. She power-jumped over, not wasting any time in coming to check on me. That's the type of person, and captain, that Naveena was. It's one of the reasons she would always be a legend in my book – not how efficiently she had slain scalies or the crazy things she'd overcome on some of the most chaotic scenes we got thrown into. Naveena always put her crew and fellow smoke eaters first.

"You're late," I said. I tried smiling, but by the way Afu frowned and blinked at me, it probably looked like I was having a stroke.

"Are you guys okay?" Naveena kneeled beside me.

"I'm fine," said Afu. "Captain Williams got nicked pretty bad by some shrapnel. How are you, Patrice?"

Patrice huffed and ejected from her power suit before falling into the seat beside me. "I don't know… what it is, but I'm burning the hell up. Like… I caught an instant flu or something."

Harribow, the rookie, put a wrist to Patrice's forehead. "You're very feverish."

"It's probably just you," Patrice said, making goo-goo eyes at him. "I've always wanted to try a white boy."

Harribow dropped his arm and turned his scared face to Naveena.

I belted out a hard laugh, like I was high. The ieiunium curate had kicked in and the icy tingles were working their way from where Patrice had coated my injured arm with the blue goop.

"What happened here?" Naveena asked, throwing concerned eyes toward me, to Afu, to Patrice.

"Coming through!" Yolanda, who I hadn't seen rush out of Jet 1, was carrying a glass container filled with fiery yellow ashes that had yet to quit burning. Ignoring our little smokie huddle, Yolanda carried the phoenix ashes to the front of the plane, securing it inside a high-tech lockbox.

"And what the hell was Yolanda carrying?" Naveena asked.

"I don't want to be flying with that stuff," Afu said. "What if it comes back?

As Yolanda attempted to explain that Afu's suggestion was impossible, Naveena put a hand to my face. "T?"

"Okay," I said, the curate perking me up a little. I could almost feel my wound sewing itself back together. "I'll tell you everything. But you're not going to believe it."

Brannigan was waiting for us in the Slayer bay when Jet 1's hatch lowered to the ground.

"What in the name of all lording fuck! Are you okay?" Then he hugged me. I didn't return it, only because I was so surprised and confused by it.

Brannigan released me and I stared at him with widened eyes. "Are *you* okay?"

"I am if you and your crew are. I've been hearing the craziest shit. You know how rumors go around the fire service, can't believe any of it. A few more days and people are going to be saying you fought a snake-haired medusa that popped out of the ground."

Goddamn, the news had beaten us back to headquarters. Smoke eaters have the biggest mouths.

"So are you well enough to tell me about it?" Brannigan asked.

I was about to tell Brannigan I'd rather do it sitting down with a cold drink in my hand, but Afu yelled for help behind me.

"Captain!"

He'd been walking Patrice down the ramp out of Jet 1. She'd told him she wasn't a grandma and could walk without his help. A few steps later, she face-planted onto the Slayer bay, knocking over a propellerhead's wheeled cart.

Everyone within the vicinity shouted or gasped. I ran over and turned Patrice onto her back, cradling her head in my lap. Her eyes were slits, but she was breathing – groaning, really.

"Patrice." I shook her shoulder. "What the hell?"

She tried to say something but it came out mush.

"Let's get her to sickbay," Brannigan shouted so everyone could here. "Now!"

Afu and Renfro grabbed different ends of Patrice's limp body and hustled into headquarters. Brannigan walked beside me with a hand at my back.

"Chief," I said, "she took some ash in the mouth. But she's a smoke eater. That couldn't hurt her. Could it?"

He didn't answer because he didn't know. He could only shake his head.

"We're going to give her a full workover." Yolanda zipped past us, spinning on her heels to jog backwards as she continued telling us the plan forward with Patrice. "Probably some antibiotics and I'm going to recommend another curate infusion to speed things along." She pointed at me, hopping backwards on the balls of her feet. "Please don't go anywhere until I've gotten a chance to talk to you about what happened out there."

Yolanda twisted back around and ran off to the sickbay.

"Why would I go anywhere?" I told Brannigan. "That's part of my crew in there."

"Come on," Brannigan said. "This is going to feel like shit – not being able to do anything – but at least you'll be there for Johnson. That blue stuff will have her better in no time. It's not your fault, whatever it is."

That's where he was wrong. If it was the phoenix ashes, ashes probably filled with poison, I'd been the one to dance a two-step on top of them and send them flying into the wind and directly into Patrice's system.

The propellerheads lay Patrice on a bed while Brannigan, Afu, Renfro and I all stood outside, watching the busy scientists through glass windows as if Patrice was a pet turtle in a terrarium. Her eyes were closed and her skin had turned a strange color – darker in most places but bright red in others. The propellerheads stripped her down to her underwear before engaging a wall of throbbing light on the other side of the glass to block us from seeing what they were doing.

"And here I thought I'd be the one getting tossed into a sick lab." I leaned my back against the glass window and crossed my arms. A heat filled my head, but it wasn't like the fever that had taken hold of

Patrice. This was a pure wad of pissed off.

"Relax, T," said Afu. "This ain't about you right now."

"I'm not trying to make it about me!" I shouted. "Patrice barely came in contact with those bastards out there today. She shouldn't be going through this."

"Everybody calm the fuck down," said Brannigan.

Naveena rushed in from the double doors at the end of the hall. She walked straight to Chief, but he kept his eyes on the sick lab, despite the light curtain.

"They tell you yet?" Naveena asked. "What they fought?"

"We'll get to that later," Brannigan said. "Not really the time."

Naveena shook her head, rolling her eyes slightly. "She'll be fine, you guys. Chief, I don't think you understand what emerged out there today. It was—"

"A fucking phoenix." Brannigan turned to her, now visibly as miffed as I felt. He even put his hands on his hips to look more intimidating.

"How'd you know about the phoenix?" Naveena said. "News travels fast around here, but not *that* fast."

Brannigan quickly dropped his hands and replaced his tough guy attitude with the face of someone caught with his hand in the vending droid.

"Yeah," I said, walking over to stand beside Naveena. "We barely said anything over the radio, and Naveena was the first person I told."

"Wait." Renfro rubbed his face, as if trying to quickly wake up. "Did you say 'phoenix'? Like the fire bird?"

Brannigan tucked in his lips and nodded.

"What the hell, Williams!" said Renfro. "Why didn't you tell me?"

"You ran off before we could, brah." Afu shrugged.

"Don't none of y'all try to derail this conversation," I said. "Chief? You want to tell me how you knew?"

He took a deep breath through his nose as he toed a piece of tile with his boot. When Brannigan looked up, he said, "I placed a camera on the front of your truck."

"Goddamn it, Brannigan!" I slammed a fist against the glass of the sick lab. "It was that black square on the grill."

I knew, somehow I knew this motherfucker was going to pull something like this on me. In my mind it would have been something a bit less 'Big Brother.' Having Naveena keep an eye on me or calling me into his office to talk every week or so would have been expected. But this?

"Now, chill out," Brannigan said. "I'm still the chief, remember?"

"Uh uh." I began pacing in front of him. "Not right now you're not. When you start spying on me, you're back to being the same asshole who stole my car and left all of us stranded at Cedar Point."

"For fuck's sake," Brannigan said. "You're still pissed about that? A dragon destroyed my house and almost killed my wife and dog."

"Your dog's a robot!"

"Still!"

Afu burst into laughter and it caught all of us off guard. For a while we just stared at him as his eyes watered and the guffaws grew louder. Then, one by one, we all were laughing.

"I missed this," Afu said. "All of us, like when we first started working together."

"I'm sorry, Williams," Brannigan said.

I looked at him, this old white dude who was like my dad here at work. "I'm sorry, too, Chief."

Secretly, I hoped all of this would bring back the old Brannigan. That is, the one who was cool with slaying monsters. Chief was beyond the regular "old," no matter what his dragon blood infusion had done for his physique. He was a born smokie, but he'd pulled some crazy shit going after a three-headed dragon and had been dropped from a height that would have killed or paralyzed anybody else. Two weeks of riding around in a psionic wheelchair and daily infusions of curate later, Brannigan came out better than before.

Hadn't done shit for his attitude, though. I could only hope that the dragon blood would heal Patrice just as good.

Yolanda came out of the sick lab and jogged over. "Patrice is resting for now. Not much you can do. You guys will want to come with me, though. This stuff is still burning."

# CHAPTER 13

Two glass containers sat on either end of a table in Yolanda's lab, both glowing like tiny infernos from their contents. One held the ashes from the phoenix, the other contained the embers from the smaug.

When the door slid closed behind Afu, Yolanda spun around with her yellow lab coat flapping open as if she was some superhero of the periodic table.

"So is it true then?" She smiled, filled with so much excitement she might have burst into flames. "Was it a phoenix?"

"Yes," all five of us said at the same time.

"Hot dog!" Yolanda drove a fist into her open palm. "I really wish you would have kept it alive. The possible—"

"We tried," I said. "At the risk of getting burned alive, too. The Sandman didn't do shit, so Patrice trapped it with the chain net. Then it blew itself up."

"Must have been some kind of defense mechanism," Brannigan said. "Maybe like when there were bumblebees and they'd die after stinging you?"

"The tranq laser didn't affect it?" Yolanda could have been talking about her collection of mold spores. "Whacky."

"More like wack," I said. "Wack as hell. The Sandman should put anything living to sleep. Not just dragons. Do you remember what happened to that one smokie on Slayer 13? Newton or somebody?"

Afu nodded. "Accidentally power jumped into the path of the laser and was out cold for nearly a month."

"This bird is obviously different," Yolanda said. "The fact that it exists is a complete anomaly. If only I'd been able to study it."

Chief took out his holoreader and set it on the table between the two containers. A hologram video of the phoenix rose above the screen. The fiery bird flapped its wings, zooming toward tiny versions of Afu and me.

"I didn't see this until Renfro and Naveena were already on their way," Brannigan told me.

I rolled my eyes.

In the holovideo, a chain net flew into the picture and caught the phoenix, throwing it into the ground. A moment later, tiny Afu tackled tiny me as the phoenix fire grew bigger despite the foam I had been dumping onto it – I hadn't even realized that was happening. Next thing you know, the phoenix burst into an explosion of flames that could have destroyed two city blocks.

We were goddamn lucky to be alive.

Brannigan shut off the holoreader as a digital Patrice was calling us ash kickers, and returned it to his pocket. "What do you make of that, Yolanda?"

The propellerhead rubbed her chin and walked around to the other side of the table. "I'm going to talk this out because it's all muddy in my head right now. We know that fire acts differently depending on the conditions and the fuel it's gobbling up to continue burning. But this," she held a hand out to each glowing container, "won't quit burning."

"It even burned up a wraith," said Afu.

Naveena widened her eyes and turned to me. "No shit?"

"Yup," I said.

"And these two are very different substances. Not just in how they look." Yolanda grabbed each container and began sliding them towards each other. "But similar in how they – ouch!"

Yolanda jerked her hands back when the containers touched. The smaug's embers flashed and died, while the phoenix ashes grew flames and filled the container.

"What in fuck?" Brannigan said.

Renfro whistled. "It's like the one container absorbed the energy from the other."

Rubbing his hands and breathing heavier, Afu said, "You know what the legend says about phoenixes, right?"

Yolanda shook her head. "Not this again."

"There was only ever one phoenix at a time, right?" Renfro said.

"Yeah," Naveena said. "But that's because it would burst into flames whenever its body was failing and would rise again from the ashes."

*Rise again from the ashes.* What if Afu was right?

We all turned our gaze to the phoenix flames. It looked like bottled hell inside the glass container.

"Told y'all!" Afu shouted.

"But that's impossible," Yolanda said. "Matter can

change, but it can't revert back. And it sure as poop can't reform into a living thing."

"Then how do you explain what we just saw?" Afu asked.

The yellow flames danced across my vision. I looked down and noticed the glow was casting shadows of us all. "Dragons," I said. "And ghosts. Hell, even the droids out there directing traffic in the middle of Parthenon City. Remember when people thought they were impossible, too?"

Naveena nodded. "She's right. I think we need to be more safe than sorry on this. Chief?"

"Right," Brannigan said. "Yolanda, we need to lock these ashes up. Somewhere fire resistant and only accessed by you and me. Can you make that happen?"

It was the first time I'd ever seen Yolanda surprised or upset. "But… but how will I study it if it's locked away?"

I could have sworn she was on the verge of tears.

"You can study the video I have and the damage to Cannon 15 when they tow it back here. If I think it's safe to do so, you can take the ashes out intermittently to do your job, but I'm firm on this, Yolanda. Okay?"

She dropped her head and nodded slightly. "I can put it in the safe-room and change the card-reader to only let in you and me. I know someone who's an expert on mythological creatures. I have to find his information. It's been a few years. Maybe some of you can go talk to him and see if he knows something that can help."

"That brings up a good question, Chief." I said. "What do me and my crew do until Cannon 15 is repaired? And what about those redneck… those volunteers who died today?"

"We'll notify their families and tell them what happened. Propellerheads on scene told me there weren't any bodies to recover since they'd been burned, eaten, or both."

"One of their bodies is still in Lake Erie," I said, remembering swimming over Wilkins' corpse.

"No use keeping this clusterfuck secret. And those idiots should have never been out there in the first place. I heard them on the video. Volunteer smokies my ass. As far as your truck and getting back to work, you can't do shit while one of your crew is lying in a sick bed anyway. Williams, you'll have to earn your new pay-grade by filling out a big ass report on everything. And I mean *everything*. I want it as thorough as you can make it. No loose ends.

"Otherwise, I'd say you all earned some paid time off for the great job you did today. Who knows how much of the state that thing would have barbecued if you hadn't been there. Oh…" Brannigan puckered his lips.

"Oh?" I asked.

"Well, this isn't really the time or place, but Sherry's been bugging the shit out of me to invite all of you out to our house this Saturday. I'm throwing a barbecue. Might as well turn it into a celebration of the ash kickers, the only smoke eater team to ever fight a goddamn phoenix. Plus, I'll have a keg."

"I'm there," the other three said in unison. Keg is a magical word.

"Don't go throwing around nicknames for us." I pinched the bridge of my nose.

Ash kickers. Ridiculous.

"I kind of like it," said Afu.

"I think I should stay here with Patrice," I said. "Going to have to cancel my DJ gig, too. So it's a no for me, Chief."

"Patrice will be there, too," Brannigan said. "I know this is scaring the shit out of you, but you've seen how fast the curate works. Look at your arm."

I did. Where a gash had been, now there was only a slight pink scar that would also vanish in time.

"I expect her to be fully-recovered by the morning," Yolanda said.

The day of a DJ gig I usually slept in so I'd have energy to go until two or five o'clock in the morning, depending on the venue. That usually didn't happen if my mama needed help with moving Daddy from his bed to his wheelchair to the toilet and back again.

But Afu said something that I'd been feeling, too. I missed this, the old team together. Even though it wouldn't be fighting scalies or running from flying wraiths, it was something I'd been craving but hadn't known I'd been missing.

I sighed and looked at Brannigan. "Can I bring my parents?"

# CHAPTER 14

"I bet you it's some damn Satanists," my daddy said from the back seat.

"Carl!" My mama's eyes about popped from her head as she spun to glare at him from the passenger seat beside me. "Don't say that word."

"What, 'damn?'"

"No, the 'S' word."

I hunched over the steering wheel a little more. I'd already been in full-Quasimodo mode since starting this joyous trek to Chief Brannigan's house. At least there would be beer and other people to distract me from my parents once we got to the barbecue.

I'd traded in my coupé for a hover-van after I'd broken up with Afu and moved in with my folks. Yolanda had generously given me the psy-roll wheelchair, the one Brannigan had been locked in on our trip to Canada. My daddy was hesitant at first and unbending against receiving any ieiunium curate, but he finally gave in on using the psychically-powered wheelchair when I assured him he could get in and out of it anytime he wanted and that I would drive him to his Friday night card game when I wasn't on shift.

The propellerheads had helped me trick out my van with an extendable ramp where Daddy could roll in and out. They even installed a holoreader into the psy-roll so my dad could watch the Feed, controlling the volume and channels with his mind. All it took with the upgraded version was a few sticky pads to his head.

The Feed is what had brought up my daddy's outburst about Satanists. There'd been another suicide arson fire. It had happened in broad daylight in the middle of a hospital while I'd been fighting the phoenix. The fire department had successfully contained the blaze, but there were still casualties. The only video of what happened showed the torcher engulfed in flames and walking into a janitor's closet full of chemicals that had advanced the blaze.

"These idiots that are blaming the new people moving to the city have got it all wrong," Daddy said. "They're just regular folks trying to get help, even if they're wanting that devil juice."

'Devil Juice' is what he called the dragon blood curate. I was conflicted on his position. An infusion would have my dad walking on his own again and breathing normally in a day's time, but I also understood where he was coming from. It was weird to put a foreign substance in your system to begin with. Given that it was the blood of the monsters that were trying to burn and eat every last one of us, you could multiply the strange factor a hundredfold.

I looked at my daddy through the rearview mirror. He was shaking his head and had his eyes glued to the holoreader.

"A few people have said these arsonists might be a

part of some cult," I said.

"Satanists!" he shouted.

"Carl Williams!" My mother put a hand to her face and leaned against her window. "We don't have to say that name. And you don't even know if that's true. I tell you something, though. Nothing has changed since the beginning of time. Fire, lasers. When I was growing up it was bullets and automatic rifles. Terrible people would walk into a church and start shooting. Or go into a school and kill babies. Evil people have been around forever. Evil people with sick minds and souls. This world needs Jesus."

This was nowhere near the conversation I wanted to be having on a Saturday afternoon. I tried to imagine how crisp and cold Brannigan's keg beer would be. My mom would have to drive us back, because the way it was going now, I was planning on getting blitzed.

Cars and trucks filled the street outside Brannigan's house when we pulled up. When I got out the smell of burning meat and kids' screaming filled the air. As a smoke eater you get used to that kind of thing but it was usually in a completely different context.

"Now you stay away from any red meat, Carl," my mom said as Daddy rolled out of the van and onto the sidewalk. "You don't want your gout acting up."

"Woman, I've lived long enough to have earned the right to eat what I want."

Rather than stay around listening to a five-minute argument, I shoved my hands into my jeans pockets and trudged toward Brannigan's backyard.

Chief was at the grill, tongs in one hand and a

plastic cup in the other while he talked to Afu and Harribow. Everyone was wearing polo shirts or tank tops. It was kind of weird to see us all together outside of uniform, even though I hung out with one or two of them off duty.

Brannigan's adopted daughter, Bethany, and a few other kids were chasing their robot dog around the party. The dog's name was Kenji and he only spoke Korean, but he was more faithful than any biological pet I'd ever met. And given that real dogs couldn't speak English either, it wasn't that big of a deal not to understand what he was saying. But I'd recently installed an automatic translation app onto my holoreader for just such an occasion.

Brannigan's wife, Sherry, walked out of the house with a tray of deviled eggs – there wouldn't be enough for everybody, given that all chicken eggs came from one of the farming skyscrapers downtown, and every citizen of Parthenon City was only allowed a dozen a week. These farms of glass and steel were the only way to get fresh produce and non-chemically-created animal products in a country with toxic soil and nothing but ashes covering the ground. Part of me felt bad for the cows and chickens stuffed on each floor, but the greater part of me would be pissed if I didn't get a burger every once in a while.

Sherry placed the tray of eggs onto a long table that had been covered with a cheap red cloth and other trays of food. Above the table, a holobanner flickered in the sunlight, saying, "Thanks, Ash Kickers!"

Goddamn it.

I walked over to Sherry. "Need help with anything?"

Her red and gray hair swung over her shoulder when she turned to smile and hug me. "Hey, Tamerica! No, I've pretty much got everything taken care of. Get yourself a drink. Keg and cups are at the end of the table there. As soon as Cole is done taking his sweet time at the grill, we should be ready to eat."

"I'm definitely hitting the keg." I gestured my head toward Mama and Daddy making their way into the backyard. "My parents came with."

"That's great!" She spun away from me as if a spider had bitten her on the ass. "Bethany! Stop riding Kenji like a horse and go wash your hands."

Little Brannigan, with fist raised to the sky as she galloped around the yard on the back of her metal steed, jumped off with a malicious laugh and ran into the house.

Back to me, Sherry grinned, as happy as she could be, and said, "I love being a mom."

At the keg, the ice-cold beer filled my cup – a golden brown with beautiful foam. Chief had gotten the good stuff. I stood there sipping on it while I got a lay of the land, keeping back before I had to start mingling with people I didn't feel like talking to, or having to explain my parents.

Patrice hadn't shown up yet. For the last few days, I'd been calling Yolanda almost constantly to see if my driver was back to her old crazy self. Yolanda was so good natured, she would have never come right out and told me to shut the hell up and let her do her job, but when she started rattling off figures and million-dollar words in reference to Patrice's condition, I knew I'd bugged her about it enough. I just told Yolanda to call me when things had gotten better.

She never called me.

I tried not to worry. I sold myself on the notion it was because Yolanda had forgotten. Knowing Patrice, my driver would probably want to make a big entrance at the barbecue – like popping out of a cake. But I didn't see any over-sized baked goods either.

Harribow was a few feet away, animated hands in the air as he talked to Naveena, who was looking at the ground and nodding.

"I read that New York *and* Boston have brought in the New US Army to handle the scalies," he said. "They won't have smoke eaters anymore."

"I can't see that happening," said Naveena. "Not here."

I couldn't either. Soldier girls and boys had their shot on E-Day, and they let us down. You can't replace an ass-kicking municipal force that can breathe dragon smoke with a bunch of messy loose-cannons more accustomed to shooting other people. It'd be like sending a cop to get a cat out of a tree. Firefighters have ladders, the police have guns. Both tools can provide a way to put a feline on the ground, but in drastically different conditions.

A slight bump against my thigh got me to look down. Kenji sat there with his rubber tongue dangling out of the side of his metal mouth; his body was gray and painted with polka dots like a Dalmatian. He happily barked once and the dark screen above his nose displayed hearts and shimmering digital blue irises.

I patted him on the head, because what else do you do to an excited dog sitting in front of you, metal or otherwise.

"*Moduga sul-e chwihaeissda!*" he said.

My holoreader instantly spoke to translate. "Everyone is getting drunk!"

"Not everyone," I told Kenji. I raised my cup. "Not yet."

Kenji was a regular at headquarters. Brannigan liked to take him along on big calls, especially dragon-caused building collapses. You never knew if someone was trapped, and the dog also helped calm down scared kids.

The robot's chest ejected a plastic bone which he snatched up and raised to me. His voice came out clear from behind the fake bone. "*Nalang nol-a, tteugeoun geosdeul.*"

Translated: "Play with me, hot stuff."

I laughed, despite being slightly harassed by an AI K9. Throwing the bone across the yard, I wondered what other irreverent bullshit the dog could say. Kenji sprinted across the yard, kicking up mounds of dirt and faux-grass. He had to have been going thirty miles an hour.

"Kenji, slow the fuck down!" Brannigan shouted at his dog, before looking around to see if Sherry had heard him cuss in front of their guests.

My mama headed over to coo over the kids. Daddy was wheeling up to the grill to park beside Chief.

Afu, seeing my father on the way, decided to move on to another part of the back yard. He'd always thought my dad hated him, but I'd never heard my father say anything about Afu one way or the other, or any of my boyfriends for that matter. He just let me wade through my own relationships by myself and then listened to me gripe or cry when they didn't work out.

I sighed and downed my beer. Here we go.

"That's not dragon meat you're cooking is it?" Daddy asked.

Brannigan, of course, laughed. But you could never tell if my daddy was joking or not, especially when it came to dragons or smoke eaters.

Chief held up a piece of meat that dripped red juice. "City-grown rib eyes. Might as well chew on one of my wife's old baseballs, but old habits die hard. Scalies have ruined enough of this country already. I'll be damned if they take my cookouts from me."

"I hear that," Daddy said, then dropped his voice to a whisper. "Save one of the big ones for me, but don't tell my Rebecca."

Brannigan nodded, the firm, between-us-men kind of head movement. "How are you, Carl? That wheelie box working out okay? Watch when you nod or move your head. I banged my chin more than twice. And I'm not going to lie, I still have nightmares about being stuck in it, but it's good you can get in and out as you please."

"I like that I only have to blink to change the TV channels." Daddy smiled then, as if he'd been holding it in and finally relented to having a good time.

All older people still called the Feed 'TV.' And my dad didn't even need to blink to change the Feed stations, he just thought he did, and I'd gotten tired of telling him otherwise.

"Glad you made it, Williams," Brannigan said as I walked up.

"Beer is good," I said.

My daddy grunted. "Don't get messy around these folks, Tammy."

I tossed Brannigan wide eyes and tight lips, a visual SOS, as I finished off what was left in my cup.

"Hey, Carl," Brannigan said. "Why don't you go find a place to park? This should be done in a minute or two and I'll make sure Sherry distracts Rebecca so you can eat your meat in peace."

Daddy smiled and zoomed off. "All right, then."

"Thanks," I told Brannigan when we were alone.

"It's a strange thing being a parent," he said. "You want your kids to be their own person, but you also want to influence them enough to not fuck up their life."

I pointed to Bethany, who picked up a deviled egg and fast-balled it into another kid's face. "You seem to be doing okay with it."

"Yeah, one can only hope."

"Is Patrice coming?" I asked.

Brannigan dropped the ribeye he'd been tonging and sighed. "I talked to Yolanda just before you showed up. She's still not any better."

I chunked my empty plastic cup into a trash can. "Thanks, for the invite, Chief, but I've got to go."

"Hold your damn horses." Brannigan slammed the grill lid closed. "You can't do anything better than the propellerheads can. I get it, you feel responsible, but you're not."

"I don't feel right, drinking beer and eating steaks while she's burning up in a sick bed. You said she'd be better. All of you. What's going on?"

Brannigan shrugged, shook his head, a man with no answers. "Yolanda said the curate isn't taking. They're filling Johnson with fluids and trying their best to keep her fever down, but nothing they do is working."

I glanced at my parents – Daddy at the end of the picnic table, smiling with the lid of his psy-roll opened like an old, gull wing car door, my mom bouncing a kid on her lap.

"I'll be back in a few to pick up my parents," I said.

Brannigan nodded. "Okay, Williams. You're a good captain."

When I turned toward the exit, a droid was walking in to the party.

"What the fuck," Brannigan said behind me.

Body painted to make it look like it wore a two-piece suit, the droid scanned the area with its head swiveling left to right – until it spotted me and Brannigan. Its leg hydraulics hissed as it lumbered over to the grill. I backed up and Brannigan lifted his grilling tongs like a weapon.

When the droid's blaring blue eyes zeroed in on me, it spoke with a digital Australian twang. "Captain Tamerica Williams."

Droids could be programmed to know exactly who was who, like walking societal archives. There weren't *that* many people left in Ohio to sort through, and the droid could scan through a million records a second.

The droid stood there for a moment, as if waiting for me to confirm.

"Yeah?" I said.

A compartment ejected from the droid's leg, where a gun would have been holstered. Brannigan threw an arm across me and slapped the droid across the metal jaw with his tongs.

The droid, not fazed at all, besides steak juice splattered across its flat face, removed a stack of plastic paper from its leg compartment and handed the bundle to me.

"You've been served," the droid said in a cheerful voice, before turning around and leaving the barbecue with heavy, clanking steps.

And that's when I remembered something. "Mother of fuck," I muttered, not caring if my mama or daddy heard. With all the chaos the phoenix had brought, Patrice getting sick, it had slipped my mind completely.

I'd never turned in the wraith I'd caught in Sandusky. It was still in my remote.

# CHAPTER 15

I should have been sitting beside Patrice, to be the first person to apologize for what she'd been through. Yolanda had done me a solid, though, setting up a live feed camera in the sick lab so I could keep an eye on Patrice through my holoreader. I'd been checking the camera at least twice every thirty minutes. Propellerheads would come in, check her vitals and mess with a computer in the room. Patrice just laid there.

It would still be better to be there in person.

But that's the thing about trying to work as a professional club DJ – if you cancel a gig, you're inevitably cancelling your career. So, waiting for my turn in the DJ booth, I sat my ass down on a stool at the neon-lit bar, between a group of loud and obnoxious patrons who were blowing glowing bubbles into the air after every hit from their vapes. One neon yellow boil floated too close to my face and I popped it with a stab of my finger.

I was surrounded by assholes and a thumping bass track.

The droid at Brannigan's party had served me a subpoena to appear before a hearing with the mayor of Parthenon City, the families of the deceased "volunteer smoke eaters" and both sides' legal representation. They were suing for wrongful death due to my negligence and also to have Mr Wilkins' wraith returned to them.

They'd gotten a copy of my incident report, so there was no denying that I'd trapped the wraith. But I never mentioned turning it in to one of the enclosures. For all they knew, Wilkins was floating around with other ghastly ghouls like himself, protecting Parthenon City with their electric glow.

*So do I own up and tell them I still have the wraith? Or do I keep it my little secret?*

The longer I sat on it, the higher chance my ass would be in a lot more trouble than it already was.

After the droid left the barbecue, Chief Brannigan had told me a hundred times that I shouldn't let it worry me. That I'd done nothing wrong and it would be crazy to hand over wraiths to the public. No judge would allow it. But he didn't know I still had it in my possession either.

He was trying to make me feel better, but the thing about people offering condolences and kind words is that it was more for the speaker than the intended recipient. When someone's in a real pit, no one can say a damned thing to get them out. They have to build their own ladder and take each rung when they're good and ready.

And I was hip-high in shit, thank you very much.

The subpoena droid had found me pretty quickly. It first stopped by headquarters and the helpful smokies who'd been on shift told it about Brannigan's barbecue. My co-workers hadn't even thought to warn me ahead of time. The on-duty folks probably just thought the droid was delivering a package or something. Then again, I thought a droid wearing a painted-on suit and riding in a smart car should have tipped them off.

It was a great idea, though, using a droid to serve subpoenas.

Most people, angry at receiving a summons, would think twice about punching a metal face, and those who might say fuck it and take a swing anyway would only break their hand in the attempt. Outside of that, the bot could take any onslaught of four-letter words in absence of fists.

"You wanna dance?"

I'd been hunched over the bar, staring at the top of my drink, when someone touched my shoulder and spoke into my ear. When I turned around, a blonde woman stood there, wearing a light-up tank top. She put her hand on my forearm as she moved her hips to the music.

"I would destroy you on the dance floor." I gently removed her hand. "Besides, I'm the next up in the DJ booth."

"Oh!" She removed a beer bottle she'd been keeping in the back of her white jeans and downed what was left. "Can you play me a song? I want to hear Melting Thunder."

"I'll see what I can do."

Something I'd learned quickly, doing these gigs, was that people have horrible taste in music, but they're also contributing to your pay for the night. You don't want to say no, but you also don't want to lie to them. So, you *saw* what you could do, and I saw myself not ever playing the cocked-up song she'd requested.

"You know," she said, breathing alcoholic funk in my face, "I've always wanted to be a DJ. Maybe you can teach me."

"DJing is nothing," I said. "You have a more impressive talent."

"I do?"

"Yeah, you can apparently pull beer bottles out of your ass."

My holoreader vibrated in my pocket. Afu was calling. I'd never been happier to see his name in digital green.

"Nice knowing you," I told Drunk Becky, and stepped over to a corner to hear better.

"I'm at the door," Afu said. "Can you get me inside?"

I put a finger in my free ear. "You break your legs or something?"

"Guy at the door says the place is at capacity."

I turned and looked at the crowd. There was barely enough room to scratch your ass let alone dance. I wasn't about to tell Afu he should have gotten there earlier and that he was on his own. No, I wanted him there with me. Not as an ex-boyfriend, and it wasn't even because he was a fellow smoke eater. I wanted him with me as a reverse wingman – someone to help keep people *away* from me. He'd also be the voice of reason, encouraging me to get up on the decks and kill it, to do it for Patrice if that's what it took to get me through the night.

"I'll be right there."

I pushed my way through the gyrating horde, shoving a path to the beat of music that sounded like lasers getting strangled by cats. DJ Asmodeus was spinning at the moment and he liked to play bangers that had the ambience of stereotyped 80s dance hits – and I mean the 1980s.

I was almost to the door when a sweaty man bumped into me, nearly causing me to set off a domino effect of dancing idiots.

"Watch it, man," I said.

The guy was coated in sweat, soaking his clothes. Even under the spastic flash of laser lights, I could see he was as pale as a leviathan's underside. He'd probably taken too much of whatever substance they were passing around the club. This wasn't a spark high, this was something a lot worse.

"You okay?" I asked. "Maybe you should go home."

He ground his teeth and squeezed his eyes shut, as if he was losing a deadly battle with constipation. "Ph… phoenix."

"What did you say?"

He turned and disappeared into the crowd.

I must have been hearing things. Some mild form of PTSD or something. A flashback. No one knew about the phoenix – no one outside my pending litigation, anyway. And it was so loud in here, there was no telling what he'd said. I shook it off and pushed my way to the front door.

Outside, Afu was at the front of a line of people who had taken to drinking from flasks previously hidden in their purses, or playing on their holoreader. The man guarding the door was dwarfed by Afu. I could tell it bugged the bouncer to have to turn away someone who could have easily thrown him into

Canada, because he was looking anywhere but at the smiling Polynesian in front of him.

I tapped the guy on the shoulder. "Big one is with me."

"Oh, good," he said, releasing the breath he'd been holding. He relaxed his puffed out chest, waving Afu in as he nervously scratched his three-day beard shadow. "Enjoy yourself, pal."

"He just call me 'pal?'" Afu asked as we squeezed back inside.

"Maybe he can call you sweetheart. Take you to the VIP area for some necking."

Afu laughed. "Beard scruff breaks my skin out."

The people in the line outside began shouting complaints, and I felt bad that the doorman had traded a giant for an angry band of club-hopping mercenaries.

I led Afu to the barstool I'd been sitting on, but Drunk Becky had taken it.

"You brought the big guns," she said, looking Afu up and down.

"And I bet you have a bull's-eye tattooed on you somewhere." I turned to Afu. "You can hang out here. I go on in about," I checked my holoreader's clock, "five minutes."

Drunk Becky clung to Afu's arm like a piece of unwanted jewelry. "What's your name?"

"He's mine," I said.

Afu snapped his head to me, raising an eyebrow so sharply it could have flown off.

"I mean, he's with me," I said.

Before shit got any more awkward, I stomped off

to the DJ booth and secured myself behind its short swinging door. Squatting in a corner, I closed my eyes and focused on my breathing. A club is not the most conducive environment for meditation, but if I didn't quit thinking about my personal shit, I'd flub the music.

"Crowd is jumping!" DJ Asmodeus said, thumbing toward the dance floor. "I'm ready for you to mix in if you're ready."

He hadn't taken off his wireless headphones – or sunglasses, for some dumb reason – so I just gave him the OK sign. Asmodeus was a thin white dude I knew almost nothing about, not even his real name, but he looked like the kind of guy who sold dragon insurance during the day.

My smoke eater power suit stood in the corner, and I stepped into it before I talked myself out of the gig. It wasn't technically against the rules to use smokie equipment for outside endeavors, but I wasn't about to advertise it in a department newsletter. The suit was all for show. It looked cool and menacing and the laser lights looked awesome bouncing off of the green metal.

As I turned on my DJ deck and connected it to my holoreader, Asmodeus introduced me.

"All right, party people! We're out here making Summer 2123 the best ever. Next up is one of your favorites. Let me hear you make some noise for Funky! Cold! Medea!"

No, I didn't pick that name. I'd been happy to spin using the name my mama gave me, but the club owner had suggested it because it sounded cool

– only to him – and it was the name of the woman from Greek myth who'd put a dragon to sleep so Jason could steal the Golden Fleece.

The crowd roared, though, when I stepped up and lifted two armored fists into the air. I jumped onto Asmodeus's last track with a thumping, steady beat – I liked mixing old school hip-hop with electronica – and turned on the hologram machine.

Two digital blue dragons swirled through the crowd and the people lost their minds. It was my signature, probably what drew a lot of the crowd out. Who could resist a real-life smoke eater playing tracks while ghostly, electric dragons danced on the floor beside you? Maybe that was another thing holding me back from leaving the dragon-catching business. I was scared that my pull as a DJ would die with it. I wanted to be a DJ, not a smoke eater who happened to play music every other weekend.

Through a few songs, I glanced over at Afu at the bar. Drunk Becky was hanging onto him talking his ear off, but he kept his eyes and bobbing head toward me. I was surprised Becky hadn't tried her magic-beer-appearing trick on him.

Goddamn it, why did I care?

I diverted my gaze to the mass of people churning five feet below on the dance floor. The sweaty drughead who'd bumped into me earlier shuffled, zombie-like, through gyrating hips and flapping elbows. His skin looked a dozen shades worse than before. Someone was definitely not having a good time.

The crowd swallowed him. Someone yelled indiscernible words from the dance floor, and then flames exploded in the middle of the crowd.

I immediately stopped the music, but the sound of screams replaced it in equal volume. It was like watching eels squirm in a drained fish tank. None of them could find space to run, so a few of them shoved others down to make room. At least three people were on fire, and everyone else was trying like hell to get away from them.

Holy shit. The flames were neon yellow.

I leapt over the DJ booth, leaving Asmodeus to cower in the corner. People pelted against my suit like fleshy bullets. To my right, Afu was pushing in from the outer ring of the fleeing crowd with a huge bucket that sloshed with liquid and chunks of ice. He'd made it only a few feet when someone bumped into his back, causing him to toss the bucket.

The water hit most of its mark but it did nothing to the flames. In fact, the fire was rising higher, almost touching the ceiling. In no time, the entire top of the club would be engulfed, the smoke would fill the room, and all the people inside would be incinerated, whether they could breathe smoke or not.

Fuck that.

I raised my foam gun into the air, hoping the arc would be high enough to coat the people who'd caught fire and prevent anyone else from ending up the same way. The sticky goop shot into the air and rained onto the flames. A few of the dancers trying to escape slipped on the foam and dropped to the floor. I couldn't help that. Besides, it was a shit ton better than catching fire.

But the foam was doing a lousy job, sizzling away

like cream on a stove top as it made contact with the
crispy forms lying on the dance floor. By the time
I realized I couldn't extinguish those who'd caught
fire, they were already dead. The ceiling caught next,
and the smoke quickly followed, banking down in
thickening layers. I looked toward the exit where
people had crammed into the doorway, trying to flee
all at once. Bodies stacked on each other five high,
where no one could get in or out.

I tried pelting the yellow flames rolling above me,
but it was too high. Blinded, coughing people kept
bumping into me, throwing off my aim. It had taken
too much foam to cover the people who'd caught fire,
and I didn't have a spare foam cartridge with me to
keep shooting.

Repeating the same thing and expecting different
results is the definition of insanity. At that moment, if
my foam wasn't doing a damned thing to extinguish
the fire, then I needed another plan, one where
pointlessly fucking around with the disco inferno
wasn't a part of it.

I hit my power jump and sailed through the dark
smoke, taking in big gasps of it before landing near
the door, accidentally crashing into Drunk Becky,
and sending her to the floor. I held a hand out to
pick her back up, but she sat on her ass, wrapping her
arms around her knees, and refused to get to her feet.

Afu pushed through the crowd as the mass of
bodies thickened near the door. "What do we do?"

"You keep these people away from me," I said.
"I'm going to relieve a little pressure."

Afu immediately stuck out both of his enormous

arms and gave me some room to work by shoving at least ten people back.

The doorway was a packed cluster of kicking stilettos and dress shoes. There were other emergency exits in the club, but in a panic, people don't think clearly. Everyone had come through the front door, so that's where they'd run to escape. They probably hadn't even noticed the other exit signs.

"Clear the way," I shouted, pointing to the group beside the door. All but one of them obeyed, so I grabbed the remaining whimpering man and shoved him toward the others.

I kicked at the wall beside the door. With my power suit's added strength, my boot made a huge dent in the wall, but it wasn't anything the building occupants could run through. A few more times I kicked, only breaking through a little each time. I was worn out, but the smoke and fire weren't going to give any of us a break, and using my lasers would have been too dangerous with so many people so close to the line of fire.

I squatted into a football player's stance and leaned my right shoulder forward.

"What are you doing?" Afu shouted.

I waited for the *ding* of my power suit and hit the jump button, crashing through the wall at what felt like a hundred miles per hour into solid rock.

Skidding to a stop on the asphalt outside, I sat up and watched the crowd burst from the extra wide opening I'd created. The people who'd been caught in the doorway were no longer trapped, although it took a few of them to realize it after the ones on top of them finally crawled out.

Afu broke ahead of the rest as they poured out of the club like rice from a busted bag. He was fast for someone so large. He hefted me to my feet and said, "Are you, okay?"

My eyes were looking into Afu's but what I was seeing in my mind were the burned bodies of the people who hadn't made it out of Club Infinity. I saw blackened heaps that couldn't be recognized as human beings any more. And I cried, falling into Afu without caring about staying upright on my own.

He wrapped his arms around me and let me cry into his chest as he held the weight of both me and the power suit. Anyone else would have toppled over.

Several feet away, the club had become "fully involved" as Brannigan would say. Which means that the roof, walls… everything… had caught fire, and anyone still inside wouldn't be coming out alive.

Sirens howled from too far away, the regular fire department responding. Dark smoke drifted across the illuminated windows of surrounding buildings as flames licked at the night sky, more orange now than the neon yellow that had started it all.

# CHAPTER 16

Club Infinity was another venue added to the list of places I wouldn't be able to DJ. Scratch that. My turntable and the rest of my gear were now spinning in the charred great beyond, so I wouldn't be performing anywhere. My lifeboat to a different career had gone up in flames as much as everything else.

I'd bought all the equipment on credit and hadn't even paid it off yet. At least I'd been smart enough to grab my holoreader, thanks to the unnatural relationship we all have with our personal electronic devices.

Life sucks.

*Don't think that way,* Mama would say. *You're alive and the same can't be said of a few folks who were there tonight.*

The fire department had finally put the fire out, although by the time they arrived, there wasn't much club left to burn. It was the first time I'd felt helpless on an emergency scene. With no dragons present, I was the one who had to stay behind the blue hologram ribbons keeping citizens out of the hot zone while the firefighters worked.

Imagine that. Me, a normal citizen. Just the thought of it made me sick. Well, that and the smell of burnt construction.

I sat on the bumper of one of the on-scene fire engines with my power suit standing beside me, answering questions first from the fire marshal, and then a detective. The fire marshal was white haired and bespectacled, could have been a mall Santa Claus come Christmas time. The detective, with a thin goatee, looked more like he could have been Satan a few months earlier. I don't know if I was much help to them. I mentioned the sweaty guy, but didn't mention what I thought he'd mumbled. The phoenix was dead and burned, after all.

The detective and fire marshal had taken Afu to the other side of the parking lot so we wouldn't get our stories mixed up, helping each other remember things and coming up with a completely imagined scenario. It was typical procedure to separate witnesses to avoid that kind of mental telephone game. Staring at the smoldering ashes and bones of the building, all I wanted to know was how this could have happened.

That guy, the sweaty one. I'd seen him in the crowd just before the fire started. On the surface, he could have been one of those suicidal arsonists the Feed kept talking about. But even if he was, how did he do it? He was coated in liquid but hadn't smelled of accelerant. It was sweat. I could still smell it on the mental wisps of memory.

Even if he'd been able to mask the smell of an accelerant, that didn't explain how the fire had grown so large so quickly. Gasoline didn't act like that, and I couldn't think of anything else that could. Was he wearing a device of some kind? No, I would have felt it underneath his clothes when I bumped into him.

"He said we're all 'Children of the phoenix'."

I snapped out of my thoughts and looked toward who had spoken; a woman in a black skirt sitting in the back of an ambulance. The fire marshal and detective were consoling her.

"And then the fire started?" the fire marshal asked. She nodded.

"Did he have anything in his hands? A button, a lighter, some kind of remote."

"No," the woman said with a cough. Black finger streaks ran down the sides of her face. The whites of her eyes had turned red. "I didn't see anything like that. He just... caught fire."

All the advances in technology, but fire was still fire. And there were a million and one ways to start it.

The fire marshal sighed and looked at the detective. He jerked his head back toward me before thanking the woman and trudging over to where I sat, cradling my holoreader and wondering if I should call my parents or Chief Brannigan first.

Great. More questions I didn't have any answers to. I fought dragons, goddamn it, not arsonists. From what I'd seen happen in that club, though, I had it easy in my career. People: those are the real monsters everyone should be worried about. A dragon burns and eats because that's what it was born to do. You can predict its movement and behavior, for the most part. They're natural. Humans on the other hand; you never knew what sick shit lay hidden between the folds of their gray matter.

"Captain Williams," the fire marshal said. "Sorry to keep you here so long, I know you've had a rough night."

"Hell, I've had a rough year," I said. "This sucks, but it's nothing I can't handle."

He hadn't seen me crying into Afu's chest.

"Right." The fire marshal cleared his throat and looked at the detective beside him like he didn't know what the hell I was talking about, but was pretending for my benefit.

"We're trying to make sense of all of this," the detective chimed in. "This is the fourth incident like this and from what we heard from other witnesses, this guy sounded like he had an agenda."

"You think it's some kind of terrorist group?" I asked.

The detective made a clicking noise out of the side of his mouth. "More like a cult."

"Should you be telling me all of this?" I asked.

"You're a smoke eater, Williams," the fire marshal said. "We don't have to hide anything from you. We just need your help."

"I certainly appreciate the interagency confidence," I said, "but I've told you everything I saw in there. I wish I knew more, but it happened so fast. It sounds like you know who did it. Hell, half the club could have called that one. As far as finding out how and why, sorry fellas, that's on you. I'm stumped."

The detective breathed out of his nose, sounding like a mixture between sigh and grumble. He sat down on the engine bumper beside me. "Your fellow smoke eater over there, the big fella, said you guys had an incident the other day that might drizzle a little more sense onto what happened here tonight."

Afu, you fucking moron.

"We were keeping that under wraps," I said. "Confidential, you understand? What did he tell you?"

"That's all he told us," the fire marshal said. "He wouldn't say anything else without his direct supervisor's approval."

"Which is you," the detective said.

I made my own grumble-sigh. "Okay, what I'm about to tell you doesn't leave this circle of three. I don't want to see this shit on the Feed later today because one of you couldn't keep your mouth shut. I know how cops and firefighters like to talk."

"You have our word," the fire marshal said.

I told them about the phoenix. Not right out of the gate. I told the whole story from when we arrived in Sandusky, met the crazy volunteer smoke eaters, and then everything that happened afterward. Who knows? Maybe in some roundabout way, having these two know my side of the story would help with my pending lawsuit.

Probably not.

They listened to everything I said, widening their eyes when I got to the part about the phoenix, but otherwise stayed quiet and treated it as normally as if I'd told them a droid had a metal ass.

"And the suspect was heard saying something about 'Children of the Phoenix'?" The detective nodded like he'd figured it all out.

"Sounds like a cult to me," the fire marshal said.

I shrugged. "It's a nice story, but it would mean he knew about the phoenix to begin with, and we haven't released that information to anybody but the victim's families, since they're suing me. I mean, *they* could have started talking about it, but we sure as shit had no idea anything like that could have existed before now. How would anyone else? That witness you talked to must have heard something through the grapevine and pulled it out of her ass. She's clearly shook. Besides, that bird is dead now, so what does it matter?"

It would matter if there were more of them. I shivered at the thought.

"So, the volunteer families could have been talking. Or maybe one of your own," the detective said. "I know how firefighters like to gossip."

"We're not the fire department," I said.

The detective shrugged. "Cut from the same cloth."

"Maybe this supposed group was the one to summon the phoenix," the fire marshal said. "And they concocted this arson spree to show devotion to their deity or something."

"Summon?" I asked. This wasn't *Dungeons and Dragons* for fuck's sake.

"Mayor Rogola did something similar," the detective said. "He used wraiths to draw dragons up. Maybe there's a group that learned about the possibility of a phoenix down below and one thing led to another and they got religious with it all."

"Guys," I said, "I'm telling you, that's not possible. I could concoct a ritual to summon a leprechaun, but that doesn't mean it would work. I mean the fire in there was…"

"Was what?" The detective wrinkled his brow.

Unkillable.

"Nothing," I said. "It was just really crazy. I've never seen anything like that."

But I had seen neon yellow fire like that before. No way in hell I was going to tell these chumps anything about, though. Not yet. Brannigan might have been convinced we were all a back-scratching group of civil servants, but until I knew why the hell some sweaty dude came up into the club shooting yellow flames like a phoenix, I wasn't going to give the cops a reason to start arresting innocent people and causing a state-wide panic.

But the phoenix was dead. Wasn't it? Something deep down told me not to count my firebirds before they resurrected, despite Yolanda's assurances.

The detective got to his feet and shoved fists into his pants pockets. The fire marshal followed and they talked in hushed tones. I might have been able to hear what they were saying if I'd tried – if I gave a damn. Instead, I turned on my holoreader to check in on Patrice.

She lay in bed while Yolanda was scrolling through holographic charts beside her. I hated that Patrice was still out of commission, but at least she had people looking after her round the clock.

Yolanda got up from her stool and turned her back to Patrice, getting really involved in whatever she was reading. Patrice sat up as if an invisible rope had been tied around her and ten people jerked on the other end.

"What the fuck?" I said aloud.

The detective and fire marshal turned to me. "What is it?" they both asked.

"Oh, nothing." I lied with a laugh and flitted a hand

in the air. "Just a dumb comedy show on the Feed."

They nodded, annoyed, and walked away as they went back to their conversation.

I stepped into my power suit and ran to the other side of the parking lot, hoping Afu had stuck around. Mostly keeping my eyes on the holoreader, I looked up only every so often to make sure I wasn't running into a fire truck or a chunk of burned dance club.

On my holoreader, Patrice turned slowly on the cot, dragging her feet off to hang just above the floor. Rising, she stood, wobbly, taking one step at a time, leaning from side to side like a zombie out for a walk.

Yolanda hadn't heard Patrice get up; she was too involved in her studies. Patrice looked like a drunken predator stalking a kill.

I shrunk the video feed to a smaller square and dialed Yolanda's number. On the screen, Yolanda fiddled inside the pocket of her lab coat, but she never got to answer my call. Patrice lunged for her, wrapping arms around Yolanda's neck and jerking her from side to side. Yolanda's holoreader dropped to the floor and skittered across the tiles before coming to a stop.

I ran faster.

Afu stood against the side of an aerial ladder truck with his eyes closed and mouth open. He snored once when I shook him and stared at me glossy-eyed, so I shook him again.

"What? What?" he said. "I'm awake."

I shook my holoreader in his face. "Patrice just attacked Yolanda."

"Say what?"

I handed him the holoreader and he raised an

eyebrow, but not in the loveable, confused way he was known for. Afu looked scared.

"We have to go," he said. "Let's take my truck."

Jogging alongside Afu, I took glances down at the holoreader. Yolanda lay on the floor. I couldn't tell if she was breathing or not. Patrice bent over the propellerhead's limp body and reached into her lab coat, ripping away a key card. When she stood, Patrice shivered. She moved toward the door leading out into the hallway, where I wouldn't be able to see what terrible thing she was going to do next.

Before Patrice left, she stopped, stone still, and raised her eyes toward the camera. She... looked at me. But the creepy thing, what sent my guts into a knot and turned my skin to ice, was that whoever was casting a death glare at the camera before charging out into the hallway, it wasn't Patrice.

# CHAPTER 17

The propellerheads answered my call on the first ring as Afu sped down the highway toward headquarters. It didn't take much to convince them Yolanda had been attacked. The drawback was protocol made them gather every scientist inside the watch room and lock it down with impenetrable titanium alloy doors.

Every smoke eater crew was out of the building. The propellerhead I spoke to said a behemoth emerged outside of Cleveland and everybody had gone, including Brannigan and Naveena – which answered the question of why neither of them had answered their holoreaders.

When Afu and I pulled up outside of headquarters, the whole building looked dark, quiet, as if nothing was amiss, a regular Saturday night out in the ashes.

"What do you think Patrice is going to do with that key card?" Afu asked as we raced up the front steps.

"I hope we find her before we find that out."

A propellerhead messaged me through the holoreader, saying they detected a heat signature on the roof. I told Afu to go put on his power suit while I made my way to the roof.

"Armor?" He opened HQ's front door and let me

through. "It's just Patrice we're talking about, right?"

"Call it a hunch," I said. "Grab my helmet while you're at it."

He nodded and jogged off toward the Slayer bay.

The only way to the roof was through a laddered hatch on the top floor, at the end of a hallway. From what I'd seen on the video feed, Patrice had barely been able to walk. How she could have gotten onto the roof was beyond me, but then again, it was even more fucked up of an idea that Patrice would attack anything that didn't have scales or ghostly tatters. I'd never heard of a fever making people go rabid. Even if that was a possibility, I'd think Patrice would be too sick to raise an arm, let alone wrap it around Yolanda's throat.

I found the ladder to the roof and took a second to breathe before climbing. It had been a long night. My armored feet and hands clanked against each rung sounding like explosions in the thick quiet of the building.

When I got to the door hatch, I raised it slowly with one hand and scanned the roof like a periscope. Patrice stood at the center of the roof with her back to me, head raised to the night sky, and her hands outstretched as if she'd recently taken up occult yoga as a hobby. Climbing onto the roof, I didn't see a pentagram drawn around her, but a jar of ashes rested between her feet.

"Patrice," I said, barely above a whisper. "What are you doing with that jar?"

She turned, only her head at first – and I seriously wondered if the damn thing would do a full 360 – but then her body followed and we faced each other, the jar of phoenix ashes now behind her.

"It's much cooler up here," she said. Her voice was calm, relaxed, as if she didn't have a care in the world.

"I'm sure you're burning up pretty bad," I said, daring a step closer. "Maybe the propellerheads can get something to keep you cool until your fever breaks."

"This isn't a fever." She shook her head and smiled. It was creepy as fuck. I'd never seen a pain-filled smile until then.

"Whatever it is—"

"It's in my head!" Her nostrils and eyes expanded as she touched her temples.

I raised my hands, palms toward her. "Okay. We're here to help you, no matter what's going on."

"None of you can help me." She was crying now.

"I want to try. You attacked Yolanda. I don't think you're in your right mind. Why did you take that key card? Why do you have those ashes? How did you even know where they were hidden?"

"I see that fucking bird, Cap. The phoenix. It's like the fire is running through my veins. I know I sound crazy, but it's like… it's like it possessed me, talking to me, even though I can't understand those damn squawks. I know what it wants. I had to get its ashes. I had to bring them up here."

This was all my fault. Those ashes had poisoned her. She was hallucinating.

"Just come with me." I stepped closer. "The phoenix is dead."

I didn't believe my own words as they came out. Something was influencing my driver, and she was too strong to let a microorganism pull her strings.

The ashes in the jar glowed brighter, throbbing and pressing against the glass. They wanted out. It didn't make any sense, but I couldn't let Patrice open that jar. I had to try talking her down. If that didn't work, I'd have to tackle her, drag her kicking and screaming back to the sick lab.

Moving faster than I would have expected her to, Patrice bent over and lifted the glowing jar above her head. "I know what I have to do to end the pain. It hurts, T. It hurts so fucking much."

"Whatever you think you have to do," I said. "I promise you, you don't have to do anything. I don't know what's going on, but I want to. We have the best people in the state, maybe even the whole goddamned country that can make you better. Don't give up, Patrice."

"I'm not giving up." Her face softened. She swallowed, even though her grimace made it look like razor blades were traveling down her throat. "I'm moving on."

She smashed the jar against the roof floor.

"No!" I shouted, but the glass had already shattered before I finished.

Flames erupted from the broken shards, engulfing Patrice so fully and quickly that I lost sight of her. The fire spread in a flash of hot neon yellow. There was no way I'd be able to withstand it once I came into contact, and I would burn for days if I did. I took off toward the edge of the roof and power jumped as the flames lashed at my boots.

My thrusters lowered me to the ground, but from that height, gravity moved me faster than I would have liked. I landed on my back, ejecting all the air from my lungs. Above me, the roof was a saffron inferno. I began to cry, but it was cut off by another wail. It wasn't a wraith. And it wasn't Patrice.

The shriek clawed through the air, nearly splitting my ears. Up from the burning roof flew a phoenix that wasted no time hanging around. Its fiery wings streaked across the night sky, still visible as a glowing blob on the other side of the thick clouds that began to gather.

Patrice.

Patrice was dead. It was all I could think about, and after the hell I'd already been through that night, there was no way I could go on. I had one job. All I had to do was keep my crew safe, and I couldn't even do that. What a piece of shit I was. But something inside me morphed out of misery and into a fury that would have given the phoenix fire a run for its money.

I was madder than fuck and I had to do something about it.

So I charged back into headquarters and shouted for Afu until I'd found him in the hallway leading to the roof access.

"What happened?" He handed me my helmet. "I thought you would have already been on the roof, and then I heard that explosion and the shriek. It almost sounded like–"

"The phoenix is back," I said. "Patrice is dead. I'm going to murder that fucking bird and this time it's going to be permanent."

My words hit Afu like a sledge hammer to the face. He fell against the wall. "What? Patrice... she died?"

"That bird got into her head somehow, Afu." The

urge to fall down and cry beside him was intense, but the roof was on fire and this wasn't the time to get leaky. I made myself stand straighter, cleared my throat. "Get focused. We have to evacuate the propellerheads and get all of the backup Slayer apparatus outside."

Afu wiped tears from his eyes with his armored fingers. "Lead the way, Cap."

Downstairs, I pounded on the sealed watch room, shouting for the propellerheads to open up, that it was me, until they finally relented and raised the titanium walls. When I told them that the roof was on fire, they tried to throw out ideas for putting the fire out, but I dismissed that shit and told them to get behind the wheel of something in the bay and drive it far enough away not to get burned, making sure to grab any tech they wouldn't want to see burned up.

Afu ran around the corner carrying Yolanda. "She's still out of it, but I think she'll be okay."

Then we were all set.

It was a mass exodus of metal and tires. I headed straight for Jet 1, because if we had a flaming bird to take down, our plane would be the thing to do it. Trouble was, I didn't have the first fucking clue on how to even drive the jet out of the bay. I snagged a propellerhead who said he knew enough to get it outside.

Sitting in the cockpit, I made sure to study everything the propellerhead did as we moved the massive plane outside, where glowing light and dancing shadows flickered on the asphalt. The fire had extended into most of the building.

Our headquarters had been fortified to resist dragon fire. This was not the same thing. The building never had a chance.

With all apparatus and staff evacuated, everyone watched Smoke Eater headquarters go down in flames. A few of us cried or cursed – most of it came from me and Afu, given how most of the propellerheads liked to keep a stoic disposition, but even a few of them showed more emotion and anguish than I'd ever seen from them before.

This was our second home, where we spent at least a third of our lives. Hell, most of the propellerheads never left. And now it was all gone.

The rising sun brought with it an armada of Slayer apparatus, a long line of them moving down the only path cutting through the wasteland ashes, back home from dealing with a three-headed dragon.

When Brannigan jumped out of his chief's truck, he lost all sense of his position, nearly pulling his hair out and charging toward the ever-growing flames until the heat was too much for even a smoke eater to take.

He turned and looked at all of us who'd escaped. "What in the fuck did you idiots do?"

# CHAPTER 18

A week later, Mayor Ghafoor allowed the smoke eaters to respond out of the few fire stations throughout the city, but that meant we were all spread out. No more of the "one building for all" approach. I wondered when the city would rebuild our headquarters. The impression I got was that some higher-ups felt we were the dumbasses who allowed our building to burn down, and that we would have to make do with what little we were offered.

Afu, the eternal optimist, thought maybe our new work environment would be a good thing, that we could get along with the firefighters who we considered our evolutionary predecessors. But when you shove a bunch of A-type personalities together in a small building, who have just a slight difference in job description… well, we had a lot of shit-talking and four-lettered shouting matches that festered into full-blown fist fights.

Usually what set it off was a firefighter making a crack about how we let our headquarters burn down. Brannigan had tried to be diplomatic and determined that both sides had started different forms of shit in each firehouse, but I was there, heard it with my own ears, and had even thrown the first punch.

On the plus side, both smokies and hose-draggers alike didn't run off and tell Mama about these brotherly scuffles. We kept it all in house, and despite the initial turmoil and confusion of whether an incoming call was for a dragon or a hover-car wreck, tensions seemed to be thinning.

Nobody likes change at first.

We got several phoenix sightings called in. We didn't doubt the validity when a citizen said they saw, "a huge goddamn chicken that looks like it ran through an even bigger bonfire."

But every time we rushed to the scene, the phoenix was gone, leaving only a few scorch marks on the ground. It was a good thing we were there though, because every single time, we found a half-eaten pile of yellow embers, and then more dragons would emerge on the spot.

Some smokies shrugged it off as a coincidence. The pessimists among us speculated that the scalies had found a way to come after us, as if they had a concept of vengeance. The realists, like me, knew the phoenix had something to do with it. It was like catnip for scalies. The way the leviathan had behaved that day outside Sandusky, waking from a Sandman nap...

Either way, the propellerheads were working their asses off, coming up with a solution to extinguishing the phoenix's unkillable fire.

We gave Patrice a nice funeral, and it reminded me that the old days weren't all fun and scaly corpses. Some of the corpses had worn power suits. Her body was never recovered, of course, because she'd burned away. So, we put together a quick memorial using her helmet. And, unlike a dragon-caused fatality, there had been no wraith. A rumor started going around, about how Patrice had somehow transformed into the new phoenix. I put a nip in that bud quicker than shit through a wyvern. Not only was it not true, but it would make me hesitate the next time I stood in front of the bird if it somehow *was* true.

I'd never seen Brannigan cry until that day at the funeral. I'm glad it was him who had to talk to Patrice's family. I wouldn't have been able to do it. Leaving earlier had probably made me look like an asshole, but I didn't care. I just couldn't handle it. I walked into my house, past my parents arguing in the bathroom as my mother tried to lift him onto the toilet. In my room, I shut the door and began punching at shelves and walls indiscriminately until I passed out on my bed in a blubbering mess.

I didn't leave my room for two days, and my parents were smart enough to let me be.

Renfro asked to transfer to my crew as driver, which bumped up Naveena's rookie to sit behind the wheel of her rig. It was the fastest promotion in smoke eater history, even counting Brannigan's and mine. Naveena had tried calling Sergeant Puck out of retirement, but in her gravelly voice she responded, "I'd rather swallow a pregnant hydra and poop out its babies!"

So Naveena was stuck with two rookies.

Yolanda and I took Jet 1 out every so often to hunt for the firebird. I always asked to ride along, learning each button and gizmo in the cockpit, the basics of flying, and a lot I didn't want to know about Yolanda. Most of it was about how she felt like Patrice's death was somehow her fault. I told her it wasn't, even though I knew it wouldn't put her mind at ease. How could a mind like Yolanda's ever be at ease? Propellerheads twirl a bit faster.

"I shouldn't have been wearing my key card," Yolanda said after explaining the altimeter. "I should have listened to Afu. He was right about the phoenix."

"Patrice would have found a way into the lockbox one way or another," I said. "The phoenix made her attack you. If it's anybody's fault, Yolanda, it's not yours."

Because it was mine.

After that, I made sure to ask as many questions about flying as I could to keep Yolanda's mind off Patrice. One day, before we set to fly out, Yolanda held out a piece of paper to me.

"What ancient shit is this?" I asked.

"It's the guy I was telling you about. Herjold. His address. Brannigan cleared it for your crew to pay him a visit and see if you can learn anything, because what we're doing now is getting us nowhere."

And that's why Renfro, Afu and I were riding quietly down Newitz Avenue, chasing another wild goose.

"I still can't believe she's gone." Afu's booming voice broke the silence, making me jerk in my seat.

More quietly, almost hoarse, Renfro said, "Yeah. Me, too."

"Yeah, well that's life," I said.

I watched the buildings fly by outside my window, but I could sense my crew's heads turn sharply toward me. If Afu's voice had been the thunder, then my statement was the lightning.

Afu huffed.

That just pissed me off. I spun around and slammed my hands on top of the truck's doghouse. "What?"

"You make out like you're some badass all the time, but I know the real you, not the front you put on for everybody else." Afu shook his head and looked away. "You're like a scared princess, building up your emotional castle walls, so nobody sees how torn up you are inside. Not even yourself."

"Don't call me a princess, you damn ogre. I'm just being real. You're the one who's always so fucking happy all the time. I take things for what they are and keep moving forward, because I have to. That's why we were never going to work out. You live in a fantasy land."

I'd never seen Afu angry. Not even while he was fighting a dragon. But right then, he lost it. "Well I sure as hell ain't happy now! I'm glad we're not together, and I'm transferring to another crew as soon as I can."

Quiet.

I thought the cab had been silent before, now it was a void.

Renfro cleared his throat. "This the house up here?"

"Yeah," I said. "Number 18. Guy named Harold."

"I thought it was Gerald," Renfro said.

"Whatever it is." I tossed the piece of paper Yolanda had given me. "I can't read her chicken scratch. She should have just sent it to my holoreader like a normal person."

Harold or Gerald's house was a bungalow pinned between "dragon proof," self-building houses on either side. I knocked three times against the polished cherry door as Renfro and Afu waited behind me.

A short, bespectacled man with a white-haired horseshoe on his head answered. "I'm not interested in buying a holostereo."

*The fuck?*

"We're not selling anything," I said.

He grunted. "Then I'm not interested in giving the imaginary friend you pray to any money either."

"Are you Harold?"

He cleared his throat. "Herjold."

Renfro tapped his fingers against my shoulder. "I told you it was Gerald."

"Herjold!" the old man said. "And who's asking?"

I still didn't understand what to call him. "If you can't tell by our uniforms, Mr Her... Ger...."

"Oh, for the love of Pete!" He removed his glasses and rubbed his eyes. "Just call me Stephen. Herjold is my last name."

"We're with the smoke eaters," I said.

"Oh, that's right. Yolanda told me you might come by. Come on in. You guys like coffee?"

"I'm good," I said.

Afu shook his head no.

"I never say no to coffee," said Renfro.

The inside of the house was old, dark and dusty. And if it weren't for the darkness, the presence of dust would have been more noticeable. Books were everywhere: on shelves along the walls, on the coffee and end tables, even stacked on the floor.

"Go on," Stephen grumbled, waving a hand toward a couch covered in, you guessed it... porcelain dolls. "Have a seat there. Just move 'em out of the way. Carefully!"

Afu, blinking with confusion, scooped up the dolls in his arms and set them in a corner. While Stephen was getting coffee from the kitchen around the corner, all three of us sat squished together on the couch.

Renfro leaned over and whispered, "What are we hoping to get out of this guy? I don't think he's left his house in thirty years."

"It's worth a shot," I said.

Afu watched the dolls in the corner as if they'd stand up and attack him.

"Hope instant coffee is fine," Stephen said as he returned with a cup in his hand. He handed it to Renfro.

"Free is free," Renfro said.

Stephen curled his lip. "Nothing in this world is free."

I gave Renfro a look, but my new engineer was focused on drinking his coffee.

"Damnedest thing." Stephen threw a pile of newspapers off an old orange chair and sat. "That mud had to be boiling hot. You didn't even wait for it to cool."

"Benefits of our condition." Renfro raised the cup to our host.

"So, what did you need to talk to me about? Yolanda didn't mention anything," Stephen asked.

"Yolanda said you were pretty knowledgeable in mythology, specifically monsters and creatures."

"Knowledgeable? Yeah, I'd say so. I taught Myth at Ohio State for most of my life. Then those damn dragons came and made us all look like idiots."

"We've encountered something new," I said.

"You've probably heard about it on the Feed."

"Bah! I don't touch all that new junk. It rots brains. Man can't even get a newspaper anymore." He pointed to the ones he'd thrown to the ground. "Those are fifty years old."

"What do you know about the phoenix?"

Stephen's eyes widened. "Wait. You're saying we don't just have dragons anymore? You've seen a real-deal phoenix?"

"We killed it once," Afu said. "Well, it killed itself really. Then it came back out of its ashes."

I pulled out my holoreader and showed him a bit of the footage Brannigan had recorded.

"Damn it all to hell!" Stephen kicked the stack of newspapers over with his foot.

I thought most people in his field would have been overjoyed to learn the creatures they had devoted their lives to actually existed. Stephen was clearly not one of those people.

"What do you want to know?" he asked. "It's probably completely crap now there's a real thing out there."

"Anything," I said. "Everything."

Stephen sighed. "Okay. So you've seen it's made of fire. Different records describe it like that while others say it was just a regular bird. But they all agree that a new incarnation rises from its ashes after it sets itself on fire."

"So, there's no way to kill it?" Afu asked.

Stephen shrugged. "Based on all the legends – and they come from all over: China, Japan, Russia, even the Native Americans had their version – it'll just rise again after it's killed. So, technically, yes, but you'll just have to rinse and repeat."

"We saw the phoenix feed on dragons. Scalies we kill have been burning to yellow embers, even when the bird isn't around. If it is around, the phoenix eats what's left of them. Even the wraiths burn away if they get too close."

"There you go." Stephen sulked. "Here I thought it was just furniture philosophy."

"What are you talking about?" I looked around at the dust-covered fixtures. His home needed furniture rehab, not just a new belief system.

"Feng shui," Stephen said. "Dragon is yang, phoenix is yin. One balances the other. Apparently, the Chinese meant it as more than advice on where to put your couch."

"So the phoenix balances the dragons?" Afu asked.

"Seems like it." Stephen spread his hands. "You all should be happy. The bird is doing your job for you."

"There's a big problem with that, though," I said. "Oh?"

"The bird got into one of our friends' heads. Made her do things. Made her release its ashes. I'm starting to think these arsons going around the city are related, too."

"There's been arsons?"

I forgot: no Feed.

"I'll tell you later," I said. "Point I'm making is, would the phoenix be able to—"

"Possess people?" Stephen leaned back in his chair and raised an eyebrow.

I felt stupid for even bringing it up, but nodded.

"There's nothing in the regular mythology about that at all."

I dropped my head. Shit.

"But…" He stood at the books lining the walls and began throwing them down as he searched. "Ah! Here."

Returning to his chair, he opened a black book titled *The Lesser Key of Solomon*.

"Is that, like, from the Bible?" Afu asked.

Stephen sputtered his lips. "Nothing of the sort. Although King Solomon was mentioned in that bogus religious text."

As Stephen flipped through the pages, Afu leaned toward Renfro. "He doesn't have to be so mad about it."

I would have loved to introduce Stephen Herjold to my parents. The fireworks would have been spectacular.

"All right" Stephen raised his finger like some great orator. He must have been hell in the classroom. "'Phenex, the thirty-seventh spirit, is a great Marquis of hell. It can only be evoked by more than one person. Any who conjure this demon must not listen to its song, and must bind it in human form'."

Renfro spit out his coffee.

"Watch the carpet!" Stephen said.

"Demons?" I said. I thought about how my daddy said it was Satanists behind the arsons. "No, that's stupid. That makes even less sense than ghosts and dragons."

Stephen raised his hands defensively. "I'm only providing information. Like I said before, it's probably all bullshit."

Patrice had *acted* like she was possessed, but I didn't believe in any of that exorcist baloney. She'd been poisoned by the ashes.

No. She'd been called. Sung to.

"Look," Stephen said. "A lot of myths have the tiniest bits of truth to them. Nanonuggets of fact. You ever play the telephone game? Or chinese whispers? Imagine what that would be like played over thousands of years. Whatever is going on, if this phoenix can affect people a certain way, there's a scientific explanation. And I'm sure Yolanda can help you figure it out."

"That's all you have?" asked Renfro.

"Yep!" Stephen stood, brushing his hands together. "And I have a chess game with my next-door neighbor in five minutes. So, was there anything else you needed?"

Afu stood. "Do you know anything about burrowing owls?"

Stephen thinned his eyes and slowly shook his head. "No."

Back in the cannon truck, we all sat there stewing in what we'd just heard. It felt like we'd listened to a lot and learned nothing.

"So," Renfro said. "Now what do we do?"

I held my helmet and stared at the shield hanging on the front. I rubbed a finger along the golden dragon head cresting the top. "If the phoenix is about balance, we'll give it some. I aim to set the scales right, and for what it did to Patrice and those jolly vollies, we're going to kill the motherfucker. Permanently."

# CHAPTER 19

Brannigan and I waited outside City Hall's main chamber room, preparing to be yelled at by either the mayor, the family of the dead jolly vollies, or both. I always wondered why they called it a chamber. A chamber is what you stick a bullet in before blasting it into a monster's head.

But that's just the way I'm wired.

"Let me handle everything," Brannigan said.

"And what if you can't?"

Brannigan huffed like he'd already thought about it a thousand times. "Well, then Mayor Ghafoor can handle the rest."

Speaking of the devil, the mayor rushed into the building with a few of her aides, who closed the doors quickly to keep out news drones that bumped against the glass like giant wasps.

"Whoo!" the mayor said, turning to face us. "Sorry I'm late. Robotic buzzards are faster than I give them credit for."

She unwrapped the scarf from her neck and didn't show any sign of sweating. It was May for crying out loud.

She shook Brannigan's hand first, then mine. "The

vampires at the Feed won't leave me alone about these terrible arson fires. Those PC First goons keep trying to ruffle my feathers. And now I'm getting complaints about a traffic light at 3rd and Asher. Shall we?"

"Do we have a minute to talk first?" Brannigan said. "I was hoping I could get an estimate on when we'll begin reconstruction of Smoke Eater headquarters."

"Chief, I'd be happy to talk to you about that at another time, because right now we have to handle a more pressing issue that your department also caused."

Brannigan blinked, clearing his throat. "We didn't cause this mess. You know this lawsuit is a joke as much as I do, so please drop the cover-your-ass, run-the-bus-over-us mentality, because it's not going to help this city or you, Tilda."

"I know the previous mayor may have been the type to do that, *Cole*, but I'm not him. I do care about our people and that means caring about those who protect them. But I'd advise you to speak to me with more respect. I've already called in the New US Army to begin patrolling the streets with this arsonist cult plaguing us. They're just itching to be allowed to handle dragons and this new… thing that's emerged."

I tensed, balling up my fists. "It's a phoenix. You can say it. And there is no arsonist cult."

The police had a lot to ask me after Patrice brought the phoenix back to life. They skewed the questions to make it sound like Patrice had been involved in this apparent cult they thought was behind everything. Such bullshit. I told them Patrice would never have gone along with that kind of thing, but they kept digging, seeing if there was ever a time I might have seen her do anything strange, illegal.

I admitted that I had seen her sacrifice a rat in the middle of the smoke eater shower room, surrounded by bloody pentagrams and upside-down crucifixes.

I can't believe I had to tell them I was kidding. Patrice was a normal, regular person. She had too much she was looking forward to, so much life left to live. A fucking sheep farm. She wouldn't have sacrificed herself for some mythical pigeon.

I don't think anyone would, but the cops weren't letting this thing go. I suggested they look into those whackos with PC First before they began chasing boogeymen.

"The army can't do what we do," Brannigan told the mayor. "Bunch of dirty mercs without a single damn to give about anyone in this state." He sighed and rubbed his face as if trying to wake up. "But I apologize. I know you're trying. We've been through a lot recently."

Ghafoor playfully slapped Brannigan on the arm, which surprised him as much as me.

"No worries, Chief. Let's get in here and take some of that stressful wind out of your sails."

I didn't think that was the best choice of words for that particular situation. Besides, it didn't make any goddamn sense.

We entered the chamber where chairs circled a long table. Some sad-looking white folks occupied one side. Brannigan nodded reassurance when I looked at him. I took the seat at the far end. Chief and the folks from City Hall took the rest.

The lawyer representing the city came in last and closed the door before saying, "All right, everyone. We don't have to drag this out." He hit a button on the underside of the table. Hologram words floated in front of each seat. "You each have a document in front of you stating the law when it comes to wraiths, and while Parthenon City and its emissaries empathize with the families of the deceased, we claim neither fault nor are we going to hand over any wraiths captured by the smoke eaters."

"You're pretty confident, Jim," the other white man in a suit said from across the table, steepling his fingers in front of him.

"It's pretty cut and dry," the city's lawyer, Jim, said.

"There is no precedent for this. The Wilkins and Harrison families are filing suit because we believe it's wrong to hold family members just because they've unfortunately become undead. They belong to their next of kin. And we see their deaths as the direct result from Captain Williams' negligence."

I couldn't have made this shit up if you'd given me a fifth of whiskey and a holoreader to write on. And a bottle of booze would have been great to calm my quivering nerves. The image of Wilkins' wraith inside my trap remote kept flashing across my mind.

Jim walked over to stand behind me. He put his hands on the top of my chair. "Do you really think a judge will agree that these wraiths could be considered to be the same people your clients knew and loved?"

"Absolutely," the other lawyer said.

Silence flooded the room as one side stared at

the other. One of the family members was an older woman I pegged as Wilkins' widow. She had the watered down blonde hair of someone who hadn't kept up with the hair dye routine, but how could anybody care about that kind of thing when their husband had died. The others in the group were about my age: a man with a buzz cut and a beard, a woman who'd done her best to dress up in a pink polo with her hair tied deathly tight behind her head.

I hadn't wanted these people to suffer, and I certainly didn't revel in it now. I'd done my due diligence over a week ago in Sandusky. I'd done everything I could.

*But you didn't turn in that wraith.*

"We told them to stay back," I said, breaking the quiet.

"You don't have to say anything," Mayor Ghafoor said. Her tense eyes told me that she really meant I *shouldn't* say anything.

I leaned forward in my seat. "I want to say something. We tried to save Mr Wilkins, but he refused to leave the house. When a leviathan emerged, it attacked him. After another one showed up and we captured it, Mr Harold and his crew showed up claiming to be smoke eater volunteers and demanding we hand over Wilkins' wraith. We told them to get out of the area and get back to safety, but like their friend, they refused, and followed us. With respect to the deceased, this was extremely dangerous and ill-advised."

The family members squirmed in their seats. Seemed like what I said rang true with how the men had lived their lives.

Jim held his hands out. "Well, there you go. They went against what the professionals told them and took their lives into their own hands."

Damn, Jim, that was blunt. He lacked a lot of tact. More than me or Brannigan, which was saying something.

The other lawyer looked at his clients, and they looked back at him. He gathered them to the side, where they huddled with sharp whispers.

When they broke and returned to the table, the families' lawyer looked defeated. "We're no longer attempting to hold the city responsible for these men's deaths."

Jim smiled. "Great—"

"But we are still going to sue for possession of Mr Wilkins' wraith."

"Why in hell would you want to do that?" Brannigan snapped. "These aren't like pets, and they sure as hell aren't going to be the men you knew before. They're going to rip you apart at the first opportunity."

*I should tell them about the remote.*

No. It would just make things worse. Until a judge signed the order, I didn't have to do shit.

Brannigan stood and the family members shrank into their seats. "You might feed me some bullshit, saying you'll just keep him in the wraith trap. Well, not only is that pointless as hell, I know for a fact that you can't take government property, even if you miraculously win this stupid crusade. So if you *really* want this wraith back, we'll gladly dump it in your front yard. And staying cooped up in your houses won't save you, because dragons will be attracted by the shrieking banshee floating among your fake petunias. They *will* come. That's a fact. They'll burn you down and gobble you up. Do you want that?"

Chief sat back down and winked at me, like he had everything under control. I stared at him with my mouth open. Another silence dropped onto the meeting, making the previous one seem like a rock concert.

The family's lawyer huffed. "I think we're done here. See you in court, Jim."

With that, he escorted the family members out of the council chamber, and when the door shut, Mayor Ghafoor spun on Brannigan.

"For crying out loud, Brannigan, what was that?"

Chief shrugged. "I was just telling them the truth."

Lawyer Jim tried to be optimistic. "I really don't see a judge granting what they want. We won today, even if it doesn't quite feel like it."

"It doesn't matter," the mayor said. "This is going to take time and money the city doesn't have. I've got much bigger fires to put out. And I mean that literally."

While Mayor Ghafoor and Jim hashed it out, Brannigan tapped me on the shoulder and thumbed toward the door. I nodded. Fuck yes, I wanted to get out of there.

In the hall, I was about to ask Brannigan about our next plan of attack on the phoenix – what we'd been doing wasn't working and I wasn't going to let another arson or phoenix-related catastrophe happen on my watch. But Brannigan's holoreader rang and the strange siren tone put a concerned look on his face. A hologram head of a long-haired man floated from the holoreader. It was Ted Sevier, the man who ran the wraith enclosures.

"Chief," Ted said. He was out of breath and clearly in a fit.

"What's going on, Ted? One of the dragons catch a hernia pushing out an egg?"

"Oh, I bet I look out of sorts," said Ted. "You probably knew something was wrong just by looking at me. That's the thing about these holoreaders–"

"Ted!" Brannigan shouted. "What's wrong?"

"It's the dragons, Chief. They're… acting strangely."

"Define strangely," Brannigan said.

"Crazy. I don't know what's gotten into them, but they're behaving more aggressively, less content. Like those loons walking downtown talking to themselves and swinging at shadows. And the dragons aren't the only ones."

"Your staff acting funny, too?" Brannigan's gray eyebrows mashed together like caterpillars as he thinned his eyes.

"You'll just have to come see for yourself," Ted said. "I'm at the eastern enclosure, but my people tell me it's also happening at the other three."

"I'm on my way," Brannigan said, before hanging up. "What do you make of that, Williams?"

"It's something to do with the phoenix," I said. "You should have seen what the leviathan was doing when that bird showed up. And we've had more dragons popping up *outside* of the enclosures, all where people have reported seeing the phoenix.

Chief, I think it's the reason Patrice might have lost her mind, too."

"Let's not jump to conclusions about Patrice." He looked at me with hope in his eyes. "You want to tag along to the enclosure?"

"You bet your ass. If only to tell you I told you so."

Outside City Hall, I was about to hop into Brannigan's truck when a chanting mob began marching around the street corner. I stood there with the passenger door splayed open.

"Come on and get in," Brannigan said from behind the wheel.

"Do you see this, Chief?"

He rolled his window down and craned his head to see what was storming toward us.

There were at least thirty of them, all dressed in black turtlenecks, carrying long laser light torches and holosigns that read "PC First" and "Throw Them Out!" At the front of the group was the mean-looking white dude I'd seen on the Feed. His fat nose and hair slicked to one side made him look like some smug, 1920s gangster son of a bitch.

Duncan Sharp. Yeah, that was the asshole's name. I remembered because I had imagined *dunking* him into a tub of *sharp* objects.

"What do these bungholes want?" Brannigan said.

"Out protesting it looks like," I got into the truck and shut the door. "They want to rid the city of all the new arrivals."

"Nazi wannabes like that won't stop at one group," Brannigan said. "They'll keep lengthening the list until we're all on it. Where does it end?"

"I'd like to not even see it start."

"Leaping lizard shit." Brannigan shook his head as we drove off. "I guess Ted was right. It's not just the dragons losing their minds."

# CHAPTER 20

The wraiths had always looked menacing and creepy floating inside the aquarium-like walls of the enclosures, but when Brannigan and I got out of the truck and stood there outside the eastern dragon pen, the ghosts were going ape shit.

They flew from one end of their encasement to the other in the blink of an eye, wailing and shattering to bits if they smashed into another wraith. Then they'd reform and go back to acting a fool, scratching against the glass and even trying to bite the wall with their electric teeth.

The enclosure was over fifty feet tall, so it was like standing outside an office building watching a shark feeding frenzy take place in every window.

I stepped closer to the section of glass directly in front of me. One of the wraiths floated down and shrieked, flexing its clawed hands and glaring at me with eyes that sparked like a busted electrical outlet. Its jaw spread so wide that it split the ethereal gray skin hanging loosely from its skull. The jaw fell off and was absorbed by the shredded bottom of the ghost's torso before it reappeared in place.

The wraith slammed its face against the glass.

"Goddamn ghosts." I ran over to join Brannigan at the entrance.

Ted Sevier opened the door and with a relieved sigh said, "Thanks for coming. Follow me."

The entryway we stepped into was meager – walls and ceiling with a polished metal shine as if we were walking through a tube of aluminum foil. A guard was posted by the wraith port, which was where smoke eaters dumped wraiths caught on dragon calls – where I should have already dumped Mr Wilkins. It was black and shaped like a robotic baby bottle. At least, that's what always came to my mind. All we had to do was stick in the pointy end of the wraith remote and press a button. Job done. The wraiths could then float around and be weird and dead amongst their peers.

That was another thing. If I had deposited the wraith here, and the Wilkins family won their suit, it would be damn near impossible to find the right ghost in the enclosure and get them out of the walls. Sure, the wraiths held a slight likeness to what they looked like in life, but it was a saggy, musty version only those with a keen eye would be able to see.

At the end of the hall we passed through another door that Ted had to unlock with a hand scan. This brought us into the dimly lit dragon observation hall, which was like being at a zoo with only one big paddock you could see into through glass that surrounded the entire dragon area.

I'd never been in here before. My crew usually left after we dropped off sleeping dragons. I hadn't known whether to imagine the scalies packed together like sardines in a can or a wide expanse of ashy terrain where dragons walked around confused.

On the other side of the glass, though, it looked like a scene from some fantasy novel. Fake sunlight poured through hologram trees as a giant, blue drake thudded through the woods, galloping on its four clawed feet like a horse trying to buck off its rider.

The drake reared on the nearest hologram tree and blasted a stream of fire into the branches. Of course, after some wobbly static, the tree went right back to being tall and serene. This just pissed the dragon off and it galloped past a group of poppers who were taking turns burrowing and then launching out of the ground to land on the back of an orange-scaled lindworm, which only had two hind claws, but a nasty tail with a tip that looked like a spiked wrecking ball. This lindworm couldn't fly away as it hadn't sprouted wings out of its side plates yet, so it was at the mercy of the poppers who continued to assault it by biting its back a few times before dropping to the ground and burrowing away to start again.

When the next popper launched out of the ground, the lindworm was ready and snatched the smaller dragon in its teeth. The lindworm's whiskers caught fire and seared the popper as the lindworm shook it from side to side in sweeping jerks.

An electric, purple scaly glided from above on short wings and slammed into the glass in front of me. I flinched and stepped away. When the dragon realized it had met resistance, it extended its neck frill and sent sparks shooting out of its thin membrane.

"What the hell is going on with these things?" I asked.

"That's why I wanted you to come see it for yourself," Ted said. "They've been acting like this since last week and its only getting worse. I'm guessing you already saw what the wraiths are doing."

Chief Brannigan made shooing moves with his arms, trying to make the electric dragon go away, even though he knew the scaly couldn't see him. "Last week, you say?"

Ted nodded. "We tranquilized one of the dragons and brought it back to the lab. Do you want to come see?"

We followed Ted into another room with a couple of propellerheads standing around a sheet-covered mound on a slab, talking about the recent droid football game. They jumped to attention when we entered.

"Let's show them your findings," Ted said.

The propellerheads each grabbed a side of the sheet and pulled it off. Lying there on a slab was a golden fafnir, about the size of a baby elephant. Its chest rose and fell steadily, heavily, and they'd placed a titanium muzzle on it as an extra precaution.

"We've had to hit this one with a Sandman more than a few times," Ted said. "Whatever has gotten into these scalies is also making it hard to keep them asleep."

One of the propellerheads took a long instrument and walked to the fafnir's back end. Raising its tail, the propeller head shoved the metal stick into, what I could only guess, was the dragon's butthole.

"Goddamn," I whispered, and clinched my own cheeks in sympathy.

The propellerhead removed the stick and said, "It

just crested nine hundred Fahrenheit."

Brannigan had been reaching out a hand to touch the scaly's chest, but jerked his hand back and said, "Holy fuck. They usually stay around four hundred, right?"

"Its temperature has been on the rise for days now," Ted said. "I never knew dragons could get fevers."

Brannigan and I turned our heads to each other, staring with worry and understanding. It didn't have to be said out loud. We were thinking the same thing: Patrice.

As we were leaving, I said, "Chief, this phoenix is doing something to the dragons, the wraiths. It fucked with Patrice when she swallowed that ash. And these arsons... there is no cult, like the police want to believe. It's the phoenix. I don't know what, but if we don't find that ugly-ass bird soon, something even worse is going to happen."

"My thoughts exactly. That's why I want to put you in charge of a special team."

The last time my position was changed, the world went to shit. But if this meant we could put an end to the fiery psychosis taking form in every ghost, person and scaly, I was down for it.

"Okay," I said.

"Good," Brannigan said. "Your focus will be on finding the phoenix and taking it out for good. Yolanda says she has some fun new toys specifically for that purpose. Also, the fire and police chiefs have asked if we could spare some folks to assist in nailing this cult they keep talking about." He raised his hand before I could object again. "We both know it has something to do with the phoenix, so that makes it your problem to solve as well."

Getting involved in some stupid investigation wasn't really on my radar. Nor was educating the folks in blue on what was really going on. But someone had to do it. "As long as I don't have to do any extra paperwork."

"No, you guys will aid in gathering information for the cops and going into any situation others can't. Flames and shit like that."

"My specialty," I said.

Brannigan clapped his hands, making it final. "I believe in you, Tamerica. Let's make sure this squawking bastard never hurts anyone else again. Tomorrow, you'll start training everyone to fight a phoenix specifically."

He started out of the door, but I stopped him.

"I do have a few conditions."

Brannigan turned, raising his eyebrows. "Oh?"

"I get to pick everyone on this team."

"Done. Send me the list and I'll make it official that you're in charge of the Ash Kickers unit."

'Ash Kickers.'

I guess it did have a ring to it.

# CHAPTER 21

The Smoke Eater headquarters lay in piles of rubble and ash a hundred or so feet away from us, but that didn't mean that our training field had taken any of the damage. I guess it's one of the benefits of having fully-customizable metal puzzle pieces stored underground. We could program it to form any type of structure: house, skyscraper, even the maze we made the rookies run through, with a mechanical dragon that was a bit slower than it used to be. Brannigan had blown it up when we were in trainee school, and the poor robot scaly had never fully-recovered.

But today was going to be all about trying out Yolanda's new gadgets and turning up the heat to see if this new shit would actually work against a phoenix.

I stood in front of Afu, Renfro, Naveena and her two smokies. Harribow still looked like a scared lamb who knew he was being prepared for slaughter but could do nothing about it. The other guy introduced himself as Calvinson, a red-haired kid who looked a lot like a guy I used to know when I first joined the smoke eaters. Hopefully he wouldn't be as cocky and get himself killed like the last dude.

"Thanks for asking me to be a part of the team,"

he said, shaking my hand.

Him and Harribow were only here because I wanted Naveena by my side and didn't think it right to split up a crew. And it wasn't like any other smokies were jumping at the chance to go after an elusive and seemingly-invincible monster.

"Thank *you*," I told Calvinson.

He smiled like I'd just given him a commendation and walked over to listen to Afu tell old war stories.

I pulled Naveena away from the others and said, "I have no idea what the fuck I'm doing. I appreciate you agreeing to do this with me. I know Brannigan put me in charge, but believe me when I say I'll be relying on your expertise a lot."

Naveena playfully punched me in my armored shoulder. "I wouldn't miss this for anything. It'll be good to nail that bastard for what it did to Patrice."

A big wad of guilt filled my throat and I looked away.

"And hey," Naveena tapped her power suit's gloves against my chest so I'd look at her, "when you've been a captain as long as me, you'll appreciate any opportunity to let someone else have the reins. You ask me, anybody who wants to be in charge all the time is the exact person who *shouldn't* be leading things. We're a team. Let's get in the game and pull off a win."

"Have you ever considered coaching little league?"

She smiled and shook her head. "I hate sports."

We walked back over to the others, Naveena's hand at my back. All of the smoke eaters I'd gathered were waiting for me to say something, to lead them. I didn't even know where to start, but Brannigan had always told me that sometimes you have to leap off the cliff and build your parachute on the way down.

I always thought that was stupid advice, because you never knew how short the drop was. But I tried.

"Okay," I said. "Welcome to the… Ash Kickers."

Afu snorted, because he knew I hated that name. He'd suggested "phoenix fuckers" but that sounded way worse.

I glared at Afu until he stood straight and shut up.

"This phoenix isn't like the dragons we've been fighting before. None of our weapons seem to do jack shit in putting out its flames. We can't even tranquilize it. All of you will have seen the video from the day we trapped it in a chain net, so you should know that it can blow itself up and come back later. So, our goal is to end it before it can end itself, and maybe that will mean it won't come back to life. That's right. None of the no-kill rules on this mission. We're back to slaying."

Renfro raised his hand. I was going to tell him he didn't need to do that, but I also didn't want the more green smokies to think they could tactlessly shout questions. I pointed to my engineer.

"You and Afu never got a chance to use your laser weapons. Maybe they'd work if we tried?"

"You'd have to get close enough to use a sword," Afu said. "Those flames stuck to Captain Williams' power suit and wouldn't go out. Have you ever seen dragonfire do that?"

Everyone shook their heads.

"Plus," I said, "the Sandman didn't do anything, so it's probably safe to say that the regular lasers or even a haymo wouldn't work. I'm not against trying those, but I'd at least like to find some way to take out its main weapon before we get laser-happy."

Harribow threw his hand up. "And how do we do that?"

A hover-van flew over the ashes, headed right for us.

I pointed to the van as it came to a stop. "Let's hope she's come up with a way."

Yolanda hopped out of the driver's seat and opened the back hatch.

I told Afu and Calvinson to go help Yolanda bring over the new toys. Since Harribow had been promoted, Afu and the new guy were the lowest smokies on the ladder, which meant they had to do more of the grunt work. Hefting cases as wide as Afu was tall, they waddled over and set them down carefully in the ash at our feet.

Yolanda smiled as we huddled around her. "This should be fun."

I was glad to see her back to herself.

Turning to the flat, metal training field, Yolanda poked at her holoreader until several sheets of metal rose from the ground and formed a small city block. Another second later, fire ignited from the top of one of the buildings and a hologram appeared over the flames in the shape of a giant hummingbird.

"Um, what the fuck is that?" I asked.

Yolanda frowned, like we were supposed to be impressed. "What do you mean? It's a phoenix."

Afu shook his head, his cheeks jiggling. "That doesn't look like a phoenix."

"Well…" Yolanda sighed. "It was the best I could do. It's just for visual aid. The main point is the fire."

She turned back to the flames and the buzzing, too-cute-to-kill hummingbird. "Those flames aren't hot enough yet."

She tapped on her holoreader and the fire grew bigger. Now, the flames hovered over our tiny, pop-up city like a blanket of fabricated hell. A greater warmth pelted my face. That was more like it.

Yolanda squatted in front of one of the cases. Two satisfying clicks sounded from the latches and the lid swung open by itself. We all bent over to see what was in it, but by that time Yolanda had pulled out what had lay inside.

"This is an Impulse shotgun," she said. "I took the same style design firefighters had been using a few years ago, but gave it a few nifty upgrades."

She cocked it and the sound made us all instinctively flinch.

"This sucker packs a wallop when it comes to extinguishing fire. It uses the same technology as your foam guns, but the foam fires in one big wad at a hundred and twenty miles per hour. Added to the foam is a sound wave emitter, and there's a concussive blast that would kill any normal fire for extra extinguishment."

Yolanda looked pretty badass hefting that large shotgun on her hip. The weapon looked like a model bazooka my daddy made back when I was eight years old, except this one was metallic gray and way too futuristic compared to the PVC pipe Daddy had used.

"So," Yolanda said, "who wants this one?"

All of our hands shot up.

"Captain Williams," Yolanda held the gun out to

me with two hands, looking eager for me to take the heavy thing from her. "Since you're in charge, I'll let you have first pick. Plus, you're used to shooting foam, so it won't be too much of a learning curve for you."

Afu groaned, the big baby.

The next case opened and Yolanda pulled out a long metal pole, as black as a dragon claw.

"Is that so Renfro can practice his stripper moves?" Naveena said.

Everyone busted a gut. The rookies, however, looked guilty about it.

Renfro laughed, too. "Y'all ain't shit."

Yolanda didn't seem to get the joke. She frowned and said, "No, but it does do this."

She pressed a button and a crescent-shaped laser blade extended from the top.

"Holy shit!" I said.

"This is a laser axe." Yolanda swung it around a few times. The blade sliced through the air, leaving behind warbles of heat, making a *phrumm, phrumm* with each pass.

"That's mine," Afu said, before anyone else could claim it.

"Well you're all getting one of these," said Yolanda. "I only had time to make one shotgun, but the axes are pretty simple to put together. And they're magnetic, so you can attach them to your power suit."

We each took a turn sticking the axes to our backs.

"Why are they better than our laser swords?" Harribow asked.

Everyone turned to look at him.

He swallowed, clearly uncomfortable being the

center of attention. "I mean, it looks awesome and all, but we already have something similar."

"It has better reach," Yolanda said. "Plus this."

She hit another button and the axe blade sparked a bolt of electricity through the air. Most of us jumped back. Afu hit the dirt, covering the back of his helmet with both hands. He didn't get back up until the sparking noise was gone and we were all laughing at him.

A stab of guilt hit me then. It felt strange to get back to usual business when everything – and everyone – had burned. But I swallowed the objection. This was good. This would tie us all even closer. That's the thing about smoke eaters, firefighters, cops, and the like. Humor is the glue that binds us. It's the single stone to stand on when the lava surrounds you.

"All right," I said. "Let's get this started. Yolanda, will you run the training scenarios?"

"Sure thing, Cap," she said. "Why don't you go first?"

I hefted the Impulse shotgun and walked onto the training field. The hummingbird hadn't moved from its chosen spot above the rooftop, and the giant flames roasting the air around it were starting to warp the top of the building.

"What's the range on this shotgun?" I asked.

"No more than a hundred feet," said Yolanda. "The closer the better, but I know that's not always going to be possible."

I'd be pushing it if I tried to shoot the hummingbird from where I stood, and I didn't want to jump onto the same building and risk getting torched. I always believed training should mirror real life scenarios as closely as possible, and I sure as fuck wouldn't get that close to the actual phoenix.

The building across the street was about a hundred feet away. I slung the shotgun onto my back with the attached sling. After a few jogging steps, I power jumped to the lip of the roof and pulled myself over, keeping the momentum going, rolling into a crouching position and taking aim at the hummingbird through the shotgun's beaded sights.

Fuck. Where's the trigger?

My fingers fumbled all over the damn gun as I tried to keep my eye on the fake phoenix. I swore at myself and brought the gun down so I could see what I had to pull to shoot the gun.

I'd had it upside down.

"You want to trade?" Afu shouted from the ground.

"Fuck you!" I readjusted and pulled the trigger.

A white ball flew across the gap between the buildings, leaving a cloudy trail of smoke behind it. The foam wad shattered the hummingbird hologram and exploded against the roof, covering the entire area like a small nuclear blast made entirely of sticky, white goo. The fire disappeared immediately.

The only thing that would have made it better is if it also contained some liquid nitrogen to freeze the bastard. I made a mental note to suggest it to Yolanda. But I was happy with my new toy.

"Hot damn!" Renfro said from the ground. "Yolanda, are you sure you can't make another shotgun? I've got to get me one of those!"

"It'll take some time," Yolanda said. "But I'm sure

Captain Williams will let everyone have a chance to use it."

"Sure thing," I said, and pointed to Renfro. "Just make sure I get it back."

"So, what are we supposed to do with these axes," Afu asked, resting one on his shoulder. "Hell, I could swing a tree branch at a hologram all day, but that doesn't mean anything."

"Oh the hologram was only for training with the foam, seeing how it extinguishes fire and the range of attack. I've got something else in mind for the axes."

"Um," Afu scratched his chin. "Like what?"

Yolanda turned toward the training city and poked a finger against her holoreader. A door I hadn't realized was there slid open at the bottom of the farthest building. I had to lean over the side of the roof to see, but all that stood there was a dark hole. Then the roar came.

I wouldn't have put it past Yolanda to unleash a living, breathing dragon on us, but out of the dark a metal claw emerged and scraped against the ground. Next came a robotic dragon head, squeaking and fumbling like it was going to fall apart before we ever laid hands on it. Scuff marks covered most of its silver body, and half its teeth were missing. After a clanking buildup within its chest, the robot dragon spit out a few measly flames that wouldn't have cooked a marshmallow. Mecha Scaly was back in business, but times had been hard.

"Oh, come on," Naveena said. "This lump of rust isn't going to give us a good fight. It can barely stand."

Yolanda huffed and tightened her arms against her

sides. "I didn't have the time or materials to build a mechanical phoenix. Besides, you'll have to catch the firebird before you can even attempt a fight. So if you want a challenge, Captain Jendal…"

Another command into the holoreader made Mecha Scaly squat. A second later, giant rubber wings fanned out from its sides. The dragon roared and leapt into the air, flapping itself to soar right over my head and the building I was atop. I stumbled backwards and landed on my ass. Mecha Scaly rose fifty feet above the training buildings circled there like a buzzard, daring us to come see if it was as rusty and out of fight as we thought.

"Well," Yolanda said to the smokies on the ground, "go get it."

They looked at each other for a confusing second, and then all five of them broke into a run, slapping hands or attempting to trip the smoke eater beside them so they'd be the first to get to the robo scaly.

I shook my head. No one likes a freelancer. And especially a glory hog.

Naveena power jumped and landed beside me on the roof, then pointed to Calvinson who'd gotten to the top of the one across the street. "Cal, shoot at it with your lasers, see if we can get it to attack us."

The rookie obeyed his captain and began shooting a burst of laserfire at Mecha Scaly, soaring high above. Calvinson's shots missed horribly, but they got the dragon's attention. First came a digital roar, then the dragon swooped down, building up speed as it launched toward Calvinson and Afu, who'd just arrived. The rookie continued shooting, but the dragon swerved from one side of the sky to the other, dodging each laser.

Something told me Yolanda had cheated, installed some kind of wise-ass program into the robot, turning it into a laser-dodging juggernaut.

Afu held out his axe and engaged it. As it flew over, Mecha Scaly attempted to chomp Calvinson, but had to divert its path when Afu swung the axe toward its side. Renfro climbed onto my building and began firing his own laser. That got the metal dragon to fly toward us instead.

"Hey! I almost had it," Afu shouted.

Instead of trying to bite us, the Mecha Scaly squeaked and hacked until a ball of flame dropped out of its mouth. A constant stream of fire would have been more dangerous. Or so we thought. When the fireball hit the roof, it blew apart, sending flames raining down on top of us.

"Shit," Renfro said, ducking under his helmet. "Yolanda must have upped its programming. I've never had this much trouble taking it out."

Naveena watched the dragon glide away and turn at the end of the street for a second attack. Stepping to the edge of the roof, she looked over and waved Renfro over to join her. "Give me some laser fire right here below us."

"Why?" I asked. I wasn't trying to hate on her mysterious plan, I just wanted to know what she was thinking.

"I want it flying right through here," Naveena said, more to Renfro than me.

Shrugging, Renfro blasted his gun down toward

the street. Mecha Scaly roared and tipped its wings to hover lower, flying straight for the shots.

Naveena put the axe pole against the back of her power suit, which magnetically drew the weapon against it with a clang. Stepping onto the roof's edge, she held out her arms as if walking the trapeze.

"Wait," I said. "What are you doing?"

Without answering me or so much as looking my way, Naveena leapt off the roof.

I ran to the edge and looked over, Naveena dropped like a boulder, just as Mecha Scaly passed under her. She landed on its back and held on with outstretched arms and legs. All laser fire ceased as every smokie watched Naveena fly around the city like a squirrel riding on the back of a crocodile.

"I've never seen shit like this," I said.

"Me either," said Renfro.

Mecha Scaly tried to bite at Naveena but missed each time as its main priority was staying airborne. With more balance than I'd ever seen in yoga videos or those stupid human tricks on the Feed, Naveena sat up and removed the laser axe from the back of her power suit. It only took one swing to bury the blade into the back of Mecha Scaly's head, even though it continued to roar and spit flames like a demented, flying steam engine as the laser burned through its circuits.

Naveena stood, using her hands to steady her. She and the dragon were circling back toward our building, and when they were about a hand stretch away, Naveena pressed a button on the axe and power jumped toward the roof. The axe's electricity ripped through Mecha Scaly and sent it churning dark smoke, plummeting toward the edge of the training field, where Yolanda had wisely chosen to run away.

Afu caught Naveena's arm and pulled her the rest of the way up. We all ran to the edge of the roof. Mecha Scaly lay in a crumpled, smoking pile. Back on the ground, everyone clapped and hooted praise. Calvinson patted his captain on the back. Harribow, who'd just come off the top of a third building, pumped a fist in the air.

"That was impressive, Naveena," I said.

"Thanks," she turned to bump my fist.

"Only one problem with it," I said. "If you jump on the phoenix like that, you'll burn to death before you can reach for your axe."

That got everyone kind of deflated, but goddamn it, it was the truth.

Naveena shrugged. "That's why you'll put out its flames first, T."

Yeah, that would be the best-case scenario. But I'd never, not in my entire career so far, been involved in a best-case scenario. They were like unicorns.

Oh no. I tried to think of something else, because if a rainbow-shitting, one-horned horse popped out of the ground, I would officially be done with this crazy line of work.

"All right," I said. "Let's have the rest of you try out the shotgun. Looks like Mecha Scaly is going back to the scrap heap."

Yolanda stood by the dead robot, shaking her head.

"Sorry, Yolanda." I turned so she wouldn't see me smirking.

I got a good view of the wasteland around the

smoke eater compound. Out on the highway, about half a mile out, a line of large metal things rolled toward Parthenon City. I had to blink a few times and then squint to make sure I wasn't seeing things.

I asked Renfro, "What's that going down the road?"

"I can see in the dark - I don't have power zoom in my retinas."

"Quit being a smartass," I said. "I'm serious. Don't you see that parade out there on the highway?"

Renfro put a hand to his brow to block out the sunlight. "Are those tanks?"

I knew it. The New US Army – what a crock of a name. There was nothing new about them. They were the same pricks from before, who'd scrambled together after E-Day and formed roving platoons, offering their services to city states with problems no one else could find the solution to. Hired guns was an understatement, they were more like a nomadic mafia. And there wasn't a smoke eater among them because they discouraged our kind from joining up. A guy I knew on Truck 8 who had looked into it and was quickly shot down.

Mayor Ghafoor, despite the controlled demeanor she put on display, had gotten desperate. She'd opened the city to wolves, and here they were storming in to town.

# CHAPTER 22

"So I have a few theories," Yolanda's hologram said.

Naveena and her crew were there in the same circle of digital green, floating above my holoreader. A one-to-one call was something that I was used to, comfortable with. I rarely participated in hologram conference calls because it freaked me out to see all those floating heads. But this was the best way for all of us to hear what Yolanda had come up with, since we had little time and a lot to do in different parts of Ohio.

As we were passing through a green light, Renfro hit our cannon truck's air horn as a tiny self-driving smart car pulled out in front of us.

"You dumbass robot!" Renfro shouted at the car and not the elderly man riding in the back. "Safe technology my ass!"

Smart cars like that had been a great idea, marketed specifically for older people whose driving ability had diminished but who still had places to go and cheeks to pinch. My folks refused to buy one. They acted like it was some form of tech phobia but I think they just liked me driving them around, a way they could spend more time with me, because Daddy certainly wasn't having problems driving the hell out of his psy-roll.

"I've studied a lot about burrowing birds," said Yolanda, "and since Herjold wasn't much help, I also looked for any myths about a phoenix preying on dragons. I didn't have much luck there, but looking at it as is, and comparing it to more recent animals, I can see how they tie together. Think of a mongoose and a cobra. The mongoose is immune to the snake's venom, so no matter how many times the mongoose gets bit, it doesn't matter, because that cobra is getting chomped when all is said and done. A phoenix is made mostly of fire, so a dragon's breath wouldn't do diddly squat to hurt it. And even if a scaly were somehow able to kill the phoenix, it would just burst into ashes and come back later."

I cleared my throat. "But the dragons aren't really in their right minds when the phoenix is around. You should see the ones at the enclosures. They're buggin' out. You look into any of that?"

Yolanda's floating head nodded. "I'm thinking the phoenix gives off some kind of frequency, much like how wraiths attract dragons. It puts dragons in a manic state, they're confused and even more violent. The phoenix attracts its food without having to go hunt."

"Wait," said Naveena. "So if the phoenix can attract dragons, could there be a way for us to attract the phoenix?"

"That's exactly what we're working on now, Captain Jendal. Very good!"

Afu stirred in the seat behind me. "But that means we're still up shit creek until Yolanda finds a way to attract some paddles."

"What about wraiths?" I said. "Could we use them to attract the phoenix?"

Yolanda froze, eyes rolling toward the ceiling. At first, I thought she might be having a stroke. Her face relaxed out of whatever thought-induced paralysis had taken over and said, "That's a great place to start. The only problem is that wraiths attract dragons. If the ghosts could also attract the phoenix, we would have seen that by now. I mean, the enclosures are a great example. The phoenix hasn't been anywhere near them."

The enclosures. "Oh shit."

"What is it?" Naveena said.

"The wraith enclosures. The dragons and ghosts are both going crazy. At best, we've given the firebird four all-you-can-eat-buffets. It'll get stronger, bigger, hotter. At worst, if the walls fail, the scalies will go on a rampage looking for the phoenix."

"Oh, boy," Yolanda said. "I'll start work on seeing if I can somehow reverse the polarity of a wraith. If any of you trap one, please rush over here to Central Fire Station so I can get to work on that."

"How do you think the firefighters are going to like a wraith in their station?" asked Naveena.

Yolanda shrugged. "They're already miffed that we're here in the first place. I don't see a ghost or two making things any worse."

I sighed. "I have a wraith on me right now."

"Oh?" Yolanda said.

It would be asking for a shit storm. If I gave the Wilkins wraith to Yolanda and the law found out about it …

Well, this was more important and I'd just stick to

the notion of it being better to request forgiveness,
because I sure as shit wasn't going to ask for permission.

"Yeah," I said.

Afu leaned forward. "But the last wraith you
caught was in—"

"Zip it, Afu." I turned back to Yolanda. "We'll
swing by after I go tell the mayor that we have to shut
down the enclosures."

"So we're not going by to talk to Ralph?" Renfro
asked.

Ralph Rankin was the detective working the
phoenix cult case, the guy with the thin goatee I'd
met outside Club Infinity. He and Renfro had grown
up together, and I was hoping to use that relationship
to get in good with the cops, put a stop to this cult
paranoia and focus on the important thing. The
phoenix was the priority, but I was also going to do
my damnedest to prevent any innocent people from
getting burned or rotting in a cell while the boys and
girls in blue slowly realized what I already knew.

"We'll have to take a rain check with the
detective," I told Renfro. "Text him and reschedule
once we stop at City Hall."

"All right then," Yolanda said. "That's all I have for
now. I'll be waiting for you and that wraith."

I ended the call and took a deep breath. As Renfro
made the turn to put us en route to City Hall, I
wondered if I'd made the right decision.

"T." Afu's voice was almost a whisper. "You never
turned in that wraith. The one that family wants."

At a red light, Renfro tuned to me. "You've had it
on you this whole time?"

"Technically it's been in the remote the whole time," I said. "And that's been in my power suit."

"Tamerica!" Renfro said.

"What?" I shifted in my seat to face him. "The family isn't going to be getting it, no matter how much they whine. And the enclosures have a ton of dead fuckers that, by the way, are going to be released themselves when we shut down the walls. I just got the jump on trapping 'em."

"We're really going to shut down the enclosures?" Afu asked.

Renfro pointed at him. "Don't change the subject."

Crossing his arms, Afu sat back, raising an eyebrow.

I sighed. "Look, with the phoenix and… and Patrice and everything else going on, I forgot. Okay? By the time I remembered, I was getting served with a subpoena. Then I decided fuck them, I should hold onto it. And now Yolanda needs a wraith, so it all works out."

Grumbling, Renfro said, "I guess you're right."

"So you're with me on this?" I looked from him to Afu. "This is just between us?"

"Yeah, I'm with you," Renfro said. "Right up until this bites us all in the ass."

A tank rolled past us on the street as we walked up to City Hall. A gunner stood at the turret on top and nodded toward us. Every instinct in me wanted to flip off this guy and everything he stood for, but professionalism won out and I nodded back, even though it was coupled with a disdainful frown.

"Fucking army," I said under my breath.

"You think they're going to take our jobs?" Afu asked.

Renfro hummed in the negative. "But I don't like the look of it. Feels like I'm in some fascist state."

"Like Texas?" I said.

We had to wait thirty minutes before we could see Mayor Ghafoor, and I sat in the waiting room the entire time, jiggling my leg and thinking about hurrying to Central Station and getting Yolanda her wraith.

Afu had been restless, too, but it wasn't until Renfro left to use the restroom that I found out it wasn't from the waiting.

"I want you to know that I'm sorry for what I said before. I'm glad to be on crew with you." He smiled with a hint of nerves.

"Don't worry about it," I said.

Lord, please don't let this be some weird way of him trying to patch up our relationship. After all, matter could never be destroyed, only changed. When fire turns a house to ash, you can't rebuild it using the same charred particles. Then again, the phoenix had kind of fucked up that scientific fact.

"I was just upset," he said. "I just want to feel like I'm appreciated. That you want me on your crew."

"I got to pick everyone I wanted to take out the phoenix. Make a note that you're wanted."

It was true. Personalities clash, but at the end of the day the only thing that mattered was if you could do the job. Afu most certainly could.

He cleared his throat. Then a second time. "I, uh, I want to take you out for dinner some night when we aren't worrying about flaming eagles and stuff."

When I widened my eyes, he raised his palms to

me in defense.

"Just as friends and coworkers. I just miss being your friend."

I tapped a finger against my knee as I thought about it. Maybe going to dinner with Afu – just as friends – would be the last push for our relationship to be fully-platonic. Closure. Closure was good.

"Ask me again when this phoenix business is behind us," I said.

"Done," Afu said. The nervousness left his smile as it grew across his face.

"What's done?" Renfro walked in from around the corner.

I hesitated to answer. Thankfully the mayor's receptionist turned to us from behind her desk.

"Mayor Ghafoor says you can go in now."

Lots of things had changed since the old mayor was torn to pieces by wraiths. The most evident was Ghafoor's new décor. Mayor Rogola had had twin Shi statues at either side of his desk, leaving the rest of the office bare. In Ghafoor's office, the statues had been thrown out and she'd lined the walls with photographs of old Ohio, when Parthenon City was once called Ashland. Seemed extremely ironic they'd traded names not long before we were living in an actual land of ash.

Mayor Ghafoor paced in front of her desk, dictating notes into her holoreader. When she saw us, she put on a smile to shame Afu and set aside her device. "Parthenon's bravest! How are things going? Are you all managing the tight fit at the firehouses?"

She must have recently slammed a jug of coffee

because she was going ninety to nothing. I paused before I spoke so my brain could catch up with her question.

"Um, we're trying to make the best of it," I said. "But we're looking forward to getting back to having our own place."

I knew Brannigan would appreciate that.

"All in good time," said Ghafoor. "So, what can I do for you?"

I waved for Afu and Renfro to take a seat in the two chairs in front of the mayor's desk. I leaned against the wall.

"We think this phoenix is driving the wraiths and dragons crazy," I said. "It's basically sending out a signal to draw them to it. We are suggesting that we temporarily shut down the enclosures until the phoenix is no longer a problem."

Ghafoor dropped her smile. If it had been made of glass, it would have shattered across the newly-waxed hardwood floor. "You've got to be kidding me."

"I'm afraid not, mayor," Renfro said.

I touched my engineer's forearm and looked into his glowing, red eyes. "I got this, Renfro."

He looked embarrassed and then nodded before leaning back into his seat.

"Mayor Ghafoor," I said, "these enclosures are going to provide the phoenix with a lot of energy."

"How?" The mayor crossed her arms.

"Well, the phoenix burns both dragons and wraiths and eats the ashes left after. That'll give it more fire power, and that's not even a pun. It grows bigger and hotter with each dragon it eats."

"So, the phoenix feeds on creatures we've been

trying to put a stop to for ten years, and you're wanting to prevent that?"

My mouth hung open as I tried to think of something smart to retort with. But she had a point. The phoenix would take care of a huge problem. Countering that, though, the phoenix was a problem itself.

Ghafoor blinked at me. "And wouldn't the dragons try to dig back underground if they had any desire to leave the enclosures?"

She had me there. The scalies were going bonkers, but they weren't trying to escape to find the firebird. I'd clearly come to the mayor prematurely, and I was looking like a complete dumbass.

"I'm not sure why the dragons haven't left. My guess is that they're affected but not to the level of wanting to find the phoenix."

"Guessing," the mayor said, nodding and walking back to sit at her desk. "I'm not going to make a decision based solely on a guess. The way I see it, if the phoenix shows up at one of the enclosures, it's saved you the time and effort to find it. I suggest you smoke eaters put units at every enclosure to be on the safe side. That way, if the dragons do finally break out and run amok, you'll be there to stop them."

"Ma'am," I said, "there are at least fifty dragons in every enclosure. Some have more than a hundred."

"I've made my decision, Captain Williams. If you find anything more concrete, more convincing, please come tell me and I promise I'll listen and change course accordingly. Until then, you have a bird to catch."

As soon as I was outside City Hall, I kicked a fire

hydrant with my heel. The pain didn't even bother me. In fact, it was welcome fuel for my anger.

A hover-car slowed as it passed in front of City Hall. A white guy in a yellow t-shirt stuck his head and two thumbs out the window. "Nice going, smoke eaters! Way to burn your own house down!"

"Fuck you!" I shouted to the car as it sped away.

"It'll be alright, Cap," Renfro said.

"I looked like a fool in there with the mayor." I spoke through clenched teeth.

"You're right, though, Cap," Afu said. "Having that many psycho dragons in one place can't be good."

"The mayor had a point, too," I said. "This phoenix eats what we've been fighting for so long. I have to wonder if it's nature's way of balancing the scales."

"Is that what these arsonists are doing, though?" Renfro asked. "Balancing the scales?"

"Those were innocent people," I said.

"Just like Patrice. The phoenix made her go crazy."

"Yeah, but why Patrice?" Tears were collecting in my eyes, but I'd be damned if they would move any farther. "Why not me or Afu? We got closer to the thing than she did."

"I don't know." Renfro huffed, shook his head. "But we can't let it be. Too many lives are at risk. We take down the phoenix, it'll put a stop to the arsons, and maybe then we can shut those PC First assholes up. I don't know if y'all have been watching the Feed, but people in this city are starting to give them support."

"It's just a fucking animal," I said. "That bullshit Herj… whatever the fuck his name was. That stuff about demons? Possession? I don't believe in that.

Certain people are affected and others aren't. We need to find out what the difference is. Maybe… maybe we don't have to kill it."

"Are you running a fever?" Afu reached out to touch my forehead, but I slapped it away.

All three of our holoreaders went off at once. I knew that could only mean one thing: dragon call.

The red flashing alert floating up from the holoreader screen said some teenagers might be trapped in FirstEnergy Stadium, where the Cleveland Browns used to play.

"Some dumbass kids went messing around out in the wastes?" Afu said. "Place is a death trap."

"Why are we getting the call, then?" Renfro asked. "That's fire department business."

I read the last line of the dispatch message and my heart leapt one way and then another. "That's why," I said, and held it up for Renfro to read.

Some wasteland scavengers had found a newer model hover-car outside the stadium. They ran off and called us when they saw a giant, flaming bird burrowing its way into the debris.

# CHAPTER 23

FirstEnergy Stadium lay rusty and folded in on itself. I couldn't imagine that anyone had scored a touchdown or eaten an overpriced hotdog here. The overpass near the front of the arena had crumbled in the middle, even now dribbling bits of concrete onto the road below. Lake Erie spanned wide and far behind the football stadium, but it wasn't a leviathan that destroyed FirstEnergy Stadium on E-Day.

I'd first heard about what happened while I was working the desk at a mechanic shop. Later, I watched video of the incident. We even broke down the chaos clip by clip in smoke eater rookie school, seeing how dragons attacked and how to evacuate on a mass scale.

Of course, they didn't know jack shit about dragons when the stadium was destroyed. It had been an off-season game between the Browns and Kansas City. Normally it wouldn't have been the kind of game to fill the stands, but most of Ohio had shown up to boo down the Chiefs, because they had worked some loophole with the NFL to allow a droid on as a player. Every Browns fan had called foul, signed petitions, posted angrily and endlessly on the Feed about how it was unfair to play a robot against flesh and blood players. The NFL saw good publicity, no matter what the majority of fans had to say about it.

It was mid-way into the second quarter when the quakes came. Huge slabs of concrete and steel beams fell over like toy blocks. That's what killed most of those in attendance, that and the stampede that followed. Then the kraken showed up.

It wasn't squid-like at all, which had always confused me. Krakens were supposed to be giant squids, right? Our instructor, Sergeant Puck, told us the name came from some ancient story about a guy fighting a monster on the back of a winged horse.

All I know is the dragon was fat and uglier than sin, scaly tendrils hanging from its head and the sides of its mouth. First, it bent over the top of the stadium like a five-year-old playing with a sand bucket. Then gallons of slime poured from its mouth and nostrils, trapping a bunch of football fans in gobs of acidic spit. Those poor dissolving people it would save for later, while it scooped up a bunch of other fleeing attendees and popped them down its throat like a clawful of candy. Players on the field were squished under its fat claws, except for the second-string bench warmers who had wisely run for the exit. Unfortunately for them, they were soon crushed by the tons of steel and stone that eventually all came down when the kraken had had its fill.

So, needless to say, I felt a little anxious being here in the flesh.

A new hover-car sat by an overturned concrete pillar. A bumper sticker said the owner was "Done with school and out the door. We're the Class of

2124!" Inside, I found a couple of backpacks and a floor covered with food wrappers, so it was safe to assume there were indeed teenage wannabe archaeologists somewhere under all the crumbled shit they used to call a stadium.

Naveena and her crew pulled up in their Slayer truck as I was scoping out the scene with my therma-goggles

"We're going to need way more smoke eaters than just our two crews," she said.

"I already requested more companies and Brannigan," I said. "But these kids aren't going to last for long if we don't hurry." If it wasn't already too late.

Naveena nodded in agreement and clapped her armored hands together. "All right. We'll take the right, you take left?"

"Done," I said.

We began our initial search, calling out for the trapped civilians, even though we didn't know their names or how deep they might have been. Shouting, "Smoke eaters! Call out so we know where you are!" usually did the trick. But after five minutes, with no other companies showing up yet, and a phoenix somewhere deep below us, I was beginning to get worried.

"Cap," Afu said, "I think we need to go deeper into the debris. We're not going to hear shit from out here."

"Renfro, you mind taking lead?" I asked. "We're going to need your vision if we don't pick up anything on the goggles."

"Yeah," he said. "Come on."

He led us up the rubble. We had to power jump

once to get over a ragged gap. Then we had to crawl
under a broken sign displaying an advertisement
for pineapple flavored soda. The farther we slid and
crawled, the darker our surroundings became. The
debris now lurched over us and blocked out the sun.
We were getting deeper by the minute.

Renfro drooped to one knee and put armored
fingers against the unstable ground just ahead of him.
"Oh, shit."

"What is it?" I asked.

"Come here, Cap," Renfro whispered. "And be as
quiet as you can."

My guts twisted. That was never a good sign.
Retracting my therma-goggles, I stepped lightly over
to Renfro and knelt beside him, looking at his fingers
and trying to see what had got him so worried. I
turned on my helmet light and saw...

...'Oh, shit' indeed.

Black oily drops had splattered the ground. It
looked like ink – if ink were made of soulless, pure
evil. Regular ink didn't give off the ethereal aura this
stuff did, and this stuff meant only one thing. There
was a jabberwock slithering through the rubble,
somewhere very close.

"Look." Renfro pointed ahead and I followed with
my flashlight.

The ink splashes followed a path that wound up
to a hole that was big enough for a van to drop into.
From where I stood, the hole looked like it led straight
down, into the middle of the collective destruction.

Renfro's next breath sounded like a gasp. "Why am
I always the one to rescue some dumbass kids?"

"Oh, man," said Afu, staring at the ink spots calling us forward. "I've never fought a jab—"

"Don't even say it!" I snapped.

Smoke eaters, like most emergency service folks, were a little superstitious, and we were already knee-deep in a shit swamp, so it wasn't like saying the jabberwock's name was going to make things any worse. But we had kids to extricate, and a phoenix. Adding a jabberwock to the mix felt like the universe was planting a foot into every one of our asses.

They were disgusting creatures. Rare, as far as dragons went, but the few times smokies had gone up against them, there were always casualties. Always.

"Come on, you guys." I slapped a hand against my helmet. "Sink or swim. Let's do this for Patrice."

That bolstered them a little bit, and maybe they were faking, but they stiffened their lips and bobbed their heads, like athletes before a big game.

I tried not to think about where I stood and the last sporting event that took place here.

Walking beside Renfro, I slung off my foam shotgun and scanned the area behind us. We circled the hole and each took a turn cautiously peering into it.

"I got nothing on my goggles," whispered Afu. "You getting anything, Renfro?"

"Just a long, dark tunnel," he said, without a single shred of enthusiasm.

"Naveena," I called over my radio. "We've got a Code J on scene. You find anything worth a damn at your location?"

"Negative," she responded. "And fuck me in the ass. I thought those things were more in Colorado's area. Send me your location and we'll catch up."

Turning on my suit's beacon, I told Naveena to stay off radio until I told her otherwise. The wrong sound could have both the jabberwock and the phoenix coming after us, and radio feedback wasn't the most subtle of noises.

I closed my eyes. My crew probably thought I was saying a prayer, but I was really trying to calm my nerves. "I'll go first. Get your axes ready, but don't turn them on unless you have to."

I swung my legs over and dropped into the hole. I landed on slick ground. My light showed the jabberwock's ink had collected in a shallow pool that covered my boots. I frowned, disgusted, and tried to shake most of it off, but the damage had already been done.

I whispered up to my crew as loud as I could without having my voice echo through the tunnel. Any time someone had tried to do that to me, it sounded like an old cat hissing at ghosts, but I didn't have much of a choice.

"Watch your landing," I said. "There's a pool of–"

Afu came barreling down. One of his boots slipped against the ink and sent him backwards into it.

"Goddamn it." I grabbed Afu by the wrist and hauled him out of the tarry pool.

Afu held out his arms and looked at his sides. Shadows deepened in the grooves of his face as he realized what he'd just landed in. He looked at me with a tremble in his lip. "What the hell?"

"It'll be alright," I said. "Just be careful and stick with us."

Renfro eased down the hole and hopped over the pool of ink to stand beside us. "Big Boy here jumped before I had a chance to tell him what you'd said."

"Oh, I didn't know you had supersonic hearing, too!" Afu mocked.

"Shhh!" I said. "Therma-goggles and Renfro's eyes only. Scan every inch as we go. The trapped kids are what we're here for. I don't give a fuck if the phoenix escapes again. But on that note, don't do anything to spook it either. I'd like to kill two birds with one stone."

"That still leaves the Code J," Afu said. "And it's not a bird."

I shook my head and moved deeper into the tunnel, hunching low and taking care with each step.

Several times the debris above us shifted and my heart almost flew out of my throat. You can't run from a structural collapse. All you can do is accept your future as a bloody pancake. We had to squeeze through a tight opening to enter what we discovered to be one of the locker rooms. It still somehow smelled like sweaty balls.

We took a break here and Renfro decided it was the best time to coat Afu's back with foam. "This might help a little," he said. "But act like you're covered in highly-flammable ink."

"I *am* covered in highly-flammable ink." Afu took a seat against the wall with his legs bunched against his chest.

If he was going to be down on himself this early, the operation was already fucked. Taking a seat beside him, I moved to put an arm around him, but dropped back when I remembered the ink.

He looked over at me and sighed. "I'm sorry, Cap."

"What's the matter with you?" I asked. "Where's happy-go-lucky Afu?"

"This is serious business. I have to step up and be serious, too. I don't want any more bad shit to happen."

This would normally have been where Naveena or Brannigan would have said that the job is always dangerous and serious, and that bad things happen even if you nail everything correctly.

But I didn't fucking feel like saying that.

So, instead I asked, "Where are you taking me on our date?"

Afu's face instantly morphed from defeat into surprise. "Date? But—"

"Don't ruin this for yourself, motherfucker. Tell me where we're going."

"Um." Afu blinked a couple times. "I was thinking about that new seafood place. They grow their own tilapia and shrimp in these huge aquariums. They even let you catch the ones you're going to eat if you want."

My change in subject was working a little, getting his mind out of the shitter. I didn't even care if it was giving him any grand ideas about rekindling our relationship. If we made it out of the fucking stadium alive, I would gladly have given Afu another shot and wouldn't feel weird about it at all.

"Shut up, y'all," Renfro hissed, raising his hand. "Do you hear that?"

Afu and I both stood, staying still and listening to the darkness. I wasn't sure whether we were listening for a teenager screaming for help, or the phoenix screeching from deeper down, or…

*Ooh… ooh… ungh…*

Even stuffed inside my power suit, my skin went icy. It sounded like a pervert stroking one out while he watched us in the dark. Hushed but biting at the same time, goblinish.

"Is that what I think it is?" I put my back against Renfro's and waved for Afu to stand beside us.

"I don't know," said Renfro. "But I don't like it."

*Ooh… ungh, ungh… ooh.*

We turned in a circle, a tri-sided reverse huddle. I scanned the walls and floor and even the hole we'd crawled through for heat signatures.

"I can't see anything," Renfro said.

Afu flicked his head from left to right. Moisture flew off of him and splattered against my cheek. I hoped it was sweat and not ink. "Where's it coming from?"

Something hit my shoulder. At first, I thought it might have been Afu gripping me for added courage, but the sound had been too wet and the accompanying smell was like a sewer rat that'd gone on a week-long booze bender.

Touching fingers to my shoulder, I drew up long, sticky streams of black sludge. I lifted my head but the jabberwock was already on us.

I shoved the others out of the way and my ink coated boots slipped on the tile as I ran toward the toilets.

Renfro started to say, "What'd you do that for?" but he stopped short, seeing all seven feet of why I'd done it. "Holy shit, it's on two legs!"

I'm not sure why Renfro had found that particular aspect of the jabberwock to be so crazy-weird, or why he had to say it out loud.

But, yeah, the jabberwock was standing on two legs and flexing long-fingered claws at the ends of its arms. That's where the human similarity ended. With no nose, and tendrils rising from four points out its head, it had protruding, bucktoothed teeth that reminded me of a rat. Its eyes had no irises, just dingy white balls stuck in its head. Standing crooked and bent on the jabberwock's back were two disgusting looking wings that wouldn't have helped an ant fly. Ink dripped from every pore on its body like rotten sweat.

*Ungh,* the jabberwock moaned. *Ooh... ungh.*

Seriously, was it trying to eat us or molest us?

"Watch its mouth," I said. "Afu stay back!"

The jabberwock jerked its head in my direction, drawn by my voice. Its pervy grunting grew louder as it pounded its feet against the locker room tile in a dead run.

Afu slid and kicked the dragon in one of its knobby knees.

"No laser weapons," I shouted. "We don't want to ignite the ink."

And all I had left was foam. The Impulse gun might have done a little damage to the jabberwock, but not enough to kill it, and just the right amount to piss it off. Plus, I was saving it for the phoenix.

Renfro jumped at the dragon as if to tackle him, hitting his power jump to put some extra force behind the punch he was about to deliver to the jabberwock's head, but the scaly spun around and caught Renfro by the forearm. My engineer cried out in pain as the metal of his suit whined under the pressure of the jabberwock's grip. The dragon lifted

Renfro off the ground and held him there to hang in front of its face.

*Ooh…*

Renfro squirmed in the monster's claw. "Let go of me, you ugly, cold-kickin-breath motherfucker!"

Renfro brought his other arm up and hit his foam gun's button. The white stream filled the jabberwock's mouth, covering its soulless eyes. It kept making that terrible grunting sound, but was now gargled against the wad of fire-prevention dripping from its maw.

"Run," I said. "We need Naveena's crew."

"It'll just follow us," Afu said, slamming a fist into the jabberwock's gut.

The punch made the dragon spew up the foam, and when it rose again to its full height it was not a happy camper.

"We need to end this here and now," said Afu, preparing for another go at the scaly.

The jabberwock slashed toward Afu. He ducked the claw, but then the dragon reared back, a hissing sound escaping from its throat, past its buckteeth.

"Afu, get away!" I ran and slammed into Afu as the jabberwock shot a loogie that looked like a piece of flaming coal. It bounced off the wall and I sat up in time to see it rolling toward my boots. My ink-coated, highly flammable boots. On contact the coal ignited my feet and I leapt up, dancing a horrible two step as I tried to stomp out the fire.

"Give me your hands," Afu said.

In the chaos, I did what he asked, not thinking about what he was planning to do. With his two huge hands, Afu grabbed my arms and swung me. My flaming boots plowed into the side of the jabberwock's head, sending it crashing into the nearby lockers.

After he set me down, I punched Afu in the chest. "What the hell was that?"

My boots still on fire, Renfro ran over and dumped a couple gallons of foam to put out the flames.

"Seriously," I said, flicking away the last of the foam. "Let's move."

"Help!" a cry came from somewhere in the dark. "We're down here."

"The kids," Renfro said, turning toward the hole we'd crawled through.

I was exhausted, and fear urged me to piss myself. My hair probably smelled like ink and smoke, and I'd promised Afu a date. And *now* the teenagers wanted to call out for help.

Groaning, I said, "Looks like we're going back the way we came."

# CHAPTER 24

"Ow!"

I'd bumped into Calvinson on our way out. Naveena and her crew stood there, blocking our way.

"Move, move, move!" I shouted.

Harribow and the others turned and booked it back down the dark tunnel. You get used to springing into action when another smoke eater tells you to haul ass. It could mean the few seconds needed to avoid getting torched.

"Y'all run into the Code J?" Naveena asked as we all filed along at a steady jog.

"Yeah," I said.

"What?" Harribow screeched. "Oh shit."

"Help!" came the disembodied cry again.

Renfro whistled for a halt. "Where is that coming from?"

Both crews stopped and listened. Harribow shook and swayed on both feet like he was considering crawling back to the surface.

"We came in the same way you did," said Naveena. "Was there another passage in that room you just left?"

"No," I said. "Locker room. Enclosed."

"What about this?" Calvinson shined his light

ahead, illuminating a small gap between two dilapidated walls.

"That wasn't there before," Naveena said.

I nodded. "Which means this shit is shifting."

"Or another dragon made that hole," Afu said.

"We have to hurry up and get the fuck out of here," I said.

"Somebody, please!" It was two of them now, shouting in chorus. And the voices were coming from behind the small gap Calvinson had discovered.

"We're going to have to break this apart," said Renfro.

The jabberwock's creepy grunting trickled through the passage behind us.

"That might weaken the top," Naveena said. Then, turning to me, "It's your call, Tamerica."

I checked behind us and then the crack. If we left now, those kids were as good as dead.

"Let's breach the wall," I said. "Carefully as all fuck."

Afu got on one side of the crack while Calvinson took the other. They were doing well to take it easy and work through the groan of debris above them, the splatter of dust that rained onto their helmets as they pried and punched. We normally would have used laser swords for this sort of thing, but Afu would have lit up like a Christmas tree.

*Ooh… ooh… ungh.*

"Hurry it up, y'all," said Renfro.

"They got this," I said. "Let them focus."

Afu yanked one final section of the wall away and crawled through without asking the rest of us if we thought it was big enough. If it was big enough for Afu…

I was the last to go through, right after Naveena. On the other side of that wall, waited a void. My steps echoed on forever into the dark. Dust trickled down, down, but I didn't know where. So I extended my therma-goggles.

We were standing in the arena. All of the football field and most of the seats were covered with rubble, but I could tell where we were from the warped field goal reaching out from under chunks of rock, about fifty feet down a steep decline.

A teenage girl stood midway between us and the field. She held a flashlight and began flapping her arms, urging us to come quick. Behind her there was a bent piece of railing, and below that, a faint yellow glow danced off the surrounding slabs of concrete.

"T!" Afu whispered. "The phoenix is down there."

The jabberwock's inappropriate groans sounded from the hole behind me. "Everyone, help me cover this up."

"That's our only way out of here," said Harribow. The yellow phoenix light glistened off of his sweat-soaked face.

"Yeah," I said. "But it's also an easy way for the Code J to get in. This will slow it down."

We didn't make it pretty. All I wanted was to block the passage. The teenager bitched at us the whole time, first thinking we hadn't seen her, then whisper-shouting that we were taking too long.

She obviously didn't know what was hunting for blood on the other side. But we did hurry down to her.

"His leg," the girl pointed toward the ground as I slid along the last bit of rock.

A boy lay there, pinned under a broken electric sign. He wasn't saying anything, and it looked like his eyes were closed.

"Hey, kid." I rubbed his chest, but it only produced groans.

At least he was alive.

"What's his name?" I asked the girl.

"Chris," she said. "And I'm Rachel. You have to get us out of here. That thing is down there."

"Shh!" I patted her arm until she shut up.

Rachel was erratic and that's not a good thing to be when you're trapped between two monsters.

"Renfro," I whispered, pointing at him.

He squatted beside me.

"You have the eyes for this. Get ready to put on a rapid tourniquet. I can't tell if he's bleeding. Unresponsive, but he's getting air. Afu and the two rookies, you lift this shit off as best you can so Renfro can pull him out. Rachel you go over there with Captain Jendal."

"I can't see anything." The girl's voice shook in the dark.

Naveena saved her the trouble by grabbing her hand and leading her away so the other smokies could work.

"Please help him!" Rachel said a little too loudly.

*Lord, kid, calm down*, I thought. *It's your damn fault we're in this mess.*

I turned toward the yellow glow on the other side of the railing, hoping Rachel's loud ass hadn't stirred up the firebird. Stepping to the railing, I peered over to snag a look.

The phoenix was asleep.

Its yellow fire crackled low and almost calmly, its head tucked under a wing and wrapped nice and cozy like a blazing avian burrito.

We could kill this fucker right now!

*Boom… boom.*

The concrete we'd used to cover the hole shook, sending pebbles of loose debris to roll down the slope. The jabberwock was trying to break through.

I chanced a look back over the railing and came face to face with the fiery eye of the phoenix.

"Guys…" I said.

The phoenix shrieked into my face, pelting my cheeks and nose with heat, blasting out my eardrums. I lowered my head so my helmet took the brunt of it.

As I slung the Impulse shotgun from my shoulder, the phoenix flapped its giant wings. Its yellow flames grew bigger, hotter like a small sun, revealing more of the surrounding arena.

I didn't waste time shouting some wise-crack, I just pulled the trigger. The foam projectile slammed into the phoenix, dead center. It tumbled through the air as its flames died down. But the fire was still there, and the bird still flew.

A crash of rocks came from behind me.

The jabberwock slithered out of the hole at the top of the stadium. Calvinson met it with a power jump and a flashing laser, but the dragon spewed a gallon of ink into his face before slapping him with a whip of its tail. The rookie flew over the squished seats and concrete, coming to a stop just in front of his captain.

"I'm fine," Calvinson croaked.

Someone's voice blipped and sizzled in my helmet. Whoever was trying to radio me wasn't getting through. We must have been deeper under the wreckage than I thought.

The jabberwock roared; no more of the *oohing* and grunting. Now it had the space and the proximity to the phoenix to really lose its shit. With its long fingers and toes, it skittered down the rocks. Renfro and I began shooting our lasers at it, although I was taking a glance over my shoulder to see what the phoenix was doing.

But the phoenix wasn't where I had left it twisting in the air, and I didn't have the time to go searching.

Zigging and zagging, the jabberwock dodged every one of our shots. Afu swung at it with his laser axe, but it slid under the blade, using its ink-soaked back to glide over the debris. The dragon didn't stop to attack Afu or even Naveena, who ran for it with her own axe. The jabberwock was coming right for me.

When it leapt into the air, it was so sudden and goddamned terrifying I didn't raise my laser in time. But the scaly sailed right over my head, dripping plods of ink onto my helmet.

I turned, following the jabberwock's trajectory and there, the phoenix hovered on the other side of the railing. It had been ready to snatch me into its fiery beak before the jabberwock clawed into its face. Both of them fell to the arena floor.

The jabberwock caught fire instantly but refused to let go of the phoenix's head, even when the bird took flight again and spiraled around the arena like a comet.

"Get the kids out of here!" I shouted, running toward the other smokies.

Renfro lifted the boy into his arms while Harribow hurried Rachel along. Calvinson, who was still spitting out wads of ink, had to grab Naveena's arm since he couldn't see. I ran past Afu. He'd dug in where he stood and kept his eyes on the battling monsters.

I skidded to a stop and turned back. "Let's go, Afu."

The phoenix twirled in the air, fast enough to shake the flaming jabberwock from its face, fast enough to throw it in Afu's direction. I saw what would happen in a flash. The jabberwock plowing into Afu, both of them going up in flames for the phoenix to feast on, seeing the only man I ever loved die in front of me.

Shit. I guess *that* cat came out of the bag. I honestly didn't know which thought was scarier.

Afu swung his laser axe at the incoming jabberwock and buried the sparking blade into its face, splitting the dragon's head and burying the blade into its throat. The jabberwock wasn't dropping off the axe, and it spun Afu around and around with it.

With a shriek, the phoenix righted itself and dove toward Afu.

"Drop it!" I ran toward him, about to power jump into the phoenix if I had to.

Afu let go of his axe, but not before detonating the electric charge and throwing both axe and dragon into the oncoming firebird. Embers exploded and rained to the ground as electrical sparks shot through the air. With a final shriek, the phoenix shattered into a shockwave of yellow flames. Glowing ashes began to fall down, accompanied by the loose slabs of concrete above us. I grabbed Afu, who stood there gawking at what he'd just caused, and shoved him toward the only way out of there. A hunk of rock that could have easily flattened him landed where he'd just been standing.

"Oh, dang!" he said, and power jumped toward the hole at the top of the stadium.

I followed him into the tunnel, dodging bits of debris that fell in our path, letting our power suits and helmets take the brunt of those we couldn't.

Emergency lights bounced down into the hole. Other crews had finally arrived. We were nearly out when the tunnel rumbled and a slab dropped onto my legs, pinning them.

"Afu!" I called, but he was already too far ahead of me, everything was too loud. He couldn't hear me. I was alone and about to be killed by a football stadium.

I didn't even like football.

"Cast!" I said into my helmet radio. Closing my eyes from the sting of blowing dust, I reached out to find a handhold, something to grab and pull myself out. But all I found was air. "Mayday, mayday, mayday! I'm trapped and can't move."

I reached and reached for something other than slick tunnel floor. I couldn't see a fucking thing. My legs were beginning to hurt pretty bad, even through the initial numbness of them going to sleep. That meant my power armor wasn't failing but had already been smashed out of usefulness.

I widened my fingers, no longer trying to get hold of anything, but hoping some smoke eater up above could see at least a part of me sticking out of the rubble, maybe even a goodbye wave if they didn't...

…When a hand grabbed my mine.

I blinked against the dust in my eyes. All I could see was a shadowy blob.

"I got ya," Brannigan's voice shouted through the rumble.

"My legs."

"They're okay. Just hold on to me." Then, "I got her. Go, go, go!"

We flew. At least, that's what it felt like. It took someone pouring water onto my eyes before I saw that Brannigan had a cable attached to his power suit and one of the Slayer truck's down on street level had pulled us out just as the jabberwock's hole crumbled like it had never been there.

Afu ran over and lifted me up into a bear hug. "I was so scared. Brannigan wouldn't let me go back in. Made me go to rehab."

I grunted against his squeeze, every inch of my body sore, but I didn't tell him to stop hugging me.

"See that, Harribow." Naveena walked over with hands on her hips, her driver in tow. "You need a girlfriend to massage your prostate. Then you can be as stout as Afu."

Afu turned to me, frowning. "Dang it, Tamerica. I knew you told!"

I didn't have time to bask in post-battle celebrations, because the battle wasn't over and I seemed to be the only one who knew it.

"Chief," I said, catching him as he was walking toward his truck. "We have to go back in there."

"You're welcome, Williams. I know you'd do the same for me any time." His sarcasm was thicker than the dirt on his face.

"I appreciate your rescue," I said, "but the phoenix ashes. They're still down there. If we don't extract them and get them to Yolanda, we'll be back to square one."

Chief opened his passenger door and poured himself a cup of water from the jug sitting in the seat.

Kenji sat in the back and gave a happy, digital bark when he saw me.

"Sherry wanted him out of the house," Brannigan said before I asked what his dog was doing here. "Bethany gets him riled up."

"Listen," I said. "It doesn't have to be Naveena's crew or mine. We just need to get it done. Send someone fresh."

Brannigan took a sip of water. "None of you is going back in there. You ash kickers shouldn't have gone in without all of these other crews here as back up."

I turned and looked at the newly-arrived Slayers and cannon trucks, an ambulance and EMTs treating the teens who had been trapped.

"But I'm not going to grill you about that," Brannigan said. "Those kids would probably be dead if it wasn't for all of you. Besides, there's no way you could get back into the stadium. All that shit collapsed and its shut tighter than Sherry when I'm in the doghouse."

"*Naneun gaejib-eul joh-ahanda!*" Kenji said.

My holoreader buzzed. Translation: "I love the doghouse!"

Looking at where the jabberwock's hole had been, I saw that Brannigan was right. Even if we were to make entry, it would be too snug and too dangerous.

"Maybe we could get the fire department to loan us a droid," Brannigan said.

"That would take too long. The ashes could reignite any moment."

"I'm not sending a human being down there, Williams."

"No, not…"

Kenji's rubber tongue drooped from the side of his mouth. The inside of his jaws looked like a deep shovel.

"Not a human," I said.

Brannigan followed my gaze as Kenji barked again.

"No," Chief shook his head hard enough it made his cheeks jiggle. "No way in hell. The rescue is over. My dog isn't…"

# CHAPTER 25

"Fuck me with flaming floss," Brannigan said as he helped me secure the camera on Kenji, the one he'd originally placed on the front of Cannon 15.

"Look at it this way," I said "now I'm not that mad you were spying on me, since we can use the camera."

"If you'd been that mad, you would have taken off the camera by now."

Kenji barked and said, "*Naneun seongyosalo naganda!*"

"That's right, buddy," I patted his head. "You're going on a mission."

Brannigan squatted in front of his metal mutt and placed his hands at either side of Kenji's face. "Now listen to me, dog, you're to get in there and grab the glowing ashes. If you sense anything dangerous, you run your metal ass back here as fast as you can. You understand me?"

Kenji barked and winked one of his digital eyes.

Afu and the others finished opening the hole as much as they could. Further in, Kenji would be on his own, with one of us guiding him via a voice program on a holoreader. Naveena took off her helmet and smeared sweat across her forehead with the back of her armored forearm.

We really needed to invest in some towels.

"We've done all we can, Chief. If Kenji is ready, we are, too."

Brannigan huffed, looked at the ground and whispered a "Goddamn it," before rising to his feet and whistling for Kenji to follow him.

Afu and Calvinson were smart and got out of Chief's way as he climbed up the FreeEnergy debris. I'd never seen Brannigan worried before. He'd always hated droids and the idea of them replacing jobs. Kenji and mecha-canines like him had replaced the dogs that had run off just before the dragons showed up, but that was different. At least to Brannigan's mind. And he might have told me that it was because Bethany loved Kenji, that she'd be heartbroken if anything happened to him, but I knew the truth: Brannigan had a soft spot for the dog-shaped automaton, and Chief would be the one crying if Kenji got buried under the rubble or, worse, if the phoenix came back and melted Kenji beyond repair or recognition.

Hell, I'd feel just as bad. I liked the dog, but this was my idea. If it went south, I'd be responsible. It would be another tick on the list of reasons why I didn't need to be a captain. Or a smoke eater.

But I stopped myself from thinking like that. Superstition and experience said that you couldn't lose your cool when you were in the heat of the moment. Success had to be the only thought on your mind.

But that didn't help the empty, twisty feeling in my guts.

I sat down on the bumper of Cannon Truck 15

and dragged the holoreader application into the air.
The video from Kenji's computer showed clear, with
only a brief jostle of static when Kenji looked at
the hole and then Brannigan, as if he wasn't sure he
wanted to do the job after all.

"You'll be fine, boy," Brannigan said. "I only wish
you could eat, so there'd be a treat in it for you after
you get back."

"*Neuj-eun bam Meogileul bogehago geolae ya,*" Kenji
said with electronic panting.

"He says it's a deal if you let him watch the
late-night Feed," I said through my holoreader's
microphone. "And the good stuff, none of that cut-
to-commercial sleaze."

"Damn it, Williams," Brannigan stared into the
camera. "I was trying to have a private moment with
my dog." He looked at Kenji. "And that's fine, Kenji,
as long as Sherry or Bethany don't know about it."

The promise of tawdry movies sent the metal dog
rushing into the hole.

"Turn on your light, Kenji," I said.

With a *click*, light filled the tunnel. The path was
clear for the first dozen feet, but Kenji stopped when
he came to a wall of metal blocking the way.

Harribow leaned over my shoulder, watching the
footage. "What's that pup going to do now?"

"Get through, Kenji," I said. "If you can."

The dog looked down at his front paws and
barked. Claws popped out of the smooth metal of his
toes with a spring-like *shing*.

"I didn't even know he had those," Brannigan said,
rushing over to watch.

Kenji used his claws to shred into the metal in front of him until he'd made a hole big enough to squeeze through. After that there wasn't much in his way, other than a few more tight squeezes he quickly maneuvered. Then he was in the main part of the arena, where we'd left the jabberwock and phoenix to their demise.

"All right, Kenji," I said. "The ashes should be somewhere over that railing. They'll be glowing yellow, so you can't miss them."

"Aren't dogs colorblind?" Afu walked over, rubbing his shoulder.

We all turned and looked at him.

"What?" Afu said.

I turned back to my holoreader. "Go on, Kenji. The sooner you find it, the sooner you can get back."

Kenji leapt over a pile of rubble and nimbly hopped down the rest of it until he got to the railing overlooking the field.

"How can he get down there?" Calvinson asked.

Naveena shrugged. "He can always jump."

"Are you fucking crazy," said Brannigan. "That's my dog!"

"And how would he get back up?" Afu asked.

"Kenji," I said. "Do you see a way down to the field?"

The dog looked left then right. It bent over and began 'sniffing' at the edge of the railing, as if the robot could actually smell. But it was one of those built-in quirks that made him more dog-like. Hell, it might have been helping him find a route, so I didn't stop him.

Kenji snapped his head up and began running. I almost thought another dragon had emerged nearby and that Kenji was running for his artificial life, but then the camera showed him coming up to a fallen and half-smashed advertisement board selling cannabis popsicles. The board extended down to the field like a ramp leaning against the top railing. Kenji had to jump over the part where the board had splintered in two, and if he wasn't careful, the whole thing would shift and fall over. Then he'd be stuck down there.

"Careful," said Brannigan, also seeing the wobbly surface of the advertisement.

"*Neoui gaseum-eul jinjeong sikyeola*," Kenji said.

Translation: "Calm your breasts."

Although I'm pretty sure he meant 'tits.'

When the dog made it down to the field, it scanned the surrounding area. I spotted a yellow glow coming from Kenji's right, and before I had to point it out to him, Kenji ran for it.

"Scoop it all up in your mouth," I said. "Then run back here like a good boy."

Naveena huffed a laugh through her nose. "You guys know you don't have to talk like that to him, right? I don't even think it was necessary to speak to real dogs like that."

"Save your shit, Naveena," Brannigan said.

Kenji stopped suddenly. He was just short of the glowing ashes and wasn't taking a step farther. Something was wrong.

"What's wrong, Kenji?" I asked.

The dog made a yipping whine, partially warbled by digital static. The video showed nothing to be worried about. Maybe Kenji was having second thoughts, considering his existence, the sudden realization, like a bomb dropped onto his chrome skull that his world could end right then and there.

"It's okay, boy," I said. "Just grab the ashes and run."

Kenji lifted a paw, hesitated to move it forward, then began taking slow steps toward the phoenix ashes.

"Something has him freaked out," said Brannigan, under his breath. "Nothing ever gets to Kenji."

The dog bent over to scoop the ashes into his mouth when the embers ignited and spread out like two fiery wings.

An avian shriek ripped from my holoreader speakers as I screamed, "Kenji run!"

Run he did, God love him. He scaled that broken Canna-Pop ad in less than two seconds, leaping over the railing as the board fell beneath his feet.

Kenji's shadow was outrunning him, swaying ahead in the camera's view, the product of the brightening fire closing in behind him. When he reached the top, Brannigan's dog leapt through the hole leading from the arena into the tunnel, and that's when the video feed shattered into snowy static.

"No!" Chief got to his feet and ran, power jumping to the hole we'd sent his dog down.

I followed right behind him.

"Fuck, Williams," Brannigan said as he stared down into the dark, waiting for any sign of Kenji. "You just had to do this your way."

Maybe I should have kept my mouth shut. Brannigan was grieving his dog – granted way too early – and I should have let him be angry. But that wasn't the way I rolled.

"I don't want anything to happen to Kenji either,

Chief. But what else were we going to do?"

"Our SOPs say—"

"Oh, fuck your SOPs!"

That shut Brannigan up… for a second. He didn't speak again until his face was redder than Renfro's eyes and a sheen of oily sweat covered it. "Now, you look here, goddamn it. I put you in your position. I can just as quickly put you back."

"You want to move us around like your private collection of chess pieces, go ahead. I ain't going to be a part of it! I should have quit before that fucking smaug dug itself out of the ground."

"Smoke eaters don't quit," Brannigan said, more sad now than angry. "Forget all of the breathing toxic smoke shit. We keep going, we keep fighting, that's what separates us from regular people."

"But now you can farm that quality out of anybody, old man. A little shot of dragon blood and you can have your pick of anyone you want. So don't get sentimental with me. I made a call. I own it. It was the best decision at the—"

Barking from the hole.

"Kenji!" Brannigan screamed into the dark.

A flashlight's glow, dim and the size of a firefly, shook left and right deep within the stadium rubble. The earth shook. Behind us, Afu, who had been rubbing the back of his leg with the other foot, fell over with a grunt. The other smokies dropped into a squat. Naveena extended her laser sword.

Toward the center of the destruction, the top layer exploded as flames shot into the sky. The phoenix had risen again. It shrieked once before buzzing over us like a jet fighter, but not low enough for any smoke eater to power jump and slash it – although Naveena tried. Then the firebird was gone. And we were back to square one. Again.

How the hell do you kill something that doesn't stay dead?

"This try-fail cycle stuff is some annoying shit," Renfro said, dropping to his ass in defeat.

Brannigan reached into the hole and pulled Kenji out, cradling the dog in his arms. "Son of a bitch, Kenji. You're one hot potato."

Dropping from Brannigan's arms, Kenji weakly trotted over to me. The phoenix fire must have really taken it out of him, but the best thing to do was to let his metal cool slowly. Rapidly cooling him down with foam or ice would have jacked his frame and circuits.

"It's okay, boy," I said, patting him on his back. I quickly yanked my hand away, sucking air through my teeth. The heat coming off him was brutal. "You tried. We'll get that damned bird next time."

Kenji's eyes winked at me and he bent over, depositing something from his mouth onto the ground.

It was a clump of glowing ashes.

"Holy shit!" I lifted Kenji and swung him around in a clumsy dance. I didn't even care how much the heat stung.

"He… did it," Harribow stumbled toward me, giving a weak smile.

"Are you okay?" I asked.

"Just a… little hot," he said, and dropped onto his face.

He didn't get back up.

# CHAPTER 26

Yolanda stood in the open bay at Central Fire Station as we ran with Harribow hanging from our arms. Kenji, barking his head off, ran ahead and began circling the propellerhead's legs.

"We need medical," I yelled.

Several of the propellerheads had been waiting with a stretcher. We placed Harribow onto it and they wheeled him off, leaving the rest of us smoke eaters standing there with thumbs up our asses. A few of the firefighters came out from their hidey holes, looking around, wondering what all the fuss was about.

Brannigan handed Yolanda a metal container. "We were able to grab some phoenix ashes. Do whatever the fuck you have to so we can finally nab this bastard."

"*Naneun geudeul-eul butjab-eun salam-ida,*" Kenji said. ("I'm the one who grabbed them.")

"Okay," Brannigan said, after hearing the translation. "Kenji scooped up the ashes. Anyway, while you're working on this, I also want to know what's going on with Harribow. Is it like Patrice Johnson?"

Naveena was exceptionally quiet, which told me she was fuming inside. If her silence hadn't told me anything, it was definitely in her clenched fists, metal scraping under the pressure.

We all stared at Yolanda, like she would give us some huge revelation. We all knew it was the same thing that happened to Patrice. What we really wanted was a way to prevent the same fiery end from happening to another smoke eater.

Yolanda caught her breath, like our stares were squeezing the life out of her. She threw up her hands, almost losing hold of the box containing the ashes. "You guys, I'm going to work as fast as I can. I really don't know anything yet. We still don't know what was wrong with Patrice."

She looked about to cry, so I stepped in to relieve some of her guilt. I was carrying enough, but I could heft a little more. "We all know you're the best, Yolanda. What do you need from us?"

Before she could answer, two black-and-white cop cars pulled in behind us. When they stepped out of the cars, I saw one of them was a droid.

"What's this shit?" I said.

"I called them," said Brannigan. "We need to have Harribow guarded."

"He's not a goddamned cult member!" Naveena finally said.

"I'm not saying he is," said Brannigan. "I'm not saying Patrice was. But this phoenix does shit to people and I'd rather have measures in place to protect him and everybody else."

When a black hover-SUV pulled in beside the black-and-whites, Yolanda said, "I'm going to get started," and ran inside.

Detective Rankin, who'd been working the cult case, got out of the SUV as it drifted to a rest on the ground.

"And this guy?" I thumbed toward the detective, giving Brannigan every ounce of pissed-off my eyes could shoot.

"He needs your help."

"Chief," the detective shook hands with Brannigan. "Sorry to hear about one of your people."

"He's not a goddamned cult member," Naveena said through gritted teeth, as if it was the only sentence she knew.

"I'm Detective Rankin, by the way," he said. "And I understand how you guys might be feeling, but we have to investigate this. We don't know if these 'Children of the Phoenix' have infiltrated your department or…"

"I can assure you that's not the case," Brannigan said. "I've already told you what we believe is happening. If you don't want to listen to reason, that's your fault."

"There's no cult," I said. "This bird is fucking with people's heads."

"And why are none of you affected the same way?" Rankin asked.

I looked to Afu, Renfro, the others. We didn't have an answer to that. Patrice had caught some of the ashes in her mouth. I thought that might have been why. But Harribow hadn't even had much action or contact with the phoenix or its ashes. Afu or Calvinson, if anybody, would have been the most likely to lose their minds from the phoenix fire.

Or me.

"Let me give you an opportunity to prove me wrong," Rankin said. He turned to the human and droid cops, motioned for them to go inside with a toss of his head.

They both obeyed as robotically as the other. I wondered what the droid would do if Harribow tried to escape or hurt somebody. I still didn't trust robots, not after what Rogola made them do to Chief Donahue.

"What do you need our help with?" Afu asked.

Rankin cleared his throat. "We need you to do some... surveillance."

"You can't be serious," I said.

"Look," Rankin said, "we've found a connection with all of these arsonists and we've narrowed down some potential additional suspects. We figure you all have the ability to withstand any... heat that might occur. And you could save a lot of people if these suspects turn out to be a part of this cult and try to burn something else. You'd be right there to stop it."

"So you want us to do your job for you," Renfro said.

Rankin gave a small laugh and shook his head, as if he couldn't understand why we would look down our noses at the opportunity to play Big Brother and violate a few citizens' basic rights. "Like I said, you have the power not to get burned, and you can go where it's smoky. It'd be handy. Plus, my people are doing their part of the heavy lifting, believe me."

"We can still get burned." Calvinson spoke up. "And the phoenix fire is hot. Hotter than our threshold."

Rankin raised his brow and looked to Brannigan.

"Should I go with my Plan B, then, Chief?"

"No," Brannigan said. He narrowed his eyes at Calvinson, too late to tell him to shut up. "We'll do this. Won't we?"

He was looking at me. I was in charge of the ash kickers. I was the one who had the whole fucking world on my shoulders.

"What's the connection between the arsonists?" I asked.

Rankin looked over his shoulder. Firefighters had slowly begun to trickle into the bay like wraiths around an ash heap.

"Not here," Rankin said. "I don't want to start a panic. Let's go inside."

"Fair enough," I said. "I still have to give Yolanda something."

The wraith inside my remote was weighing me down. The quicker I could give Wilkins to Yolanda, the sooner I didn't have to worry so much about the ghost's family taking him back and doing God-knew-what with him.

The propellerheads had closed off part of the fire station and had placed one of the scientists outside a sliding glass door to prevent looky-loo firefighters from sneaking a peek. The guard was a nervous looking blonde woman with thick red glasses. She held a stun pistol and breathed a tsunami of relief when she saw us coming down the hall.

"Oh, thank God." She opened the door for us. "I hate playing security guard. Please, please come in."

The other side of the glass looked like a squished version of the propellerhead watch room at our old headquarters. Harribow was on the stretcher behind a curtain hung to provide only the tiniest amount of privacy. Both cops who'd entered earlier stood outside the curtain at parade rest. The human cop was dressed in the dark blue of a Parthenon City beat cop, while the droid had a police shield etched into its chest.

Yolanda was on the other side of the room, clenching her shoulders tight, clearly uncomfortable with the tight working conditions and having to squeeze by her coworkers.

"All right," I said to Rankin. "What's the connection between all these arsons."

"Dragon blood," Rankin said with a nod.

Yolanda looked up from her holoreader, face squished as if she'd bitten into a lemon.

Rankin continued. "Autopsies show that every person of interest, whether they'd moved from another city or not, all received dragon blood infusions within the last six months. That's too big of a connection to ignore. That's why we want you to be on their tail. They'll have smoke eater abilities and who better than you guys to step in if something happens?"

"Right," said Naveena. "Who better to stalk a five-year-old cancer patient? What is this Orwellian bullshit you've got us doing, Brannigan?"

Rankin shook his head. "We've vetted these suspects pretty thoroughly. They're recent imports and–"

"So you're aligning with those PC First scumbags," I said. "They're not from here so they're obviously terrorists."

"I don't agree with those fascist bastards," Rankin said. "Not one bit. But it's hard to ignore the evidence. We're thinking these cult members got DB infusions to be able to withstand hot and smoky conditions so they can do whatever morbid shit they're into. No offense to you guys."

Brannigan held up a hand, in an attempt to calm us all down before we had another fist fight with a different branch of public service. "I wanted us to assist in this because I know we'd do it the right way. Because we care about people." He bobbed his head at Rankin. "No offense."

Rankin shrugged.

"And if we don't agree," I said, "what's Plan B?"

"The New US Army," Rankin said, without any hesitation or regret.

Shitballs. This was going to happen one way or another. Brannigan was right. If we walked away and tried to hunt the bird without anything to go on, we'd risk losing not only time, but citizen lives because the army wouldn't give two shits about saving any of our citizens. They'd be targets, and targets were to be eliminated.

"Perhaps," Yolanda's softened voice broke through the tension, "it's the dragon blood itself that's causing these individuals to lose their minds and… essentially burn the house down."

"That doesn't make any sense," said Rankin. "I thought dragon blood cured people. Made them better, stronger."

"Well, it's not just the blood, but the reaction the phoenix causes in those with dragon blood running through their veins."

Holy shit. That was it. That was the key. Patrice

and Harribow had both been given ieiunium curate to become smoke eaters. They hadn't been born to eat smoke, and that made them susceptible to the phoenix's influence.

"The way the dragons are acting at the enclosures," I said, "I believe it. Think about it, Rankin. What if there is no cult? Just a bunch of sick people like Harribow in there. Like Patrice."

"It's too organized," said Rankin. "We know what criminal group behavior looks like. That guy at the club the other night. He said he was one of the 'Children of the Phoenix'."

"He was out of his mind, sick, and probably saying all kinds of weird shit," I said. "You're only seeing what you want to see. It's easier to create an enemy to go after. It's a lot harder to realize these are victims. We wanted to cure shit so bad, we didn't look at what could happen when we put monster DNA inside of us."

Brannigan turned away from us suddenly. "I… I have to go. I have to get Kenji. I have to see Sherry."

He left without saying anything else. His wife had received dragon blood after she was attacked by a droid. Brannigan himself had been injected with it for two solid weeks. The good news was that Chief believed my side of things, but the bad news was that both he and his wife could turn into crazed human bombs at any moment.

Rankin decided Brannigan's leave meant he could take on the role of leader. "Now, look, Captain. I'm not going to entertain this crazy theory. Thousands of people in this city have received dragon blood. Parthenon would be a goddamned inferno by now.

Has your chief gotten close to the phoenix?"

"Close enough," I said.

"And he's fine. He's not going to spontaneously combust."

"Not necessarily," said Yolanda.

"Y'all," Renfro said. "Rankin is a good man. I've known him for years. He's good at his job. I say we at least give him a shot."

I looked at Yolanda who only shook her head slightly.

"It's your call, T." Naveena folded her arms and chewed on a nail. "I'll support your decision one way or the other."

I looked at Harribow lying on the stretcher, looking like a lobster with the flu. If I had known being a captain involved this many difficult choices, where you could only go left or right and not both...

...But that wasn't true.

Nobody said I couldn't follow Rankin's suspects and work with Yolanda on reversing what the phoenix was doing to them. And, like Rankin said, who better than us to do it? Better us than some shithead mercs.

"We'll do it," I said.

Rankin nodded. "Good. Can you start tonight?"

I groaned and the other smokies looked back at me with tired eyes, slouching and ready to crash into a bed. "We just fought two monsters at once, Detective. We could use a break."

"Tomorrow night, then," Rankin said. "Meet me at police HQ, say, eight o'clock?"

"We'll be there." I crossed my arms. It was time for Dick Tracy to take a hike.

Rankin took a deep breath as if he'd just survived some harrowing battle, and nodded. "All right then. I'll leave you to it."

He walked away, taking a few seconds to look over Harribow lying on the stretcher before leaving the building. We all watched him through the window as he reversed his hovering SUV and sped off to fuck with someone else's day.

"Are you sure about this, Tamerica?" Afu asked.

"What's done is done," I said. "You guys go on. I have to talk to Yolanda about something."

Renfro and the rest walked out, but Naveena hung around in the doorway. "I told you I'd support you one way or the other. Just don't make me regret it."

She was gone before I could bolster any confidence in my decision, but that was just how it was going to have to be. I didn't like it any more than them. But, like Brannigan always said, when have to eat a shit sandwich, best to do it as quickly as possible.

"I promise I won't let the same thing happen again," Yolanda told me. She wrung her hands and looked into my eyes like I was going to slap her.

"I know. That's not what I want to talk to you about. I've got a wraith for you."

Her face brightened. "Oh! That's great. That'll speed up the work."

I took a breath through my nose, smelling the stale, dusty funk of the firehouse. "Yeah, thing is. There's something about it you need to know. Something you have to keep to yourself."

"You didn't do anything untoward did you?"

I'd never heard anyone in person use that word

outside of a spelling bee.

I shook my head and took out my wraith remote. "See, I trapped this sucker when those wannabe smoke eaters were getting in our way fighting the leviathans and the phoenix. The other wraith burned up, but I'm thinking this one is still good. But…"

"This is about your legal predicament." She blinked and waited for me to respond. Casual as a cucumber.

"Right. Some people might come around and try to take it. That's why you have to work faster than you ever have before. It's only a matter of time before they find out it's here. Do we understand each other?"

Yolanda took my wraith remote. "I've got the ashes and a wraith. Now all I have to do is figure out how to reverse the wraith's frequency to get the bird to come to you. Check back with me in a day or two."

I smiled, despite everything that had happened. "You're the best, Yolanda."

She walked over to cabinet and tossed me an empty wraith remote. "I know."

When I walked outside, my fellow smokies were watching something going on down the street. I made my way around the cannon truck to see what had grabbed their interest.

A couple of military hover-vehicles that looked like metal tarantulas had veered onto the curb. Four soldiers surrounded a man in a short-sleeved shirt and slacks, just an ordinary man, and they had him up against the wall. One soldier was patting him down, while the others aimed laser rifles at his back, save one soldier who held a young boy, no more than twelve, by the collar of his t-shirt.

"What the fuck is this?" I asked Naveena.

"This guy was walking with his son, or whoever that kid is. The army pulled over and began searching him for no reason."

The boy wasn't crying, but he was close enough to it. His dad was telling him everything was okay, but the soldiers told the man to shut up, pretty much killing the notion that everything was indeed 'okay'.

I legged it down the street, toward this bullshit on full, public display.

"Where are you going?" Afu asked.

I turned back to the ash kickers while staying in motion, back-pedaling. "Are you just going to stand there and watch this mess?"

Calvinson, whose teeth were still stained with jabberwock ink, said, "But they have guns."

"I don't give a fuck." I turned round again and ran.

Feet hitting pavement behind me helped my courage a little, but my stomach was already in a knot and I began thinking of who would take care of Mama and Daddy if these assholes shot me in the street.

"Whoa!" The first soldier who noticed me moved his rifle toward my chest. "Stay back."

The other soldier turned her weapon on me, while the man who'd been patting the civilian down looked over his shoulder as casually as if I was a plastic bag flying by in the wind.

"What do you think you're doing?" I asked, taking out my holoreader and quickly hitting record on the video app. The soldiers looked at my upheld holoreader and, in unison, looked to the soldier who'd been doing the frisking.

So, he must be the one in charge.

"This is army business," the frisker said. "Move along."

"Like hell," I said. "I'm Captain Williams with Smoke Eater Division. And what you're doing is illegal. You're not the police and I doubt this man has done anything to warrant your harassment. So maybe *you* should move along."

"I'm Colonel Calhoun," the man who'd been frisking said. He gave me a smug smile, showing a silver-capped front tooth. "And by order of Mayor Ghafoor, we have every right to search any person we deem to be a potential threat to this city."

The civilian pressed his back against the building. His lip bled.

"My dad and I were on the way to the ice cream shop," the boy said.

Calhoun tucked his lips and glared at the kid, almost as if he was jealous of the prospect of Dippin' Dots. Then he smiled and straightened his uniform. "We're all trying to do the right thing, Captain."

"Then start right now," I said. "Let 'em go, and maybe I don't report this little incident to Mayor Ghafoor."

"None of you are going to have jobs for long," said one of the other soldiers.

Calhoun laughed as if the soldier had been telling a tall tale, but the one who'd said it looked as serious as could be.

"Look, just let us do our duty and we'll let you do yours. That's fair isn't it?" Calhoun said.

"Fair?" I raised my voice. "I can show you fair."

One of the other smoke eaters grabbed my arm. It was Naveena, who whispered, "Let's go, Captain."

Her eyes held restrained anger. She hadn't been trying to betray me, but that's exactly how I felt.

Calhoun brushed off the shoulders of the man he'd just been forcibly groping and, very roughly, ruffled his hand through the boy's hair.

"You look a little young for a captain," he said to me. "What did you do to get promoted so fast?"

"Me?" I said, with a smile full of venom. "I've got a great ass and know how to kick ass, too." I bent to the side, overdoing a look at Calhoun's rear end. "You don't seem to have much of one, so you must be great at sucking dick."

"Cap," Afu said, clearing his throat. "We got to head out, yeah?"

"That sounds like a great plan," Calhoun said. "Go protect us all from the scary monsters rising from beneath. Meanwhile, we'll be doing the grunt work, making sure every citizen here supports the greater good."

With a grand draw of his arm, Calhoun let the man and his son go as his soldiers cursed under their breath and hiked it back to their tarantula-looking shitmobiles.

I turned the other way, broke through the line of smoke eaters. They'd been behind me, but they sure as hell didn't have my back. "Thanks for the support, guys."

"That's not our jurisdiction, T," said Renfro. "I can handle flames and dragons, but I can't live through a laser to the head."

They all followed me to Cannon 15, where I opened the captain's door, but didn't get inside.

I huffed and turned back to the others with hands on my hips. It was something Sergeant Puck would have done right before giving us all an important speech.

"The scalies didn't burn away our decency, right? I mean, they can take our houses and ash, the dirt we stand on, but I thought we were at least upholding some basic principles in this dump of a country. The shit that just happened was wrong. And you all know it. This notion that it's good to sacrifice freedom for security, it's been kicked around since before Brannigan's old ass was born, and I'm tired of seeing it thrown at us again and again every time something bad happens. That's not us. And now we've got the cops having us follow people around like some fucking Gestapo agents. What's happened?"

I didn't expect an answer. I was just regurgitating my mind, no, my heart onto the pavement between me and the other smoke eaters. And I was too tired to cry.

"Better us than those assholes back there," said Afu. "Ay, Tamerica?"

"Yeah," I said, beginning to nod. "Let's wrap this phoenix shit up so we can run these army bastards out of town."

Afu pulled me to the side as the others went their separate ways. "This might not be the right time, but…"

"But what?"

He rubbed the back of his neck. "Well… we don't really have anything to do tonight. Kind of in limbo, you know? So, I was thinking, how about that date?"

# CHAPTER 27

"Fish out, fish it out!" Afu moved his arms as if he was the one holding the net, like he could help steer my hands to catch the slippery shrimp at the bottom of the tank.

"Just give me a damn minute!" I said.

I'd worn a red dress, one Afu had bought for me back when we were an item, and some matching pumps I'd borrowed from Mama. It wasn't the most ideal attire for bending over any fish tanks, trying to catch our seafood dinner, but I'd forgotten Afu had mentioned it was that type of restaurant. I was better at catching dragons anyway – in any outfit.

Afu had shown up in a blazer, jeans, and solid gray t-shirt. We'd met outside the restaurant, *McCaffrey's Catch 'n' Fry*, because I thought him picking me up would make it too much of a date.

The squirmy shrimp I'd been hunting ran into a corner where I nabbed him with the net. "Gotcha, you little bastard."

I scooped it out and dropped it into the metal basket the restaurant had provided.

"This might take all night," Afu said, as I handed him the net. "I can't eat just one shrimp."

"Go for a lobster. They're way slower."

"Yeah, but they cost way too damn much."

"Then maybe you should have taken me to McDonald's."

He shrugged and began going for one of the bigger lobsters.

After thirty minutes of failing to grab enough food for dinner, we requested the staff do the catching for us and took our seats near the big window overlooking Parthenon's midtown.

Afu took a sip of water. "How can we catch a phoenix if we can't even catch a crustacean?"

"Maybe we should have brought the others here, made it a training exercise."

He reached out and grabbed my hand on top of the table. "I just wanted this to be the two of us."

Pulling my hand away, I pointed to the black candle on our table. "I like the color choice. Most fancy restaurants like this have white candles. Nice touch."

"I'm worried about Harribow," he said.

And I really wished he hadn't. It was already taking all I had not to feel like shit for having a night out while yet another one of our people lay in a bed surrounded by propellerheads.

"I'm worried about Brannigan," I said. "And everybody else who had the curate. How do we protect them?"

"By killing the phoenix."

"Yeah, but how do we do that? We can't just let everyone burn. We told them the dragon blood would save them. Now, it's just another thing to wipe us all out."

"You think that's really the thing going on?" He stuffed a slice of bread into his mouth and ate the whole thing in one bite. "Is that why we're not going crazy and bursting into flames. How can that bird make the blood do that?"

This really wasn't the conversation I wanted to be having.

"I don't know," I said. "It's like a detonation, I guess. It was only supposed to be for the dragons, but we fucked it all up. I mean, Yolanda has always said we can do what we do because we have a little dragon DNA. I always thought it was bullshit."

"So... non-smokies don't have, like, a biological filter?"

"You're getting too scientific for my pay grade. Either way, we'll get this figured out." I grabbed a slice of bread from the basket and dragged a buttered knife across its surface.

"This phoenix has gotten me thinking, though," he said.

"Hmm?" I kept my eyes on the bread, raking the butter here and there like a Zen garden.

"About new beginnings. Old things being reborn. Like... you and me."

I dropped my knife.

"You know," he said. "How things can burn down but come back to life. It's kind of beautiful."

Setting the bread aside, I cleared my throat. "I know you're trying to be sweet or romantic or whatever, but it's probably not the best analogy to use right now."

"Oh." He looked out the window. "Yeah, I guess you're right."

"I'm tired, Afu. I was so burnt out with catching dragons. I wanted something more exciting. But like they say, be careful what you wish for, because I got more than I can handle."

"But you're doing great. I wouldn't want any other captain."

I nodded. "That's right. I'm your captain. And this…"

Waving my hand over the table, even as the waiter brought over our seafood, I realized had been a mistake.

"I have to go, Afu."

"Go? Our food just got here. I was going to take you to the arcade."

A lump formed in my throat. Tears stung at the corners of my eyes. I felt like shit. I wanted to have a good time with Afu. I wanted to be open to raising our relationship from the dead. But I just couldn't. I suddenly felt the weight of everything, like it had always been there, but I only just figured out that it was suffocating me. Like a frog put in a pot, the heat turning up ever so slowly till the damn thing is boiled.

"I'm sorry," I said, and left him there at the table.

I slammed the door of my parents' house and stomped up the stairs to my bedroom.

"Tammy?" My mama called from the living room. "Are you okay?"

No, I wasn't okay. And I sure as hell didn't want to talk about it.

I flung myself onto the bed and buried my face into a pillow. Blindly, I grabbed the remote to the holostereo and kept hitting buttons, surfing through music: a smooth jazz R&B groove, a dark rock song about selling your soul for love. Other beats, other melodies, searching for the right tune to drown myself in. None of them fit. They all just pissed me off, so I turned the stereo off and screamed into the pillow until the silence of my room won out.

Three knocks came from my door before it opened.

"Tamerica," my mama said. "Can I come in?"

I stayed still. After a few seconds, the weight of Mama's body sank onto the edge of my bed.

"Did your date go bad?"

I turned over, showed Mama my red eyes and wet cheeks.

"Oh, baby," she said. "What's wrong?"

"It's too much, Mama. The world is crumbling and everybody expects me to keep going. To lead them. I'm supposed to be strong. I'm supposed to fight the bad stuff. But I can't."

"Of course you can. You're my girl. You can do anything."

"You're not helping!"

My daddy called from the first floor. "What the hell is going on up there?"

"Everything's fine," Mama called back. "Finish your robot show."

I closed my eyes and let the tears fall wherever they wanted. Mama didn't say anything for a long time. But I could hear her breathing. She began rubbing a hand up and down my arm like she used to when I was a little girl.

"I remember when you were in fourth grade,"

she said. "You were always a big girl, but always so beautiful and happy. But this one day you came home crying. They were having a field day the next week and some mean little boy told you that you'd never win the footrace because of your weight."

"Charlie Gunther," I said. I'd heard the little bastard had grown up to die on E-Day.

"I never remembered his name," Mama said. "But what I do remember is coming to your room, just like now. I wiped your tears and you told me all about it. Do you remember what I said to you?"

I vaguely remembered. Keeping my mouth shut, so I wouldn't wail, I lay there waiting for her to tell me.

"I told you that you were the strongest, most resourceful creation on God's green earth, and that you could do anything that you put your mind to. I told you that giving up would only make that little boy right, and that if you gave it your best, you could have that mean little punk choking on your dust. And do you remember what happened after that?"

"I trained with everything I had, ran every day. When we had the race, I smoked that bastard and everybody else."

"You came home with the trophy," Mama said. "And I told you to never, ever forget what you did. And I guess I'm here tonight to remind you. You were born special. You were called to protect people who can't protect themselves. Nobody said it was going to be easy, baby, but let me tell you something: my daughter, my Tamerica, doesn't give up."

I sat up and hugged my mama. I cried some more, but this time it was because a determination had seized me and I told myself I was never going to give in. Not to the phoenix, the dragons, or anybody else. I soaked my mama's shoulders in tears, but she didn't seem to care.

"Thank you, Mama."

"Sink or swim, baby." She patted my back, the way only mamas can. "Sink or swim."

# CHAPTER 28

The police officer at the front desk shot a blast of cold air into his face from the tiny fan gun in his hand. It wasn't doing much for him; poor guy was basically raining onto his holodesk. Fat drops flew from his forehead and chin, sailing through hovering digital keys and splashing against the screen. The sweat typed out gibberish.

"Damn this summer," the officer said. "Worst one I can remember. Sorry, our air conditioning is being repaired."

I looked to Afu and Renfro at either side of me and shrugged, not feeling whatever heat was punishing the cop and everyone else in the building. "We're smoke eaters."

"Lucky you," he said, wiping away the hologram keyboard like it was vapor in the air. "What can I do for you?"

"We're here to see Detective Rankin," I said.

"Oh, right, right, right." The officer stood and put a half-eaten burrito in his mouth. He gave us a summoning wave and mumbled over his food. "He's out back. Follow me."

The officer led us past tired looking human police at

their desks and a couple of droids that were doing twice the work in half the time, typing up fifty-page reports in less than a minute. One day we were going to have a droid-novelist and no one would be able to stop him.

After a long walk down a short hallway, we came to a large blue door that looked more like a loading gate. The officer pressed his thumb to a pad and the door lifted outward.

Rankin stood there, puffing on a bubble vape, but quickly popped the green orb he'd blown into the air and, like a hot-heeled Houdini, swapped it out with a metal toothpick.

"Oh, you're here," Rankin said.

"Eight o'clock, like you said." I shook his hand.

The desk clerk swallowed some of his chorizo and waved as he walked back inside. "I've got more pounds to shed sitting in this goddamned inferno."

The loading door closed and now it was just the detective and us smoke eaters under an orange street light behind the tall, blue building the cops called home.

"Where's the other captain and her crew?" Rankin asked.

"They're short a guy," Renfro said. "Captain Williams asked them to work on looking into any phoenix sightings while we do this thing for you."

I gave our surroundings one more glance. Felt like Jack the Ripper would pop out from behind a trash can. "So what's with the secret squirrel shit, Rankin? Why are we out here?"

"It's just the few of us who know about this little operation. I don't want the press getting wind of it and I sure as shit don't want to hear about all the legal hoohaw from any desk riders."

I pinched the bridge of my nose, feeling a headache coming on. "Are you saying you conned us into something illegal?"

"No, no." Rankin rolled his metal toothpick from one side of his mouth to the other. "Well, not really."

"Good lord, Ralph," Renfro said.

"Mayor's approved it," Rankin held his hands up in defense.

"That doesn't mean shit to me," I said. "She also approved the army to roll in here and rough up innocent people."

"And I'm trying to prevent more of that," Rankin said. "That's why I came to you first. I'm stretched thin and out of options. And more than likely this isn't going to produce any results, so you have nothing to worry about."

I groaned. "Just tell us what to do."

"Alright," Rankin said. "Pull out your holoreader."

He sent a file from his device to mine. Afu and Renfro squeezed in beside me to get a look. A white man's picture appeared in the air. He was somewhere in his twenties, fresh-faced and probably grew up in a cul-de-sac. He looked like many things, but a cult member wasn't one of them. Then again, neither did any of the other supposed arsonists.

Rankin pointed his toothpick at the man's face. "His name is Terrence Blithe."

"He looks harmless to me," said Afu.

Rankin shrugged. "He just moved here from New York. He's got a record, but only some minor protesting stuff, nothing I'd normally worry about, except he's also some kind of whiz with pyrotechnics. He did all of the fireworks for New York's big events. Plus, he also recently received a dragon blood infusion and likes to attend group meetings for his various interests. I mean, a lot of meetings. Like, he has an addiction to them. Too bad there's no such thing as a Groupaholics Anonymous."

"That doesn't sound like enough to go on," I said. "And *everybody* loves fireworks. How did you find out so much about him?"

Rankin rubbed the back of his neck. "We have our ways."

"Never trust the police," I said under my breath.

"Are you sure you want us doing this, Ralph?" Renfro said. "If this blows up in our face..."

"You're just going to keep an eye on Blithe, okay? Look at it this way, if you're right about there not being a cult, then we can move on and you can tell me you told me so. Oh, and I should tell you not to engage him, unless it's to save somebody's life. Fair enough?"

I huffed. "Alright, where can we find him?"

"So what's the more bullshit job?" Afu asked me as we sat, wearing our power suits, and crammed inside an SUV the police department had provided. "Nabbing dragons alive or this?"

"This," I said, staring down the street at the community center Terrence Blithe had entered forty-five minutes before. "At least with the dragons we didn't have to wait around for them to finish their Art of Wood Carving class."

"I always thought about taking a cooking class," Renfro said.

Afu hummed. "Me and Tamerica went to one about a year ago. It was fun."

I glanced at Renfro out of the corner of my eye, waiting for him to make a face.

The cooking class *had* been fun. Afu and I had made ravioli with alfredo sauce, which confused the instructor, who'd told the class to use marinara. That's just what we were like, especially together – always coloring outside the lines.

I kicked the floorboard. "This is so stupid."

"Class is letting out," Renfro said.

I turned and watched the clusters of people making their way down the community center steps. Most of them were older ladies, so it was easy to spot our prey.

"Okay," I said. "There he is."

"I still think it's going to be pretty obvious he's being followed," Afu said. "This SUV is bright white."

"That's why we have the best driver in the department behind the wheel. You can be covert, right?"

"I guess," Renfro said.

He waited until Blithe had walked around the corner and started the SUV. We eased into a slow speed until we came to a red light. Blithe kept walking in the dark by himself

"He's not getting into a car," I said.

Renfro hummed. "Nice night for a stroll?"

We made the block, and Blithe passed us, now headed in the other direction. We parked across the street in a fire lane outside a twenty-four-hour gym.

"This is going to be a long night," Afu said.

A black hover-van pulled up and three people

wearing ski masks jumped out. Blithe was able to get out a blip of a shout when the masked men put a silencing bag over his head and threw him inside the van.

"What the fuck!" I said.

"Looks like we weren't the only ones looking for Blithe," said Renfro.

"Does this mean he really is in a cult?" Afu asked.

The van sped off.

"No, but this means our job has gotten a shit ton bigger than surveillance. Follow that van, Renfro."

The van was speeding, but not so much that it would draw notice from any patrolling cop cars.

"They're taking the freeway to South Parthenon," Renfro said. "You still want me to follow?"

If we didn't, and these masked people did something to Blithe, we could be charged with something. Negligence? Failure to Act? I'd feel like shit one way or another.

"Yes," I told Renfro. "Get in another lane until you see them taking an exit."

"Maybe these guys are the real cult and they're trying to take Blithe out so he doesn't draw attention to them."

"There's no cult, goddamn it!" But now I wasn't so sure. "Anyway, we won't know shit until these creeps get to wherever they're going."

"You going to call the cops in on this?" Renfro asked.

I knew I should.

"Not yet," I said.

"I don't know if that's a good idea. This isn't what we signed up for."

"Renfro, I'll let you know when to call Rankin.

Let's just see where this goes."

The van exited the freeway and Renfro slowed to follow behind. I had him stop at the corner while the van zoomed farther down the street, turning onto a path leading to the abandoned lumber warehouse.

"I don't like this," Afu said. "Creepy van. People in masks. Now a run-down warehouse. This is some horror movie shit."

"Says a guy who fights monsters for a living." I tried to smile, but this was giving me a weird feeling too.

"Dragons are easy," Afu said. "People are the scary ones."

"Renfro, stay here. Give it ten minutes and then call the cops. Me and Afu are going to go get a better look."

"Aww man!" Afu leaned his head back in defeat.

"I can do that, Cap," Renfro said. "But are you sure you don't want to wait until the cops get here first?"

"If this is the cult the cops keep droning on and on about, I want to see it for myself. And you and I both know how slow PD response is. If Blithe is in danger, I want to stop it."

Renfro nodded. "All right then. As long as you aren't just trying to be a hero."

I left my seat and waited in front of the SUV as Afu took his sweet ass time.

"This is kind of exciting, isn't it?" I said.

"Sometimes I just don't understand you," said Afu.

"Come on, you big wuss."

Afu sighed and followed me toward the warehouse. We had to follow the chain link fence surrounding the property for about a hundred feet before we came to the path leading in. The hover van had been left just outside a wooden door that looked like it had been repeatedly assaulted by termites and spray paint.

Keeping low, we moved across the lot and stopped at the van. They'd locked it and no one was inside from what I could see. That left the warehouse itself.

"Do we have to go in there?" Afu whispered.

I drew my fingers across my throat and put them to my lips. Smoke eaters didn't have any official hand signals, but I'm sure he understood that I was telling him to shut the fuck up.

Outside the warehouse's front door, a sign had been posted in red and white:

WARNING! This property is protected by armed droids.

Afu jabbed a worried finger at the sign, but I shooed it away. The sign had probably been put up when the warehouse was still open. Nothing to worry about.

Removing my helmet, I put my ear to the door. Afu raised his brow, asking if I heard anything. I shook my head. No voices, no screaming Terrence Blithe, not even footsteps or a cough. I opened the door slowly to keep its creaking swing to a minimum.

Pitch dark lay before us but I wasn't about to turn on a flashlight and kill the stealth we'd been fortunate enough to have. Afu's heavy footsteps would end that eventually.

I stepped into the warehouse and Afu shoved his way in to stay at my side.

That's when the floor fell beneath us and we dropped like bowling balls. And it didn't matter how silent I'd been before, because as I fell through the bottomless dark, I screamed and screamed and screamed.

# CHAPTER 29

Darkness has a way of distorting time. Falling, too.
So when you combine them, it can feel like a million
eons while you drop to your death.

But my ass landed on some kind of metal slide and
I was zooming around curves before I fully realized
what was going on. Afu's giant feet kicked me in the
head, and he was moaning as loud as I was screaming.
By the time we'd reached the bottom of the slide,
I'd composed myself enough to stop screaming and
roll out of Afu's way as he barreled off the track. A
light was coming from somewhere, because I could
actually see the floor in front of me. An electric
chirping made me and Afu look up.

Two droids stood over us.

"Trespassing," they said, pointing their arms at our
heads. Laser guns sat on their robotic forearms, the
barrels throbbing with green light, aching to be shot.

"I knew we should have listened to that sign," Afu
said.

I held my hands up so the droids could clearly
see them with their digital blue eyes. "We're smoke
eaters. Just doing a precautionary sweep. We heard
there might have been a dragon nearby."

The droids didn't move, didn't speak. All I needed was an opening and then I could blast them with my laser arm while Afu used his sword. But we were still on our asses and the droid's had their weapons inches from our faces.

"Oh, there are plenty of dragons down here," a human voice said from behind the robots.

A masked man walked toward us, carrying a laser lantern on the end of a stick. Three other people in black masks appeared behind him. They were carrying pistols instead of torches.

"Thing is," the man who'd spoken said, "there's even more *rats* down here. On your feet, smokies. And out of those metal suits."

"What?" I didn't know who the fuck this guy was, but I'd be damned if I'd be bossed around by some prick with a sock on his head.

"I said get up and get out of those tuna cans!"

Afu stood up before I did, but he was flexing his fists and looking to rip the man's head off. Both the masked people and the droids aimed their weapons at him.

"Don't make us force you," the leader said. I got to my feet and popped open my power suit.

Afu shook his head. "Tamerica…"

I put a hand on his shoulder. "Do what they say."

With a groan, Afu unlocked his suit and stepped out. Two of the masked goons ran behind us and knocked the suits over.

"Take their helmets, too," the masked leader said. "We don't want them calling for help."

Our helmets were ripped off. One of the creeps put mine on their head and tapped it with their pistol.

The leader laughed. "You picked the wrong party to crash, Big Man and Little Girl. But maybe we can have some fun with this."

"What the fuck is going on here?" I asked. "The cops know where we are. They had us tail the guy you kidnapped. Don't do anything stupid."

The others looked to their leader, lowering their pistols an inch.

That's right, be worried, you dumb dickweeds.

"Lady," the leader said, "who do you think told us about ol' Terry Blithe in the first place?"

Never trust the police. Goddamn it, I knew this whole thing stunk, but I was just so eager to do the right thing.

"So I'm guessing you're not the arsonist cult," I said.

"We're the ones who are going to make sure they don't burn anything ever again. You and your souped-up dragon Slayers haven't been able to do jack shit about it yet. And the army, hell, those guys are crazy!"

In the dim light of the laser torch, I stared at the leader's eyes poking out from the two, ragged holes in his mask, trying to figure out who he was.

"Who are you people?" I asked.

"Enough of this back and forth," he said. "Move them to the pit."

Afu looked at me, no longer pissed, but worried. I was right there with him. Nothing called "The Pit" could ever be a good thing.

They marched us down a dark path where rivulets of sawdust trickled onto my shoulder. There was brighter light and noise at the end of the path. We were somewhere deep under the warehouse, but these clowns had rigged it up to their twisted specifications, a fun house of horrors. A trapdoor and a slide? Who the fuck thinks of that?

When we got to the larger area at the end of the path, I stopped so I wouldn't fall off into "The Pit." The room looked like an underground circus, full of other masked people stomping their feet on shoddy stands. A portable electric generator rumbled off to the side, powering yellow-tinted work lights that had been strung up to illuminate what lay in the center of the room.

"The Pit" was a small circle that could have been a miniature version of FreeEnergy Stadium. Terrence Blithe stood below us, up against the wall, gripping it with both hands and moving his terrified face from one fist-shaking creep above him to the other. The masked audience was shouting, almost chanting, but none of them said the same thing. Some shouted, "Our city!" while others hollered at the top of their voices, "Burn 'em out! Burn 'em all out!"

This whole damn scene was too crazy for my mind to comprehend. No doubt, I was scared shitless, but my fear had a conjoined twin in the form of unadulterated rage.

The people at our backs shoved me and Afu into the pit.

We landed on cold dirt. I was able to roll, smoothing the fall. Afu landed flat on his front.

He coughed and brushed dirt from his face. "What the hell, man!?"

I grabbed his arm and helped him up.

Terrence Blithe scooted against the edge of the arena to get closer to us. "What's going on? Please help me!"

"Just relax," I said. "We'll get out of this."

What I really wanted to tell him was that we were in as much shit as he was. But public service workers don't have that kind of luxury. We had to be the ones who remain calm. It can get really fucking annoying.

"Why are they doing this?" Blithe asked.

"You're not in a phoenix cult are you?" Afu asked.

"What?" Blithe said. "No! Wait, you mean they think I'm one of those arsonist people?"

"If it makes you feel better," I said, "they probably just don't like you because you're an immigrant."

"But I'm an American!"

"A New Yorker. An immigrant to Parthenon City." I looked at Afu. "You know who these assholes are, right?"

Afu glanced at the churning bodies above us, who might have been foaming at the mouth if their masks weren't concealing their faces. "It's those PC First jokers."

I should have recognized that voice behind the mask; the way he'd said "rats."

"Brothers and sisters," Duncan Sharp's voice boomed over the rabble.

He stood above us on some kind of rinky-dink podium, and I noticed that, below him, and directly in front of us, was some kind of doorway in the arena's wall.

"Brothers and sisters," the leader said again until they'd all quieted down. "I thought we were going to have a nice time, gathering together and ridding this city of one more leech. But fate had other plans. If you'll look into the pit below you, you'll notice that we have two new visitors."

The masked crowd booed.

"They came into our house," the leader said, "wearing their fancy armored suits, wielding their high-tech weapons. I take that as a threat, don't you?"

Pissed-off cheers responded.

"They say they're smoke eaters, the same people who are supposed to protect us, not intimidate us. But they want to protect the people coming to *our city*, taking our food and healthcare. Clogging our streets with their filth. Look at them down there in the pit. They don't look like smoke eaters to me. Do you know what they look like?" Sharp paused for effect. "They look like rats!"

The crowd began chanting, "Rats, rats, rats," over and over.

Sharp raised his arms. "Let's show them what we do to rats around here."

The door I'd spotted in the pit's wall opened in front of us. Afu grabbed my arm as Blithe put himself behind us, using our bodies like a shield for whatever was coming out of the door.

I focused on getting my breath under control while I searched the dark in front of me. Glowing green eyes appeared, blinking and staring back at me. Black smoke began to flow from the door, followed by a low, rumbling growl.

Several of the masked assholes in the stands above us began to cough. They pulled out pocket respirators and secured them to their noses and mouths, having to lift the bottom of their masks to do so.

"Blithe, cover your mouth with your shirt," I shouted over my shoulder.

It wasn't ideal, but this was dragon smoke, and a

thin bit of fabric was better than nothing. Whether Blithe covered his face or not, I didn't know, I couldn't keep my eyes off the door.

A large, clawed foot shot out of the dark and landed with a heavy thud. It was emerald green, the scales glistening under the arena's work lights. Next came a green snout and a head covered in white horns. The dragon snorted and jets of black smoke shot from its nostrils, filling the pit.

Above us, several of the PCF people leaned over the edge of the arena with stun poles. The ends sparked with electricity, causing the scaly to growl and jerk its head away before cowering lower. It had firsthand experience with those poles. How many people had been where we stood, facing the same scaly?

In an instant, the dragon shot out of the door. Blithe screamed through his shirt behind us, but Afu and I stood our ground. The scaly must have wanted a chase, because it stopped short and hunched down, trying to get a read on us.

It was a wyvern, meaning it only had two legs. Its wings had been cut off, leaving only charred stumps where it had most likely cauterized the wounds itself. I slew dragons for a living and even I thought that shit was cruel.

"Blithe," I said. "Stay back and let us handle this."

"You don't even have any armor!" he said.

"He's right," Afu said. "We're practically naked."

"Yeah, well, if this thing is going to eat us, I don't want to make it easy."

The wyvern roared and dug its claws into the dirt. It charged. It snapped its jaws toward me, leaving its neck open for Afu to grab hold of. Heaving Afu a few inches off the ground, the wyvern tried to lift its neck and pull away. I began wailing on its head, dodging its teeth with every punch. Smoke blasted from its throat and into my face, but I inhaled it as easily as spring air and blew it back at the dragon.

Afu grunted under the strain. "This approach isn't going to last long."

"I don't what else to do without our…"

The wyvern's slimy, green tail squirmed between Afu's legs.

"Watch out!" I screamed.

The dragon's tail snapped like a whip, slamming into Afu's nether regions and sending him sailing into the far wall of the arena. I dove out of the way as the scaly did a death roll in the dirt, blasting fire from its mouth indiscriminately.

"My nuts," Afu said in a puny, high-pitched voice.

I sat him up and grabbed each side of his face. "Are you okay?"

"I'll live."

The PC First assholes were chanting, "Burn the rats!"

I looked up and glared at Duncan Sharp. His head bobbed up and down as if he was laughing under his dingy mask and respirator.

I'd give him something to laugh about.

"How strong are you really, Afu?" I asked.

"Huh?" He scrunched his face, annoyed that I wasn't more concerned about his balls.

I made like I was kissing his cheek and whispered my plan into his ear.

When I pulled away, Afu shrugged. "I'll give it try."

Behind us, Blithe was cowering where we'd left him, and the wyvern had just taken notice. It was gearing up for another charge, so I fought against my exhaustion and ran.

Jagged teeth came inches from Blithe's head before I slammed into the wyvern. I hadn't hit it hard enough to knock it over, but it was enough to save Blithe a decapitation. I raised my arm to follow up with a punch, but the dragon twisted its neck around and bit at my hand. I flinched and nearly fell over. I turned and ran toward Afu who'd ripped off one side of the arena door, holding it like a shield.

"Now!" I shouted.

Afu dropped into a squat and placed the metal sheet on top of him, creating a make-shift ramp. The PC First mob shouted chants of murder as I hopscotched over flames that flew at my heels and ran onto the metal door. The wyvern followed. With a jump, I landed as hard as I could onto the edge of the ramp. Afu helped to heave from the bottom, and like a catapult, we launched the wyvern, still blasting flames, into the stands.

Duncan Sharp's mask caught fire. He screamed as he beat his palms against his burning face, fumbling through the crowd to get away from the dragon. The other assholes weren't as lucky as their boss. The wyvern flattened two of them as it rolled over to get to its feet, then snagged another guy in its mouth. The one being eaten kicked their legs violently as if it would do any good. Once the dragon bit down, it put a stop to those dancing feet. A few chews later and there was no more of the masked person, legs or anything else.

The wyvern spun around to look for more snacks, and when it did, its massive tail crashed into a handful of people trying to make a run for it. A few slammed into a wall or the stands at the other side of the arena. One of them fell to the dirt in front of me, but their back was smoking and they didn't get back up.

"Thank you!" Blithe grabbed my arm with two hands.

"Don't thank us just yet," I said. "We still have to figure out how to get out of this death trap."

"Might as well go through that door." Afu pointed toward the blob of darkness the wyvern had come from.

But we hadn't taken half a step when two droids marched through the door with their guns raised, laser sights forcing me to cover my eyes. They weren't going to hesitate this time. I spread my arms, as if to shield Afu and Blithe. And that's when the firing started.

One of the droids' heads exploded in a shower of metal and electric sparks. The other took an assault to the middle of its torso.

It was able to let out a final word: "Rats!"

Damn. The PC First bastards had even corrupted the droids with their xenophobic bullshit.

I ducked and darted my head around to see where the shots had come from. Cops flooded into the room, chasing masked people through the stands, and backing away when they saw the wyvern crushing wooden seats and running amok.

Renfro and Detective Rankin charged into the pit.

"Good thing I called the cops about five minutes sooner than you told me to," Renfro said.

"Assholes took our power suits." I pointed to the

dragon in the stands. "You think you can handle that wyvern by yourself."

"On it." Renfro gave me a two-fingered salute and power jumped toward the scaly.

Rankin sucked on his metal toothpick so nervously, I thought he might stain his teeth gray. "I swear I had no idea this was going to happen."

"Their leader, Duncan Sharp, said something about how the cops gave them a heads up on Blithe," I said.

Blithe wobbled over, arms wrapped around his chest. "Serve and protect, my ass!"

I put a hand on Blithe's shoulder. "Settle down, sweetheart. Anyway, Rankin, that's some terribly deceitful shit if you ask me. Are you in with these PC First people?"

"What!?" Rankin spit out his toothpick. "Hell no! I rushed over here with the few on-duties I could grab. I thought it was the cult. You saying these are those crazy people with the shitty haircuts?"

I squinted, looking into his eyes, seeing if I could spot a liar inside. But I was pretty sure after a few seconds that Rankin was on the up and up.

"If you're done trying your wannabe psychic shit on me," Rankin said. "Let's get your power suits back to you and see if we can find this Duncan Sharp."

"If he survived," I said, following Rankin, "he'll have one hell of a burn on his face."

Behind us, a heavy thud hit the arena floor. The wyvern had been knocked out.

Renfro hopped down from the stands, dusting off his hands to show a job well done. "You two couldn't handle one measly wyvern?"

# CHAPTER 30

Outside the warehouse, the cops had rounded up a fair amount of the PC First creeps and sat them in a row in the gravel. They went up and down the line one by one, removing their masks.

I didn't recognize any of them, just their look – the same sleazeball Nazi hair and faces filled with unwarranted disenfranchisement.

"Any of these punks our guy?" Rankin asked me as we looked over each one.

I shook my head.

"Where's Duncan Sharp?" Rankin asked the line of perps.

They stared smugly at the detective, staying silent.

"We're going to find him soon enough anyway," Rankin threatened. "And all of you can rot in a holding cell for all I care. Then, you'll likely be charged with attempted murder. Still don't feel like cooperating?"

The guy at the end of the line looked to his compatriots for a second, wondering if any of them would fold, but when he saw they remained statuesque and uncooperative, he went back to doing the same.

Rankin sighed and turned back to me. "He'll turn up eventually. Between you and me, I don't know if we'll have enough to charge him when we finally nab the sonofabitch. And if he gets some dragon blood, that burn on his face you told me about will be healed and nonexistent. Did any of these shitheads actually say they were with PC First?"

I stopped to think about it, a swell of anger rising from my gut as I realized the answer. "No," I said. "But he called us rats. That's how I knew for sure."

Rankin took out his bubble vape and let a glowing ball escape from his mouth. "That's not promising. But I'll try."

Yolanda was calling. I turned away from Rankin and picked up my holoreader.

"I've figured it out," she said.

"The wraith?"

"Come get a gander." She hung up with a satisfied smirk on her face. I took it for some good news. Finally.

Rankin asked to come along, saying he had some more questions for me and Afu about what went on down in that warehouse. I think he just wanted to take a look at a wraith up close and personal and see if our propellerheads had come up with a way to make his job easier. Maybe he'd finally given up on his cult theory.

Back at Central Fire Station, we walked in and paid our respects to Harribow lying in the cot. He hadn't improved, but he also hadn't gotten worse, so that was hopeful. Naveena and Calvinson followed behind us.

Yolanda stood next to a containment cylinder big

enough to hold Afu and then some. A dark sheet covered it. Yolanda held her hands out like she was an illusionist's assistant.

"Any word from Brannigan?" I asked Naveena.

She shook her head. "He won't answer my calls."

"Yeah," I said. "Me neither."

"I'd stop by his house, but I know that would just piss him off."

"This dragon blood thing has got him spooked," I said.

"I don't blame him. You think the mayor will put a stop to the infusions?"

"I don't know," I said. "But if I know the people of Parthenon City, once the word gets out, there's going to be a bunch of scared people. And people do stupid things when they're scared."

Yolanda huffed. "I'm not going to stand here holding my arms up like this forever."

"Then pull the goddamn sheet off!" I said.

With dramatic flavor, Yolanda grabbed the edge of the sheet and ripped it away.

Wilkins' wraith clawed at the cylinder's glass, floating around at high speed, looking for an opening to get through. The ghost shrieked and gnashed its teeth. It was also no longer the eerie white that wraiths were known for. This wraith had turned a very deep sunset color.

"It's..." I tilted my head as I stared at it. "It's orange."

"Precisely," Yolanda said.

Afu laughed and pointed. "It looks like a Halloween decoration."

"I reversed the polarity," said Yolanda. "Watch."

She went over to a locked case and brought back a jar with the phoenix ashes inside. The embers roared to life, the flames reaching, stretching toward the wraith inside the cylinder.

"Hot damn!" Renfro said.

"So now you can draw this bird out of hiding?" Detective Rankin said, fiddling with the metal toothpicks in his hand.

"I believe so," Yolanda said. "The wraith should attract the phoenix, but I have to warn all of you: dragons will still be drawn by the bird if not the ghost. I suggest wrapping things up before you're swarmed with scalies."

"You sure this is going to work?" I asked.

"There's only one way to find out. Right?"

The doors burst open behind us. We all turned with a jolt to see a middle-aged woman wearing jeans and a tank top, standing there beside the lawyer representing the dead Sandusky volunteer's families. It was Mrs Wilkins. Two cops stood behind them, looking visibly uncomfortable.

"We'll be taking that wraith into our possession," the lawyer said.

I made myself as wide as I could, hands on my hips. "Like hell you will."

The lawyer held up his holoreader and displayed a shit ton of digital pages in the air. "We have a warrant, signed by the honorable Judge Linda Mayhue." The lawyer turned to his client. "Is that Mr Wilkins' wraith inside that container?"

"He looks like a rotten tangerine," the woman said, choking up, "but that's my Johnny."

Yolanda raised her hand as if she was going to ask for a hall pass. "I understand this is a sensitive issue, but we're needing this wraith to apprehend the phoenix that's been terrorizing Ohio. It's a matter of state security that—"

"Save it," Jim the lawyer said, raising his own hand, but more like a crossing guard halting any further discussion. "You," he pointed to Detective Rankin. "You're police. Tell these people that we are well within our legal rights to take possession of the deceased."

We all looked to the detective.

He swallowed. "Um, I mean. It's not really a body or anything, but... if they have a warrant, you guys have to hand him over."

"This is bullshit," I said, but I'd known this day would come eventually, I'd just been hoping the phoenix would have been dealt with already.

"I think we should have the city's lawyer present," Renfro said.

"No," the lawyer shook his head. "We already had our back and forth with the city. Place Mr Wilkins' wraith in a device for transport and hand him over. We have police here with us as you can see, just in case you decide not to be cooperative."

"You guys are crazy," said Afu.

I patted him on the chest. "It's okay, everybody. Yolanda, do what he says."

The propellerhead twisted her lips and huffed sadly through her nose. She took one last look at the orange-glowing wraith that was spinning around the cylinder like a fiery tornado. Yolanda plugged a wraith remote into the box at the bottom of the containment cylinder and pressed a button. Like vapor being sucked up by a vacuum, the wraith zipped into the remote with a final *schloop*. The make-shift propellerhead lab got a lot quieter.

Yolanda handed the remote to me, and I quickly gave it to the lawyer before any bad ideas could crawl into my mind.

"Thank you," he said, and with great care, placed the remote into his client's hands.

The woman turned to us and held the remote like a club. "Johnny wanted to be just like you. I can't understand why. All of you are terrible people. You got him killed and kept him from me. You can't just use people to get what you want. I don't care if they're alive or not."

Tears began streaming down her face.

The lawyer put his hands on her shoulders. "Come on, now. It's over. Let's go."

And they did. Harribow, laying in the cot, squirmed and moaned all zombie like when they passed, causing the woman to flinch and nearly drop the wraith remote to the floor. Harribow calmed down after they'd gone, but it got me worried that we weren't going to find a way to fix him in time. The rest of us standing in the lab said nothing for a few minutes.

Until Calvinson spoke up, "So, I guess we need to go to one of the enclosures?" He fiddled his hands inside his pockets. "You know, to get another wraith."

"Calvinson!" Naveena shouted.

The rookie stiffened, widened his eyes. "What?"

"You're a fucking genius."

He smiled, showing tiny teeth and making his

freckles scrunch together.

"It'll take me some time to repeat the process," Yolanda said. "But I don't see any other option at this point. The firefighters here yelled at me the last time I reversed the polarity. It killed the Feed while they were watching some droid foozeball game."

"Fuck them," Naveena said. "They were probably the ones who called that lawyer."

"Right," I said. "We all go together. I'm not going to have another situation where we're caught without backup. Let's meet up back here in three hours."

I turned to leave.

"Where are you going?" Naveena asked.

"Getting some sleep." I sighed and looked over my shoulder. "Then I'm going to go check on Brannigan."

# CHAPTER 31

The next morning, Brannigan's truck was parked in the driveway outside his house. He turned the garage into his personal art studio – he'd shown me some of his paintings the year before, and I thought it was a good thing he was great at being a smoke eater, because he was shit at painting.

Sherry wasn't home. A sigh of relief left my lips as I walked to the front door. This would have been harder if Mrs Brannigan was here. She'd hoard her husband away and never let him leave the house. She hadn't wanted him to be a smoke eater in the first place, although she got over it eventually. But now that there was an added threat of him turning into a flame puppet for the phoenix, there was no way she would let him back as chief. Which made me wonder if he'd even told her what was going on.

I knocked on the door three times but no one answered. I called Brannigan on my holoreader but had the same result.

"I know you're in there, you old motherfucker!" I shouted. I looked around at the neighboring houses, hoping I hadn't been so loud to cause someone to call the cops on the crazy black woman trying to break down the Brannigans' door. "So, let me in and let's talk. Or are you too chickenshit?"

After that, I heard heavy footsteps coming closer until the front door swung open. Brannigan was already walking away into his living room.

I stood on the front step and watched him take a seat on the big pleather couch in front of a Feed screen. Softly, I closed the door behind me and then joined him on the couch. The Feed was showing a commercial for dragon shelters. This company would come to your house, dig a hole in the backyard, and put a titanium box inside for your family to crawl into in the event of a dragon emergency.

It didn't make much sense to me, seeing how dragons came from beneath the ground, and it would only make it that much easier for a dragon to munch on a husband, wife, and their two-point-five kids, but people were dumb enough to buy that kind of shit, so hooray for capitalism, I guess.

"Where's Sherry?" I asked.

"She took Bethany and Kenji to her mother's house in Wisconsin. I had some propellerheads fly them out in Jet 1."

"And she didn't wonder why you were sending them away?"

He shrugged as the Feed went back to the daily news program.

I turned to face him. "Chief, you're a born smoke eater. We're thinking there's no reason to be afraid of–"

"I had dragon blood pumping into my veins for two weeks while I was in that fucking robo-box. Anyway, it's not about me. Sherry received an infusion, too, and I have Bethany to think of."

"But you're still here," I said. "You didn't go to Wisconsin. So this can't be you quitting."

He laughed under his breath. "Funny you should be the one talking to me about quitting. Wasn't long ago you said you were thinking of getting out."

"Yeah." I nodded. "But I realized that there's shit in this world that will never work itself out alone. And there's only a few of us who can make things better. We need you, old man."

His next words were soft, the voice of defeat. "No, you don't."

"Yes, goddamn it, we do!" I jumped off the couch and leaned over him.

"I'll end up like Harribow and Patrice. I'll burn and take others with me. It's better I stay here. Alone."

I took a step back to get a better look at him. "Do I need to put you on suicide watch?"

He scoffed. "I like myself too much to off it. I figure if the phoenix flies over and turns this dragon blood running through my veins into zombie juice, at least it would just be me and the house getting torched. I was working on chaining myself to the bed when you showed up."

"You're not a fucking werewolf, Chief."

He shrugged. "Same principle, right?"

I shook my head. "You know, part of me thinks that this phoenix is actually a good thing. Or would have been if we didn't go fucking around with that blood. I know we couldn't have predicted any of this, but... the thing eats dragons. It could have ended the whole problem for us. And because we were so hungry to take humans to the next level, all these people are feeling the wrath that was supposed to be for the scalies. It's a shit show."

"That's humanity for you," Brannigan said. "We try so hard to fix one problem, we end up creating one even worse. Listen, I need you to do me a favor. Can you promise me you'll do it?"

"Depends on what it is."

"Damn it, Williams. Promise me."

I swore, rubbed my hands across my face and paced around Brannigan's living room before walking back over to him. "Fine. What is it?"

"I want you to put Naveena up for smoke eater chief. No one should argue with it. She was going to be next in line anyway."

I could have strangled the old, stubborn bastard.

"You are going to be fine. You hear me?"

"Either way," he said. "You promised. Don't fuck with your promise. Not one you make to me. I'll come back and haunt your ass. And not like a wraith. I'll sing old country western songs while you try to sleep every night. It'll be hell. Now, say it back to me. What are you going to do when you get back?"

I rolled my eyes. "I ain't playing with you."

"What are you going to do, Tamerica?" he said, more sternly.

"I'll put Naveena up for chief."

"Okay," he nodded and relaxed into the couch.

I was glad, at least, that I had provided some kind of comfort to him. It was like he was already dead, and I had the singular curse of hearing his last wishes from beyond the grave.

What a disappointment. I'd looked up to this man. Thought he was the most badass smoke eater to ever live. He was like a second father to me and to everybody else on the job for that matter. And now he was giving up without a fight.

On the Feed, Duncan Sharp, leader of PC First, appeared on the floating screen. I forgot what I was about to say to Brannigan and listened in to the broadcast.

A voice over said, "The activist group, known as PC First, will host a benefit tonight in support of volunteer smoke eater families who recently lost loved ones to dragons. Duncan Sharp spoke with us this morning at the Parthenon Convention Center where the gala will be held."

Mrs Wilkins stood beside Duncan Sharp as he spoke to a group of news drones and curious citizens. Something big and covered by a tarp stood behind Sharp as he snarled out his diatribe.

"Mayor Ghafoor has recently suggested putting a stop to dragon blood supplies because the rats invading our city have put fear into her and those too weak to see that the problem isn't our medicine, but those who would seek to take everything we've worked hard to achieve. So, tonight at the first of many fundraisers, we are going to be providing infusions to any natural citizen of Parthenon City for a low cost that will benefit the families who lost brave heroes trying to protect us. And what's more, we'll show you what the so-called professional smoke eaters have done to this poor woman's late husband."

"No way," I said, but I couldn't take my eyes off the screen.

Sharp turned to the tarp behind him and ripped it away. There, in a glass container only slightly different from the one Yolanda had been using, floated Wilkins' wraith, radiating orange light and acting a fool for all the Feed cameras.

"This is your chance to see a wraith up close and personal," Sharp said with a grin.

Mrs Wilkins frowned at that, but she was too deep in this mess to argue with the carnival side show Duncan Sharp had turned her husband into.

"These dumbasses are going to bring the phoenix right on top of them," I said, wanting to throw something against the wall. "And everyone there with an infusion is going to catch fire and blow the place up. It's going to be chaos!"

Brannigan sniffed. "Then it looks like you have some work to do."

Yeah, just put it all on me.

"I've got to go," I said, and hurried toward the door.

"I'm proud of you!" he called from the living room.

I stood there at the front door, one leg outside, trying to think of how to reply. I'd never thanked Brannigan for everything he'd done for me, from rookie school till now. I wished I could have said I was proud of him, too. But I wasn't. I *used* to be. Now, there was nothing left to discuss. Sometimes you just have to let people bury themselves, because trying to dig them out will only put you six feet under as well. I had no intention of throwing in the towel, not while the phoenix was still flying over Parthenon City. Words meant jack shit to me. Actions were what proved things, changed things. I should have told Brannigan where he could stick his pride.

But I closed the door and didn't look back.

"What do you mean, stay indoors?" my daddy said from my holoreader. "We never go anywhere. That barbecue at your boss man's house was the last time we left the house. I might as well call your mama The Warden."

I was a mile out from Central Fire Station. The night was looking like a potential shit storm and I wanted to give my parents a call, just in case it was the last time I'd get to talk to them.

"I'm just saying that some crazy people are going to make things a lot worse and I don't want you or Mama going out."

"And you expect me to sit here calmly while you're out there?"

It was a fair question, but that's exactly what I expected him to do.

"You're either bursting into the house crying or out there gallivanting with monsters and Satanists. Tammy, you just need to come home."

"There's no cult, Daddy."

"I know what I know."

Naveena and the other ash kickers stood outside the fire station. I had to get off the holoreader, so I swallowed down a few tears and told my daddy, "I love you."

"Tamerica?" He must have heard the tremble in my voice, but I didn't give him a chance to go on.

I hung up.

"Let's giddyup," I shouted as I jogged toward Cannon 15.

"Where we headed?" Naveena asked.

"Eastern enclosure." I didn't forget the promise I'd made to Brannigan. Far from it. Seeing Naveena should have urged me to tell her everything. Instead, I decided Brannigan had asked me to deliver an emotional bomb, and I needed my crew's focus intact. I locked into my power suit and kept my secret.

The gauge on my right forearm showed the suit's power charged and ready to go. I grabbed a laser axe and flicked it on, taking a few practice swings and listening to the satisfying sound of the blade going *phoom, phoom* through the air.

"We'll snag a wraith and bring it back here to Yolanda. Then we need to haul ass to the convention center downtown."

"What the hell's going on over there?" Afu asked.

"I'll tell you on the way to the enclosure."

Yolanda walked out of the fire station. "You're going to need the wraith once I've finished with it."

"I'm with you there," I said. "But that dumb woman is showing off her dead husband so a bunch of neo-Nazis can inject more people with dragon blood. I'm pretty fucking sure we'll be able to find the phoenix without a problem."

"The wraith isn't just to attract the bird," Yolanda said. "You're going to need the reversed polarity to destroy it."

I dropped my axe and it sizzled against the asphalt. "And when were you going to let us know that important little detail?"

"That lawyer interrupted me. Plus, I had to look over my data a bit more. You're going to have to release it from the remote at a close range to the phoenix. But… that might be a little dangerous."

Afu snorted. "Is anything about this job not dangerous."

"This part is especially so," Yolanda said. "Because the phoenix may explode."

"And probably come back again like the resurrecting bastard it is." Naveena shook her head.

"Not likely," said Yolanda. "This explosion may be a teensy bit on the… nuclear level."

You could have heard a dragon scale drop out there on the fire station's front pad. Renfro's jaw fell open.

"The fuck?" I said.

"It's a very slight possibility," Yolanda said. "Maybe a little more than slight. Slight and a half."

"Will it kill the phoenix?" Naveena asked. She licked her lips, a nervous twitch Brannigan had always thought was a form of flirting. "And I mean for good?"

"Most definitely," Yolanda said. "But it might vaporize you as well, if you're too close. Nuclear or not."

I grabbed my helmet and sat on the truck's side bumper. "There's got to be another way. I'm not going to blow up the city just to kill that goddamn bird. The mayor would fire us all and put the army in our place if I even offered her the idea."

"Don't have to tell her anything." Naveena looked at me from the side of her eyes. "Do ya?"

"I don't see another option," Yolanda said. "I've

been using this reversed polarity idea on Harribow and it seems to have stalled any further degradation."

Renfro's eyes got as big as dinner plates. "*He's* not going to turn into a nuke is he?"

Yolanda shrugged. "I don't think so."

I groaned and put the laser axe back into the truck, slamming the bin door shut. "We've wasted too much time talking about this. Let's roll."

Calvinson got into the driver's seat of Slayer 5 while Naveena got into the seat beside him. We were down too many smoke eaters for them to find a temporary replacement for Harribow, and it wouldn't feel right if we did. It was a silent reminder of what we were working so hard and fast for. I got into my seat and swallowed against a rise of bile in my throat. Afu buckled in. Renfro started the truck.

I could feel it in my gut and in my bones, even before we left the fire station: this was going to be a long night.

We weren't far from the enclosure when Renfro said, "Um, Captain."

I looked up from my holoreader. I'd been staring at the blank screen, hoping Brannigan would message me, saying he was on his way to take the lead.

"What is it?" I asked.

He didn't say anything; he pointed toward the night sky just ahead of us, just above where the enclosure would be. I sat forward and bent my neck to see what he was trying to show me.

A fiery streak flew across the purple and pink sunset. It had wings, and if I held my head out of the window, I would probably hear the phoenix's tea kettle screech sounding out over the ashen wasteland.

"Pedal to the metal," I said.

"Um…" Afu said.

"What now?" I turned in my seat to look at him. He'd crawled to the other side of the truck and pointed out the window.

"We're not the only ones heading for the enclosure, Cap."

I squinted as I looked outside. On a parallel road a quarter mile away, the last bit of sunlight struck against long metal barrels and rugged treads. Army tanks and spider vehicles were kicking up ash as they raced toward our same destination.

Our truck's holoreader buzzed with a flashing red screen. The words floating in the air turned my skin ice cold: NORTH, WEST, AND SOUTH ENCLOSURES HAVE BEEN BREACHED. DRAGONS ESCAPED.

# CHAPTER 32

*Kaboom!*

The tank at the front of the army's cavalcade fired at the phoenix. The bird spun in a fiery spiral and dodged the cannon shell. It turned away from the enclosure and shrieked as it sliced through the air. The army vehicles were now on the menu.

"All right," I said. "If those idiots want to fight the phoenix, let them. It'll give us time to grab a wraith and get the hell out of here."

Renfro slid Cannon 15 to a stop outside the city's last remaining enclosure. As soon as I got out of the truck, people flooded out of the enclosure's front door, running to their cars and speeding away as fast as they could. I tried to flag down a few of them, but they only bathed me in their headlights before veering out of my path, ash flinging from their fleeing hover-thrusters.

I spotted Ted Sevier fumbling for his keys outside a burgundy coupe.

"Where are you going?" I grabbed him by the arm.

He looked like a cornered animal, eyes red, face covered in sweat, trembling inside his navy blue blazer. "We've lost control. The other enclosures have fallen. You've got to do something. I'm getting the hell out of here."

I didn't understand the gibberish coming out of his mouth. "What do you mean you lost control?"

The walls of the enclosure shook as something very large and very heavy slammed against the other side of it. The wraiths inside the walls attacked the glass, slashing it with their claws and even attempting to bite it.

I turned back to Ted. "Did everyone get out?"

"Yes. Yes, I think so."

I released him and he quickly got into his car and drove off.

Radioing the other ash kickers, I said, "Something's gone wrong with the enclosures. If we're going to—"

"Tamerica!" Naveena's voice blasted through my helmet. "The phoenix is heading right for you!"

I turned and looked skyward. The firebird dive bombed toward me like a loosed arrow.

As I flattened myself against the ground, the phoenix's scorching wings sailed overhead. It cruised to a stop just in front of the enclosure and hovered there, staring at the ghosts trapped inside the glass.

With a heaving flap of the its wings and a squawk for good measure, every wraith inside the enclosure exploded into flames. The walls now contained an inferno. Then, like gunshots in the night, cracks began to ripple through the enclosure's glass.

"Renfro!" I shouted into my helmet. "Set up the cannons right now! This enclosure is about to bust. Everyone, we need to take the defensive. Surround and drown. Don't let any of these fucking scalies get past us!"

I turned back to put eyes on my crew. Instead I found an army spider vehicle gliding over the ash. A turret gun rose from its top, and then fired two rapid blasts. Blue laser streaks flew over my head. The first shot passed just under the phoenix's right wing and slammed into the enclosure wall. It shattered, billows of glass and flames. The second shot hit the phoenix in the middle and sent it hurdling through the fire, into the enclosure.

I covered my face as shrapnel pelted my helmet and power suit.

"You fucking idiots!" I shouted.

"We didn't do anything!" Afu said over the radio.

I'd meant it for the army and their careless-ass attack, but I realized only my crew could hear it.

Multiple angry roars came from behind the smoke and flames. A scaly foot broke through and landed just in front of me. I looked up to see a white, crystalline dragon head looking down at me from at least fifty feet up. Training and adrenaline kicked in as I fired a few rounds at the scaly, the lasers striking the translucent spikes protruding from its cheek bones. My efforts only chipped off a few pieces of the spikes and made the dragon flinch slightly, as if the lasers were houseflies buzzing around its face.

Then, with a snarl, the dragon opened its mouth and showed me a sparkling blue light at the back of its throat.

Well, you don't see that every day.

Still flat on the ground, I hit my suit's power jump. The thrusters threw me across the ground. I didn't go far but it was enough to dodge the scaly's attack which came out as a blinding cone of cold energy.

"It's a fucking ice dragon!" Naveena shouted through my helmet. "Get out of there, T!"

I scrambled onto my feet and ran for the cannon truck as the ice dragon slammed another foot where I'd been lying.

"Shoot it!" I said between huffing breaths. "Shoot it, goddamn it!"

"Which one?" came Renfro's voice.

Movement to my right.

I looked over to see a lindworm stampeding alongside me, seemingly unconcerned about my presence and just happy to be sprung from jail. At my left, poppers sailed in and out of the ground like cresting dolphins. The sky above me, dark already from the fledgling night, darkened even more from the mass of flying monsters filling the air with their flapping wings.

The phoenix flew over, carrying a small drake in its talons and zooming fast and far ahead of the horde of flying scalies. They were all heading for the heart of Parthenon City.

When the lindworm reached the army spider vehicle, it jumped on top and began biting at the metal and shooting blasts of flames. It took only seconds for the dragon to rip away the top hatch of the spider like a ragged can of tuna fish. A man's screams came from inside and continued when the lindworm dropped into the vehicle and thrashed so hard, it looked like it would topple over.

"Lower the cannon, Renfro," I said. "Get back in the truck. We've got to get downtown."

Renfro hurried to lower the cannon as Afu chugged his huge legs and jumped back into the truck.

I climbed into my seat as an army tank rolled up and shot at the ice dragon. The booming tank fire made me cover my ears, but it didn't seem to do shit to the giant scaly, besides making it stumble a bit and then roar almost as loudly as the cannon. A blast of ice covered the tank and when the freezing light had subsided, what remained was a frosty tanksicle.

The ice dragon took a single flap of its icy wings to leap into the air and came down right on top of the frozen tank. The metal shattered as the tank flattened under the ice dragon's weight. It would have been bad enough for the dragon to call that the end of it, but it grabbed what remained of the tank in its claws and flew off toward the city.

Renfro jumped into the driver's seat, nearly chomped by a passing electro scaly's snapping teeth.

"Drive!" I said. "Follow the dragons."

"Where are they going?" Afu asked.

"They're following the phoenix. And the bird is going to be heading for the convention center because those PC First fuckheads are going to put our orange wraith on full display. And that wraith is the only thing we have left to kill the phoenix."

Over my helmet radio, I called for a full response to the city, every damn smoke eater we had, no matter if they were on another call or off duty and halfway through a bottle of whiskey. I told the propellerheads to keep sending out the emergency response calls until every smoke eater in Ohio acknowledged that they were on their way.

A dragon that looked like a rhinoceros bullfrog slammed my side of the truck. Renfro twirled the steering wheel to keep us all upright, but we were skidding hard and plowed into a group of wyverns. Scaly blood and guts splattered across the windshield, but Renfro, being the consummate professional he was, simply turned on the windshield wipers and smeared the gore into a thin paste across the glass.

Several thumps racked the top of the cannon truck. I tried to look up from my window but could see nothing besides the edge of a heaving bat-like wing. The truck heaved and for a moment our wheels weren't touching the ground.

"Can you shake this thing off of us?" I asked Renfro.

"Hold onto your butts." He whipped the steering wheel to the right.

The force threw me into the door, then Renfro pulled the same maneuver to the left and my seat belt nearly choked me. Poor Afu in the back was being tossed around like a marble in an empty soda can.

"Damn it, Afu!" I shouted. "How many times do I have to tell you to put your seatbelt on?"

"Dragon still has us," Renfro said.

Again, the truck lifted off the ground for at least two seconds before the wheels touched back down again.

"On second thought," I pointed to Afu, "get on the roof and chop this fucker's legs off if you have to."

Afu nodded, secured his laser axe to the back of his power suit and moved to climb out of the window.

"Wait!" I stretched myself toward the back of the cab and grabbed Afu by the metal collar of his power suit. I kissed him, kissed him like I'd never kissed him before, and like I never would again.

When I pulled away, Afu was grinning as wide as a Cheshire cat.

"Now get the hell up there," I said. "I'll try to cover you with some laser fire. Stay in radio contact. Renfro, try to stay smooth, but don't let up on the gas."

My driver nodded and my smoke eater climbed out of the window.

"Holy Jesus!" Afu's voice crackled over the radio. "This thing is huge."

"Don't worry about killing it," I said. "We just need it off our truck."

I lowered my window and began to lean out. The ground surged a few feet away, launching a popper out of the ground. I blasted the dragon with a few lasers and dropped it midair. Our truck's rear dual wheels ran over the dead popper, and the ensuing bump tossed all of us like ragdolls. Seeing it from my side mirror, the dragon burst into yellow embers in our wake.

"Fuck, man," Afu said. "Watch your driving!"

I placed my ass on the open window and looked toward the truck's roof. Afu clung to the emergency light bar. Above him, the blue dragon I'd seen galloping in the enclosure flapped its massive wings, eyes focused on the city.

"I'm going for it," Afu said. "Keep her steady."

On wobbly legs, Afu slowly began to stand. He reached over his shoulder and brought out his laser axe. The sound of the laser must have caught the dragon's attention, because it roared and tried to lift the truck again.

Fight or flight hit Afu hard and, thankfully, he

chose to bury his axe in the nearest scaly limb. Blood misted across Afu's face and helmet but he kept hacking until the dragon let go with its claw dangling by a thin strand of flesh. In its retreat, the scaly attempted to snap its teeth at Afu, but I was ready with my haymo grenade.

Streaks of blistering light sliced through the dragon's neck and Afu leaned away to avoid being cut by the haymo's propellers. The blue scaly burst into embers before it ever hit the ground, and our speeding cannon truck made it look like we were releasing an armada of fireflies off our roof.

"Ouch, ouch!" Afu slapped at his power suit. "Hot shit!"

"All right," I said, giving Afu a thumbs up and a smile. "Get back in here."

I had Renfro slow the truck to let Afu climb back in and then it was back to speeding after the dragons and the phoenix.

"Where's Naveena?" I asked.

"We're over here," her voice said.

I leaned forward to look past Renfro and saw Naveena's Slayer truck tearing across the ash to get on the road behind us.

"Dear God," Renfro said as he looked ahead. He was able to see the horror better than all of us with his red eyes. But even I saw more than I cared to.

Parthenon City was lit up like a glistening jewel in the night, and roaring, clawing, and flapping their way between us and nearly a million innocent people was the largest stampede of dragons I'd ever seen in my life.

# CHAPTER 33

"A two-headed purple thing just flew by my window."
Mayor Ghafoor was panting from my holoreader.
"What's going on out there? Where are the smoke
eaters?"

"We're on our way," I said. "You need to evacuate
the city."

"Do what?"

"Evacuate the city," I repeated. What part of that
did she not understand?

Ghafoor's hologram wrenched her face into a
scowl, as if I'd given her a big spoonful of medicine.
"I… I can't do that."

"You're the mayor, goddamn it! Have the army get
people out, since you're so keen on using them. I'm
telling you one last time, there are hundreds of scalies
headed right for the city, the phoenix on top of that. If
you want to go down as the last mayor of Parthenon,
that's your fuck up, but I won't let you get people
killed because you didn't want to do anything."

Ghafoor's digital green eyes stared too long. I
had other things on my mind besides talking to the
mayor, something that shouldn't have taken more
than a minute. I almost thought there was a glitch in

the network and her image had frozen, but then she closed her eyes, sighed, and said, "Alright. I'll do my job. You just do yours."

And then she was gone, hanging up like an angry teenager.

I groaned. "This is why I prefer dealing with dragons over politicians."

"Well, we've got plenty of them on our hands now," said Renfro.

He parked Cannon 15 at the corner of Main and St. George, where a smart-car had been squished and thrown onto its side. The few citizens who'd seen the dragons coming were running back into office buildings or trying to drive off in their cars. I didn't know which option was worse, but the people still out in the open were in Shitsville.

I opened every bin on the truck and surveyed the arsenal at our disposal. A loud roar and a crash of glass made me jump but I resisted the urge to turn away. Gawking at the destruction wasn't going to fix it, but cutting into some dragon flesh might. I attached a laser axe to my back and slung the Impulse foam gun over my shoulder.

Afu met me at the front bumper with his laser sword extended and an activated axe in his other hand. "What's the plan?"

Renfro joined us as Naveena and Calvinson jogged over from their Slayer truck. That's when I got a lay of the land.

Firelight reflected off shiny steel and darkened windows from multiple points. Dark smoke drifted into the moonlight from somewhere deeper

downtown. Growls, roars, and squawks echoed
down the streets, while scaled shadows swooped to
disappear around corners or nosedived to snatch
some unlucky bastard off the sidewalk. Bulging
shapes stomped over cars like living monster trucks.
Something large had slammed into buildings as if
they were made of toy blocks. A fast food restaurant's
electric sign crashed to the ground, shattering in a
cascade of plastic and electricity.

I was in over my head.

How the fuck was I supposed to tell these people
around me what to do when I'd never experienced
anything like this? There's a controlled chaos to every
dragon call, a burning of adrenaline, a constant worry
in the back of your mind that you might very well
fuck everything up, even if you give your damnedest.
But this... this was a goddamned apocalypse.

I looked at Naveena, who held her laser sword
at the ready while waiting for my orders. Passing
the ball to her would be the right move. It's what
Brannigan wanted. She had more experience, no fear.
She'd make every dragon in this city her bitch and
never break a sweat.

I don't know if she saw the fear in my eyes, or just
believed that this was my moment, my time to pass
through the fire, because she nodded to me and said,
"You got this, T. What do you want to do?"

Fuck it. Let's do this.

"Alright. Renfro and Calvinson, you guys man your
guns. Renfro, you can stay put here. Blast anything
that you think you have a good shot at. The phoenix
is going to make it difficult to keep these bastards

unconscious, so, if you can, use your laserfire to finish them off. We also need your eyes to spot any danger we might not see. That goes for everybody. Stay in radio contact, and if you see something, for the love of sweet baby Jesus, say something. Calvinson."

The rookie jumped at his name. He was shaking in his power suit.

"You paying attention?"

"Yes, ma'am." He swallowed.

I pulled out my holoreader and brought up the city's map. "I want you to get on the other side of this mess, or at least as best as you can. Stage your Slayer at... 7th and Chester. Do like Renfro and blast these sonsabitches at will."

"But," Calvinson said. "But if they don't stay asleep, my suit has a sword. Not a laser gun."

"Then you're going to be getting a lot of exercise getting on and off that truck."

Calvinson took a slow breath to calm his nerves.

"Just be safe," I said. "As soon as other companies arrive, I'll send them over to you, but until then, you're on your own. We all are."

"What about us?" Afu swung his axe through the air.

"You, me, and Naveena are going on foot. We'll make our way to the center of the city until we get to the convention center."

"But that's like two miles away," Afu said, eyes widened.

"Yeah," I said. "And we're going to slice through every fucking dragon we see on our way there. That's the plan, people. We're ditching the standard operating procedure and getting back to slaying. We don't have the time or people to worry about being humane. Does anyone have a problem with that?"

They all shook their heads. Naveena grinned.

"What?" I asked her.

"Nothing, Captain. I wouldn't change a thing. Sink or swim."

"Sink or swim," we all responded.

"Help!" a man screamed above us.

A flapper – an ugly pterodactyl-looking dragon – swooped around the block, carrying a man dangling upside down in its talons. He was wearing a gray hoodie, and jeans that were about slip off his ass and drop him into the pavement.

"Got him!" Afu said.

He climbed on top of the truck and power jumped toward the scaly. The flapper got out a screech before Afu slung his laser axe through the air and severed the dragon's legs. The civilian fell, but Naveena had already run over and caught him in her arms, cradling him like a baby.

Naveena set the man down saying, "Get the hell out of the city and tell everyone you see the same."

The man ran off, repeatedly saying, "Thank you, thank you, thank you!"

The flapper spiraled into a descent until it smacked into a fire hydrant and lay there, bleeding and shrieking. If we didn't hurry and shut it up, more flappers would be on their way to defend one of their horde. Afu wasted no time and removed the dragon's head with a swipe of his sword.

I grabbed his axe off the street and handed it to him. "Let's try not to toss away the only things that are going to keep us alive tonight."

"You got it, boo." Afu winked.

We didn't have time for me to tell him to keep the endearments to himself, so I began running down the street. Calvinson drove off to his destination and Renfro shouted good luck to us as we rounded onto St. George Avenue.

The way ahead was clear of people, dragons, and otherwise. At first I was glad for the break, but then I realized that meant the scalies and the phoenix were closer to their goal then we were.

"We can take Third," Naveena suggested. "It's downhill, so we can power jump to the next block."

Breathing heavy, I gave her a thumbs up. When we got to 3rd Street, we were greeted by roars, but they weren't coming from dragons.

At least a dozen people, some pulling at their hair or ripping their shirts off, rushed away from us down the hill. They looked like regular folks fleeing for their lives, but that thought was quickly put to bed when one of them burst into flames and kept running.

"Holy shit!" Afu said.

I power jumped toward the woman, who began throwing her flaming arms around as if she were fighting off a ghost. My landing got her attention along with the rest of the soon-to-be-flaming crazies.

I blasted the woman with my foam gun, having to hold her back with my other arm as she took swipes at my helmet. It was hard not to look into her burning, angry face, so I coated it with foam. In my periphery, the other pyro-zombies were moving in on me, running like they were in a hundred meter dash and ready to rip my throat out.

The first one to reach me pulled me away by the shoulder. When he grabbed the Impulse gun the strap pulled against my throat, choking me. I bent low and twisted around to face him. My first extinct was to blast the fucker with my lasers, but I had to stop myself. These were innocent people – phoenix crazy as they were – I couldn't kill them. But my hesitation got the man, screaming at the top of his lungs and face flushed red, to launch himself at me as if he were a dragon. I blocked his attacks with crossed, armored arms. He bit at my face and clawed against my metal. Taking out dragons was easy. How the hell was I supposed to incapacitate another human without blowing a hole through him or slicing off an appendage?

A high-pitched howl rang down the street. Afu flew in and ripped the wild man off me. With a quick jab to his jaw, Afu dropped the civilian to the street.

Naveena dropped in between us and looked at the man lying on his back. "Damn, Afu."

"What?" Afu said. "He's still breathing."

I squatted over the woman I'd covered in foam. "Well, she's not."

Carefully, I lifted her chin to see if that would open the airway, but her chest remained still. There was nothing we could do for her. Emergency triage protocols said that anyone who couldn't breathe on their own was considered dead. Black tag.

There was nothing to tag, though, because a second later the woman's body smoldered into ash and blew away with the next gust of wind.

"My God," Naveena said. "What are we going to do?"

"Hey." Afu looked around the street. "Where are the other—"

Five more crazies ran out from behind a smoking car and jumped onto Afu, dog piling him and bringing him all the way down.

"Oh shit, oh shit!" Afu screamed.

Naveena extended her laser sword and stepped forward.

"No!" I said. "These are people. Just grab 'em."

"And then what?"

The pile of people clawed with their hands and gnashed their teeth like wraiths that hadn't shed their skin yet. They covered Afu so I couldn't see him anymore. I rushed to grab the one on top, but stopped short when one of them in the middle burst into flames.

"Afu!" Naveena charged in where I had hesitated.

Then the whole pile exploded. Every one of them turned into a human bonfire. I blasted the pile with my foam, while Naveena grabbed them, one by one, and chunked them off Afu.

I couldn't breathe. My heart beat so fast that it felt like my entire power suit was thumping, about to fall off from the quake of my pulse.

Then the pile rose, and Afu stood up, covered in foam and soot, tossing the last dead psycho from his shoulders.

Afu spit and wiped his mouth with the back of his armored hand. "Why is it always me?"

Above us, in adjacent skyscrapers, windows blew out, churning fire into the night. Out of one, a flaming human shape fell, twisting in an almost beautiful ballerina twirl before it hit the street, scattering flaming guts and body parts across the street. They soon turned to ash.

The city shook. Cracks rippled through the asphalt under our boots.

A wave of exhaustion coated me like syrup and I took a knee, holding on to the side of Naveena's power suit so I wouldn't fall over in the rumble.

The bottom three floors of the tallest building near us exploded in a shower of concrete and steel. A roar stabbed my ears, and there, clawing out of the toppling building, was the ice dragon.

"Take cover!" I shouted, and began running the other way.

Afu and Naveena followed as clouds of crushed skyscraper filled the air, the street, everything in front of and behind us. I couldn't see shit, and my smoke eater lungs only helped so much against the particulates.

"Afu! Naveena!" I shouted.

"Here!" they both said.

Afu was somewhere behind me and to my right. Naveena sounded like she was a mile away, her voice echoing from my left.

The street shook with heavy steps, the unmistakable sound of a dragon on the move, getting closer. A growl followed it. It was on the hunt.

"This is Captain Williams," I cast through my helmet radio. "We are in desperate need of reinforcements. Where the hell are you guys?"

"We're almost to the city," someone responded. "This is Captain Kiesling. ETA, two to three minutes."

Fuck, Kiesling. We could be squished, frozen, and eaten in half that time.

"I need the first unit on scene to assist Slayer 5 at 7th and Chester. Everyone else get your ass over to 3rd Street. You can't miss it."

"10-4," Kiesling responded.

"Where is Brannigan?" Naveena asked.

*What great timing.*

I coughed as I felt my way through the fog. "He ain't coming."

"What!?"

White, icy light flickered throughout the debris cloud like lightning, followed by the thunder of a scaly roar. A thick whooshing came next, slow at first, but building speed. The smoke began to clear, and I was glad to finally be able to see farther than my arm could stretch. But the improvement in visibility was dashed against what I was now able to see.

The ice dragon's blue and white head appeared first. Teeth like icicles hung over its lips. Dark shadows at each side of its body heaved up and down and when the clouds gave way, it showed me what I already knew. Dragon wings. The thing was about to go airborne. All four of its claws were already off the street.

"Renfro!" I shouted into my radio. "We need you to aim toward 3rd Street. We're about to have one take flight."

"Kind of busy right now," Renfro said. Heavy breath and laser fire accompanied his voice through my helmet.

With another roar, the dragon flicked its tail and rose twenty feet higher. It sailed over our heads, wings blasting us with an air current that almost tossed my helmet off. It turned the corner and was gone, heading for the convention center.

"After that dragon," I said.

"We can't outrun it," said Afu.

I looked around the street. One of the few hover-cars parked on the curb hadn't been crushed. Its door was splayed open. The engine looked to be running.

I pointed toward it. "Afu, you drive. Me and Naveena will ride on top."

# CHAPTER 34

The small car hit a bump in the street, nearly throwing Naveena and me off the roof.

"Goddamn it, Afu!" More than likely he couldn't hear me, but I said it all the same. "I just remembered you can't drive for shit."

Ahead of us the ice dragon's tail, which looked like a crystal fan at the end of a snow-covered log, flicked from one side of the street to the other, smashing into office buildings and concrete pillars of parking garages.

"Get us a little closer!" I shouted.

Afu stuck his head out of the window. "Huh?"

I pumped my arm toward the dragon. "Closer, closer!"

Afu swerved around an over-turned city bus, but the rest of the block stretched ahead without a single obstacle. I squeezed tighter against the roof as the little-hover-car-that-could launched into overdrive. We passed under the dragon's tail, keeping pace under the part where some icy testicles could have hung. The scaly's claws were only a few feet ahead of the car, and a casual back kick of either leg would rip through the metal and kill all three of us.

Naveena tapped me on the shoulder and yelled

through the wind. "Let's power jump! Get on top of it."

"Why are you always wanting to ride these things?" I asked.

"On three!" Naveena climbed into a squatting position and held out three fingers. By the time I got to my own feet, Naveena had folded down one finger, leaving two to go.

The ice dragon breathed its fury down the street as smatterings of people screamed and ran. Sheets of frost formed on windows. A few unfortunate souls had gotten blasted by the dragon's ice beam, turning into macabre snow people after the light passed over them.

When Naveena lowered her final finger and the ice dragon's tail swooped over our heads to the left, she shouted, "Now!"

Both of us hit our jump buttons and sailed into the air. Our trajectory should have put us dead center on the back of the scaly's neck. But its tail swung back as we flew through the air, slamming into me first, then Naveena. We soared together in a tangled girl ball of smoke eaters. I managed to grab onto her, unsure which part it even was. I just wanted something to hang onto. The world spun out of my control as I tumbled into the unknown.

Something hit me… or I hit something. We'd definitely connected with a window. I remember the initial smack of a smooth surface, followed by the cymbal crash of glass that sliced my cheek. After a few rolls of my helmeted head smacking against the floor, I crawled, aching, to my feet. We'd been whacked through a window and now stood inside a darkened office filled with cubicles.

"You okay?" I asked Naveena, who groaned from the ground, still flat on her face.

"Yeah. How 'bout you?"

"I'm sore as hell, but never mind that. We have to stop that dragon."

Naveena sighed. "There'll just be another dragon after that. They never stop."

I helped her to stand. "Yeah, but that's our job, remember? Plus, the others aren't that big or icy."

"That frosty fuck is halfway to Canada by now."

A crash and a roar came from the nearest window.

"No, it's not," I said.

Afu broke in through my helmet radio. "I got ahead of it. But it's turned around and it's chasing me now."

Outside, the ice dragon was making a circle around the building. The top of its ice-clustered head crested the lowest part of the window. If it kept circling around…

"Come on." I slapped Naveena's armored chest and ran for the wall.

"How are you going to—"

My lasers bit into the bare wall, chewing through the sheetrock like a dragon through wet toilet paper. With an elbow raised in front of my face, I went through the wall and out the other side, stumbling a bit, but quickly regained my footing and picked up speed.

"You're crazy as fuck." Naveena laughed and zoomed past me.

Skinny girls piss me off.

She broke through the next wall without even having to slash it with her sword. I zipped through the hole she'd made, and entered a corner office. Its window looked onto the next street over, where the convention center stood a few blocks away, glistening with bright yellow lights like a beacon to all scalies great and small.

"This it," Naveena said. "Now or never. What are we gonna do?"

The ice dragon's roar grew closer, even the beat of its wings shook the window in front of me.

I removed my laser axe and smashed out the closest pane. The night air blew in, but it did nothing to cool me off or calm me down. Keeping my eyes on the broken window, I said, "Remember when we were training and you pulled that stupid stunt with Mecha Scaly?"

"Hey, wait—" was all I heard Naveena say.

I backed up a few feet, ran, and leapt from the window. The ice dragon was nowhere close. In fact, I'd jumped the gun, hoping my power suit would notice the shift in gravity and engage its thrusters to slow my fall. On the street, Afu sped below me, but I only caught a glimpse. The ice dragon's head filled my vision.

I landed with an *oof* that knocked the air from my lungs. My body began to slip, but, flailing my arms, I grabbed the ice dragon by the horns – which is difficult with an axe in one hand. Fucking scaly was frigid to the touch. Its scales freezer-burned my face, where the window glass had already sliced. It was like riding an angry popsicle. The cold sucks ass. I would have taken the phoenix any day over this wintery bastard.

Knowing something was wrong, the ice dragon flicked its wings backward, heaving to a stop midair. I squeezed the dragon horns tighter. One slip and I'd fall toward a squishy death.

Say what you will about dragons, but they're great at multitasking. The ice dragon hovered there above the street, beating its wings while it wriggled its head to and fro, trying to catch me in its teeth or knock me off.

Dragon horns still in one hand, I took a swing with my axe. Missed. I was better at shooting, but with my laser arm committed to holding on for dear life, I really didn't have a choice.

My next swing found dragon flesh and lobbed off a big hunk. The frozen mass fell and smashed against the asphalt like a block of ice. Instead of blood, frosty blue water flowed from the wound. I raised my arm for another whack.

Behind me, the dragon's body heaved. Naveena landed just behind its wings, and with a scared but wild smile, she began clumsily slashing.

"How did you get here?" I dug in, hacking and swinging my axe in a frenzy. Slaying a dragon by yourself is scary shit. When you have someone at your side, especially someone like Naveena, it dulls the fear a little, knowing that if you go down fighting, you at least won't be alone.

The dragon, unable to keep itself aloft any longer, dropped to the side, plummeting toward the street and tossing both Naveena and I off with a heavy dusting of shaved ice.

The ground shook as the dragon crushed a couple cars and the awning of bus stop that had been advertising flame-resistant clothing for the fashion-conscious.

When I hit the ground, I rolled and forced myself

to keep rolling to stay out of the path of the collapsing dragon. I covered my head and waited for the sounds of destruction to fade. When they had, I turned over and looked up to Naveena's outstretched hand.

"Now, that," she said, "is slaying a dragon."

What was left of the ice dragon melted instantly into puddles of yellow, glowing goo.

"And *that*," I said, "is just nasty."

Afu and the tiny car whipped around the end of the street and pulled up in front of us. He squeezed out of the driver's seat and said, "If we keep doing this kind of stuff, we're never going to make it to the convention center."

There were no clouds in the sky, but a yellow streak of lightning flickered overhead. It was made of fire and death. Instead of thunder, an avian shriek ripped over the city. The phoenix had been called, whether the people inside the convention center knew or cared, and it had reached its destination.

# CHAPTER 35

While all the people who'd come out to the convention center could be called dumb, at least a handful of them weren't dumb enough to stay inside while the city crumbled around them. The phoenix dropping onto the roof must have been the final motivation for the smart ones to flee, because when we pulled up in the hover car, they were rushing onto the street, like stuffed trash-bags in their gowns and tuxes.

Other smokies had arrived in a big, black and purple Slayer truck, and were doing their part to take down dragons that were running around, ruining these slightly-less-dumb people's evening.

A small electro scaly cornered three civilians against the building – two men and a woman in a flowing, off-pink dress. The woman stood out front, spreading her arms against the men in an attempt to protect them, clutching her glittery hand purse as if it was a magical dagger. But it wouldn't protect them from the dragon or the sparks of electricity shooting from its extended frill, striking the ground, closer and closer like whips of lightning as the scaly moved in for the kill.

The dragon rasped, building up a ball of current inside its throat – its attack call. I launched myself between the trio of people and the dragon, and put a few rounds of lasers into Sparky's face. Its head exploded with a shower of gore and electricity. When I turned around the three who'd been cornered had run off without so much as a "thank you for your service."

The ground shook behind me, bringing with it an intense wave of heat. With wings spread, the phoenix looked at all of the smoke eaters. It cocked its head to the side, curious, and I wondered if it remembered us, remembered we were a threat.

"Let's get inside," I said, low.

The phoenix blasted us with a screech that could have easily taken my helmet off.

"Everyone inside!" I turned and ran.

There were plenty of doors for us to go through, but all of them were blocked with people shoved against the other side. I shoved all my weight against the door but only budged it a crack. The idiots pressed against the door stared at me with wide eyes and red faces. How many of them had dragon blood running through their veins? I wondered. How many had just received a fiery death sentence?

The sight of the phoenix caused the mass of people to back away from the doors. The smoke eaters charged in... but so did the phoenix.

Fire filled the building, glass showering us, heat bursting against my face. The doors weren't there anymore. As the flames depleted, a screech sliced through the smoke. Human screams responded. The bird had shrunk in the blast. While still big enough to swallow me, now it could dive into the convention center.

And, of course, the fucker did.

The phoenix snapped its beak toward me. I backed into the crowd, knocking them over like bowling pins. Kicking feet and screams covered me as everyone tried to scramble away from the phoenix's enormous head. One of the other smoke eaters attempted to douse the phoenix with her foam gun. That got the bird distracted enough for me to get upright and help those still on the ground to their feet.

"Get to the back exits," I told them.

They rushed to do as I said, but it was like wading through a river of molasses. A few of them began to moan, and that's when the chain reaction of human combustibles started.

The first ones to burn were those closest to the phoenix. They didn't get time to go crazy first. The ones nearest to me, further in to the convention center's foyer, howled and started what looked like an aristocratic mosh pit.

Women removed their high heels and beat them against smoke eater helmets and armor. Afu had to hoist a man, smoking from his nostrils, over his head and toss him out of the way. Men I'd just helped to stand swung fists at my face. More and more of the crowd began to explode like fireworks, filling the crammed space with smoke. The phoenix thrashed, breaking away chunks of metal as it forced its way in to the building.

There was nothing we could do for these people. Not while the phoenix was still around. Not while the wraith we needed waited behind the doors on the other side of this horde of flaming assholes.

"We've got to get to the wraith," I said.

Naveena punched a fiery man in the face, sending him flopping backwards into a group of crazies. "I thought that's what we were trying to do."

"Afu!" I shouted. "Clear us a path!"

He turned away from the group he'd been trying to keep off him and bulldozed his way through the crowd. Naveena and I followed, punching and shoving as we went. The other smoke eaters followed behind us until we'd made it inside the banquet hall. The last smoke eater shut the door and leaned against it.

"Calm down," Duncan Sharp said through a microphone. "Everyone, please. We're very safe in here and the dragon blood infusions will help us survive this."

Fat chance.

The people still in the banquet hall were doing everything but calming down. They were hiding under tables, pulling at windows on the other side of the room. When a dragon flew by outside, they backed off and ran to find another means of escape.

On the stage, Duncan Sharp stood next to the Wilkins family, while the dead man's wraith flew in crazy, orange circles inside a containment cylinder. The room, filled with tables and chairs and a big, holographic banner reading, 'Parthenon City First!' had enough room for a couple thousand people, but only a third of them remained.

"Shut it down!" I ran for the stage.

Men and women who were dressed more militarily ran toward me with outstretched arms.

"If you think a bunch of dragons can't stop us," I said, "do you think you really have a shot?"

They backed off as I climbed my way up to the stage.

"I need that wraith right now. Otherwise everyone here is going to die."

Sharp was fuming, but he somehow forced a grin to his face. "You're the only reason all of this is happening. If you'd just done your job—"

"I'm trying to do my job!" I snapped. "The phoenix is here because that orange wraith attracted it. And it brought a shit ton of dragons in tow. Everyone here with dragon blood in their system is in danger of going crazy and bursting into flames."

"Please help us," Mrs Wilkins said. Her eyes filled with tears. She wanted off the Duncan Sharp train and saw me as the only landing pad passing by.

The doors to the foyer rattled violently enough that the hinges almost came off.

"We can't hold them back for much longer." Afu strained with the other smoke eaters to keep the doors closed.

Duncan Sharp shook his head. "They can't do anything for us."

I got in his face. "You seem to know a lot about rats. Well, if you don't stand down, you're all going to be stuck in here, frying like rats in an oven. We're the only ones who can do anything. So step out of the way and let me work."

A tinny *clink* came from behind Sharp.

Mrs Wilkins stood next to the wraith cylinder which had been given a hefty whack. She hefted a microphone stand over her shoulder like a club. "If my Jimmy can save us, then I'm letting him out. He'd have wanted it."

She swung again.

"No!" Sharp shouted, leaping for her.

But he wasn't fast enough. Little old woman had a hell of swing. The microphone stand connected against the cylinder's glass and the whole thing shattered. Sharp tried to peddle backward but ended up on his ass instead.

The orange wraith clawed past what remained of the cylinder and flew straight for Sharp. I could have let the wraith have him, tear him apart while the rest of us got the hell out of there. But smoke eaters are sworn to protect everyone, even assholes like him.

I ejected my wraith remote and sucked up the ghost just as its tangerine claw swiped for Sharp's face. He lay there for a second, still in shock. With trembling lips, he stared at me. All I gave him was a nod.

The doors to the foyer burst open. Smoke eaters ran for cover as fiery civilians and a couple of confused but excited dragons broke through.

"Afu! Naveena!" I said. "Break those windows. We have to get everyone out. The rest of you slay the dragons."

They moved quickly, breaking open the windows and helping folks who'd already gathered around them out of the window. The rest of the smoke eaters began dousing the pyromaniacs with foam or slicing off dragon heads.

Duncan Sharp decided he wanted to do things his way and ran for the foyer doors.

"Sharp!" I called out. "Stop!"

A group of crazies that hadn't yet combusted grabbed him in the middle of the banquet hall. As he screamed and I began running to help, the phoenix burst in, fashionably late to the big hoorah.

"You want this, you ugly bitch?" I patted the

pocket in my power suit where I'd returned the wraith remote.

The phoenix couldn't have cared less. No longer drawn by the wraith, it was now looking for an escape like everyone else. It began flapping its wings.

The pile of crazies on top of Sharp had gotten taller. He managed to squeeze his face out and grit his teeth. The side of his face, where he'd recently grown new skin, ignited and turned the whole stack of bodies into a pyre of flames.

The phoenix broke through the ceiling. Huge pieces of concrete pulverized the fiery mass of people below, along with Duncan Sharp trapped beneath them.

The smoke eaters who'd been taking care of the dragons rushed for the windows and everyone who'd had enough sense to do what I'd told them made it out of the convention center with only a few scrapes and burns. More Slayer trucks arrived, as did the fire department. Above us, the phoenix broke free of the building and sailed high to the top of a nearby skyscraper. There it stayed. I could see its flames flickering from the street.

"I'm so tired." Afu dropped to a knee, heaving gulps of breath. "Please tell me we're done."

"Come on, big boy," Naveena said, even though I could hear the exhaustion in her voice. "For Patrice and Harribow and every damn person in this city."

I was wiped out, too. Adrenaline helps a lot, but there's a threshold you cross, where no amount of chemicals in your system can help you keep going.

But we had a job to do.

Afu groaned and got to his feet. "Why can't this

fucking thing fly to Arkansas or something?"

"When did you become such a sack of whiny balls?" I asked.

He laughed. Naveena did, too. I was too tired and worried to laugh, but I did grin and help Afu stand.

Kiesling ran by. I stopped him with a weak wave of my hand. "Cap, hold up a minute."

"What, Williams?" he said through gulps of air. "We got a mess on our hands."

"I'm passing command to you."

His mouth hung open and he stared blankly as if I must have been joking. Lord knows he didn't wake up that morning, expecting to be in the middle of this conundrum, let alone be in charge of it.

"You'll do great. It's just clean up from here." I hoped anyway. There were still plenty of dragons roaming the streets and people set to explode.

Naveena, Afu and I hurried as fast as our tired bodies would let us. We stopped in front of the skyscraper, craning our necks to see how high the building rose.

"Afu," I said. "I hate to tell you this, but we're about to face the worst thing yet."

"The phoenix?"

"No," I told him. "Stairs."

A black SUV with purple emergency lights swerved around the debris and stopped just behind us.

Wearing his power suit, Brannigan got out and strapped on his helmet.

I'd be lying if I said I wasn't glad to see him and it must have shown on my face.

"What?" Brannigan said. "You didn't think I'd miss a party like this did you?"

# CHAPTER 36

"And we're taking the elevator," Brannigan said as we entered the lobby. "We don't always have to do things the hard way, Williams."

"Thank you, Chief." Afu looked like he wanted to grab Brannigan in a hug.

Brannigan punched the elevator button and turned to Naveena. "You been taking care of things, okay?"

"This is Williams' show," said Naveena.

Brannigan scrunched his eyebrows as he looked back to me. "You didn't tell her, did you?"

"Tell me what?" Naveena asked.

"Nothing," I said.

The elevator doors opened and Brannigan stepped inside.

"What were you supposed to tell me?" Naveena wasn't letting it go.

"That Sherry and Chief are getting a divorce and he wants to know if you still have feelings for him."

"I never had feelings for him!" Naveena crossed her arms.

"I never said that at all," Brannigan said. "Goddamn it, Williams. If you're going to lie, at least make up something believable."

I smiled and stared at the holographic floor numbers rising higher.

"Captain Williams and me are back together," Afu stated, like a proud little boy who got a smiley face sticker on his science project.

"I kissed you," I said. "That doesn't mean we're back together."

"Give her time, big guy," Brannigan said.

I spun around. "Are you guys in the same situation I'm in? We've got a phoenix to kill and this wraith might cause it to explode and permanently paint our shadows against the walls."

"I don't think the roof is going to have walls," Afu said.

"You know what I mean. I'm trying to figure out how we can get out of this thing alive."

Brannigan stuck out his hand. "Hand me the remote."

"What?"

"The wraith," he said. "I'll hold onto it."

"Chief, you shouldn't be getting close to the phoenix. You know as well as I do you could go crazy and burn–"

"How did you just address me?" Brannigan asked.

"I…"

He hadn't drawn back his hand. If the old bastard was wanting to showboat and take all the credit, fine. He could have it, but I wasn't going to have his death on my conscience. Patrice filled that space enough as it was.

"Chief," I said.

"Right." Brannigan nodded. "And as your chief, I'm giving you a direct order. Wraith remote. Now."

I huffed and ejected the remote from my pocket. With a slap against his open, armored palm, I relinquished the wraith trapper.

"All right," he said. "This is how we're going to do it. I'm going out there first."

I tried to object, but Brannigan lifted his hand and stopped me before I could even get a word in.

"You three are going to stand back until I say it's all clear." He studied the laser axe in Afu's hands. "You mind if I give that a try?"

Afu handed it over. "All yours, Chief."

Brannigan tested the ax's weight in his hands. "Nice."

The elevator dinged and opened to the top floor.

"All right," Brannigan said. "Sink or swim."

The only way to the roof was from a flight of metal stairs at the end of the hallway. The phoenix's shrieks rumbled through the ceiling, shaking the tiles. One of the tiles dropped to the floor behind us and we all turned with laser blades extended.

"Why are you guys so jumpy?" Naveena swallowed and retracted her laser sword.

I'd been somewhere like this before, that night I'd climbed the roof of Smoke Eater headquarters to face Patrice. Fear hit me like a cannonball in the gut, but I wasn't afraid of the phoenix. I was scared that I would just be repeating the past. That I'd be stuck in the same terrible déjà vu and wouldn't be helping anybody. That I'd be failing once again.

"Chief," I said. "I've got this Impulse gun. I can go out there with you as back up. At least to–"

"No, Williams." Brannigan said.

"Chief's right," said Naveena. "The bird might

be right at the door, and if we have to lose someone, better it be someone already at death's door."

Naveena tried to smile, but it felt forced. Brannigan only shrugged.

We came to the door and I put a hand against it. "I can feel the heat. Even through my power suit. I don't think this is a good idea."

"This is our shot," said Brannigan. "We're smoke eaters. We can stand a little heat."

My hand began shaking. I felt powerless, useless, tied up in something I couldn't get out of, kind of like how Mrs Wilkins had been scooped up by PC First and made to have her husband be the undead voice of a cause she probably didn't give two shits about.

Brannigan took hold of my arm and eased me out of the way. "Just give me two seconds."

I stared into Brannigan's eyes. He didn't say word. With a firm hand, he grabbed the door handle and pulled.

As Brannigan went through, I got a quick glimpse of the phoenix on the other side, arching its wings in a defensive posture. Then the door closed and the sound of a metal pole scraped against the door.

"Chief?" I called.

I tried the door but it wouldn't budge.

"Brannigan, open the door!"

Afu and Naveena tried to help me open it, but he'd shoved the laser axe through the door handle on the other side. We couldn't get through.

"Back up," I told Afu and Naveena. "I'm going to blast through this fucking door."

"Williams." The heavy door muffled Brannigan's

voice. "I'm about to release this wraith and if Yolanda was right, like she usually is, this is going to set off an explosion. I'm ordering all of you to leave now."

"You stupid, old fuck!" I cried. My knees buckled. And here I thought I couldn't have been made to feel any weaker.

I grabbed the door handle again. Naveena and Afu tried to pull me away, but I wouldn't let go.

"I'm going to keep the bird occupied until I know you're on the street," Brannigan said. "If you try to break through the door, I'll release the wraith and we'll all be barbecue. This city needs you. Don't disappoint them. Don't disappoint me."

I let go of the door. For a while I didn't even try to run away. Afu dragged me until we reached the first step leading down to the top floor. By that point, I had no choice but to move one foot in front of the other, picking up speed gradually, as if Brannigan was a big wad of glue I had to force myself out of.

"The stairs will be faster," Naveena said.

How could they go along with this? Why weren't they trying to stop Brannigan? It was like they wanted him to die.

"Why? Why?" I kept mumbling as we ran down the stairs, taking entire flights in a jump. "He's the Chief," Afu said. "We can't stop him."

In the lobby, Naveena had to push me along as Afu ran ahead of us and, ever the gentleman, held the door open for us to pass through.

"Goddamn, I'm burning up," Brannigan's voice came through my helmet. "This bird isn't going to stick around long. Are all of you on the street yet?"

I couldn't respond. Giving him the affirmative would mean he'd release the wraith and be gone from my life forever.

"Tamerica." Naveena grabbed my arm, urging me with her tensed eyes.

I wanted Naveena to make this all go away, to find a way to stop it, an alternative where nobody else had to die. But all she must have seen was that I wasn't going to respond to Brannigan's message.

Naveena took a deep breath and cast from her radio. "We're out of the building, Chief."

"I'm proud of you guys," was the last thing I heard Brannigan say over a wraith's shrieks.

A second later, the top of the building exploded in a ring of electric fire like I'd never seen before or since. The old bastard had actually gone through with it. Flaming pieces of debris rained down from the roof, like glowing snow.

We told all of the Slayer trucks to move out of the way and stay back. All the smokies watched the top of the building burn like some morbid fireworks show.

After a while, everything got so quiet I could hear my heart thumping inside my power suit. No flaming bird flew from the skyscraper. No smoke eater spoke over the radio – we were keeping the channel clear to hear if Brannigan had somehow made it out of there in time. But after twenty minutes of silence we knew: the phoenix was gone, and our chief with it.

I went to the roof with the cleanup crew. For safety reasons, they'd shut the power down and we had to take the stairs. I didn't mind. It was a form of penance I had to pay for letting Brannigan sacrifice himself. It was a drop in an ocean of pain I had planned to put myself through. I was never going to forgive myself, not for this one.

The three floors below the roof were completely demolished. We couldn't make it to the roof because there was no longer a roof to get to. The cleanup crew told me there was no possible way anything could have survived the blast. I told them they didn't know much about our chief. For over an hour they appeased me, letting me turn over charred hunks of metal and concrete. But everyone has their limit. They finally closed down the scene and all but dragged me back down to the street.

Afu and Naveena had refused to come along. They already knew what I was still denying.

Calvinson and Renfro were there when I walked out of the building. Outside the hot zone, where crews had put up hologram caution tape, the street was bustling with smoke eater and firefighter crews. Even a few army vehicles had shown up. Soldiers stood around with laser rifles hanging from their shoulders, looking on as if they thought they could have done a better job.

Renfro gave me a big hug and I fought the urge to just cry into his power suit. Ash-covered metal isn't the most conducive for sobbing your grief into.

I pulled away from him when my holoreader rang. It was Yolanda.

"Harribow is awake," she said. "He's doing great, all things considered. A complete turnaround. I want to run some more tests, but I'm thinking this means you guys were successful?"

"Brannigan did it," I said.

"Wonderful. I hate to ask you for anything more, but if you can, I'd love to get any residue from the phoenix. It might help us be better prepared if any more show up in the future."

Fuck that, I thought.

I shook my head, emotionless, a hollowed out hunk of flesh. "There's nothing left."

"Oh," Yolanda said. Her hologram head tilted in a concerned lean to the side. "Well, no matter. I'll see you all when you get back."

She hung up and I stood there staring at a blank screen. It was almost like some part of me thought I'd be getting another call. Additional orders from an old man I didn't know I'd miss until it was too late.

People talk about the five stages of grief as if they're levels of a videogame, like you go from one to the other, in a progressive linear fashion. I wasn't goddamn Mario. I was feeling every single stage at the same time. Maybe that's what it was really like and over time, if you were lucky, they'd start to drop away one by one, like dead scales.

"Captain," Renfro said. "The clean-up crews should have everything under control now. All of the dragons are ash."

"And the pyro people," said Calvinson.

Naveena glared at him.

Renfro cleared his throat. "Anyway. I'm sure you have a big report to type up. Definitely some rest is earned. And we have to elect a new…"

His words drifted off. He couldn't say it, but we all knew what he was about to tell us.

"He named Naveena chief," I said.

My fellow captain's eyes widened. She crossed her arms and turned away. "It's too early to be talking about this."

"You guys can talk about it all you want, whenever you want," I said. "Because I'm done."

"I know." Renfro dropped a hand to my shoulder. "Like I said, we all need a good rest before we handle anything else."

I shook my head. "No, that's not what I mean. I'm quitting the smoke eaters. I'm out."

"T," Afu stepped toward me with his hands outstretched, but stopped short. He realized I was serious.

"You can't let this force you out," Naveena said. "This isn't like you. Now's the time to fight even harder. That's what Brannigan would have wanted. Smoke eaters don't quit."

"I'm not a smoke eater anymore."

"None of you are."

We all turned at the woman's voice.

Mayor Ghafoor stood there with Colonel Calhoun and a few of his army thugs. "I have never seen such a disaster, not even E-Day can compare. You have all let this city down. You've let me down. I cannot in my good conscience entrust our safety to your organization any longer."

"What are you talking about?" said Naveena. "We stopped this mess from devolving into a full scale clusterfuck. Your army goons made it worse. That Duncan Sharp asshole, too."

"Colonel Calhoun has given me his report,"

Ghafoor said, "and I saw firsthand how things happened from the news drones."

"The Feed?" Afu said. "Really? They don't get anything right. Everybody would be dead if it wasn't for us."

"There's going to be an investigation," Ghafoor continued. "And I'll be involved every step of the way. I intend to see that official charges are brought against Smoke Eater Division. The evidence I've seen is enough. I'm afraid of what the whole story is going to reveal."

"She can't do this, can she?" Calvinson asked us.

I said nothing. It was only fitting this blob of bullshit would come down on us, without Brannigan around to carry the weight.

"Listen!" Ghafoor stamped her foot into the cracked asphalt. "As of this moment, you are to relinquish all apparatus and equipment. All operations are terminated, along with your positions. Get this through your heads, people: the smoke eaters are no more."

# ACKNOWLEDGEMENTS

I've never written a sequel before. This was certainly a learning experience, but, overall, it was a hell of a lot of fun.

I first want to thank readers like you. Your enthusiasm for *Smoke Eaters* helped make this book a reality, and I can't express enough how much you mean to me.

I want to thank Steph O'Neil, Laura Adams, Marc Morris, Rachel Noel, Derek Arsenault, Laurie Bell, Matt Shileikis, Sean Little, and Eddie Moore for being fantastic beta readers, and sorry to those decimated by the ending. Here's hoping for Book 3!

Marc Gascoigne and Lee Gibbons created a fantastic cover that completely outdoes the first, which I never thought possible. Paul Simpson, who edited *Ash Kickers*, was phenomenal to work with. He truly made this book shine, and, after copyediting *Smoke Eaters*, finally got me to eliminate modern references, like *Predator* and *Where's Waldo?*

Thanks to Gemma Creffield for taking on the publicity end, as well as the copyedits. Odds are, you heard about this book because of her. And that goes for everyone at Angry Robot Books.

Finally, I want to thank my wonderful wife for

putting up with me. With every book, especially during the edit, I become a strange, obsessive weirdo. Lisa, thanks for being there and supporting me. I love you more than a dragon loves ash.

# ABOUT THE AUTHOR

Sean Grigsby is a professional firefighter in central Arkansas, where he writes about lasers, aliens, and guitar battles with the Devil when he's not fighting dragons. He grew up on Goosebumps books in Memphis, Tennessee, and hosts the Cosmic Dragon podcast.

By the same author...

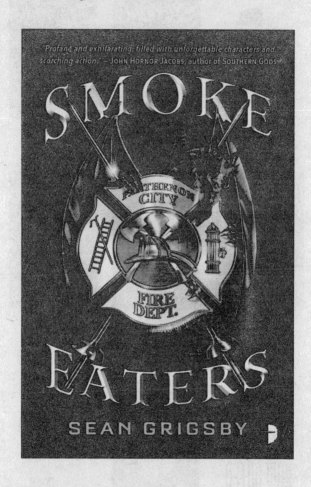

**ANGRY ROBOT**

We are Angry Robot

angryrobotbooks.com

**SILENT HALL**
N. S. DOLKART

**AMONG THE FALLEN**
N. S. DOLKART

**A BREACH IN THE HEAVENS**
N. S. DOLKART

## Science Fiction, Fantasy and WTF?!

**THE BULLET-CATCHER'S DAUGHTER**
ROD DUNCAN

**UNSEEMLY SCIENCE**
ROD DUNCAN

**THE CUSTODIAN OF MARVELS**
ROD DUNCAN

@angryrobotbooks

**THE INTERMINABLES**
PAIGE ORWIN

**MOONSHINE**
JASMINE GOWER

**AN OATH OF DOGS**
WENDY N WAGNER

# *UNDER THE PENDULUM SUN* BY

# JEANETTE NG

## PAPERBACK & EBOOK
from all good stationers and book emporia

Two Victorian missionaries travel into darkest
fairyland, to deliver their uplifting message to the
godless magical beings who dwell there… at the risk
of losing their own mortal souls.

*Winner of the Sydney J Bounds Award, the British
Fantasy Award for Best Newcomer*

*Shortlisted for the John W Campbell Award*